AN UNDEAD CHRISTMAS
A ZOMBIE ANTHOLOGY

EDITED BY
ANTHONY GIANGREGORIO

Table of Contents

FOREWORD

Instead of rambling on about zombies and Christmas and how much fun it all is, I decided to toss in the following story about Santa Claus and a small boy named Timmy. Though there are no zombies in it, I hope you like it. Merry Christmas.

THE "REAL" SANTA CLAUS

ANTHONY GIANGREGORIO

Timmy had awoken to something but he didn't know what it was. Then he heard it again.

Snorting, and bells…like jingle bells?

He glanced to his clock on his nightstand and saw it was two hours past midnight.

It was Christmas!

Finally!

There was more noise and then there was the sound of something landing heavily in the living room. Muffled curses soon followed.

"Dad?" Timmy said softly. Maybe his father was putting out the presents for the next morning. He couldn't wait; he'd asked for the new Xbox and also a BB gun. He didn't think he was going to get the BB gun but hey, he'd asked anyway when sitting on Santa's lap at the mall.

More muttered curses and a loud *thunk* came to him and he slid out of bed, curious to see what was making so much racket. He made sure to take his stuffed bear Willie with him of course; just in case he needed protection. Willie might be stuffed, but he had courage and was strong and protected Timmy every night from the monsters under his bed.

As he tip-toed into the hallway and made his way past his parents' bedroom, he peeked inside. His dad was snoring like he was a lumberjack and the shape of his mom was right next to him.

That was weird. If his parents were both still sleeping, then who was making so much noise?

No, it couldn't be, but then again…

Timmy pulled his head away from the bedroom door and began running down the hallway, and realizing he was going too fast, he tried to put on the brakes. He began skating across the hardwood floor, his socks allowing him to 'ice skate.' He slid right into the back of the couch and fell onto his butt.

"Huh? What the hell was that?" a voice said and Timmy rolled over and quickly pushed up tight against the back of the couch. A shadow loomed over him a second later, as someone inspected the area behind the couch, which was lost in the shadows, and Timmy was well hidden.

"Huh, must be gettin' jumpy in my old age."

The shadow retreated and Timmy let out a soft sigh…he was safe.

More noise came to him and he heard the Christmas tree ornaments rattling as the man put items under it. The moon was high this night and the pale glow filtered into the room, casting everything in a yellow pallor.

Timmy, his heart in his throat, slowly raised his head over the back of the couch, so he could see who was in his house, and at the same time—with both hope and wonder—praying what he thought was happening was coming true.

If someone had been watching the couch, they would have seen Timmy's face slowly appear, like he was on a rising platform. His hair was first, followed by his forehead, then his eyes popped up from the top of the couch. Timmy's eyes went wide when he saw before him, standing in front of the Christmas tree, a man in a red suit with white trim.

(Author's note: *Yeah, I think we all know who this is so I'm not gonna go into all that 'bowl full of jelly junk' or his 'round belly' or his 'white beard' ect. I think you get it.*)

So anyway, back to Timmy.

Timmy's eyes were wide as he stared at Santa. He watched with wonder as the man worked, placing presents under the tree.

But the more Timmy watched Santa work, the more something seemed *off* about him.

For one thing, he smelled like cheap liquor. (Timmy knew this from when his dad went on business meetings and came home late. He would tuck Timmy in and his breath always smelled the same).

Another thing was Santa kept swearing as he worked. Timmy wasn't allowed to say those words but he knew them well from hearing his father use them. Not all the time but when something bad happened, like his dad was hammering in a nail and he missed and hit his thumb instead. Or Timmy had left one of his toys lying around on the floor in the living room or hallway and his dad accidentally stepped on it, or there was the time Timmy had left his bicycle in the driveway and his father had backed into it, scratching the bumper of the family car.

So yeah, Timmy knew those swear words well.

Santa went over to the milk and cookies on the table and picked up the glass of milk and took a big bite of one of the cookies. He winced as he sipped the milk—as if he didn't like the taste—and after dropping the cookie back to the plate, he reached inside his suit and pulled out a silver flask. Popping the top with his teeth, he poured something that Timmy didn't know was

Vodka into the milk. After putting the flask away, Santa took another sip of milk and this time smiled...widely.

He went and sat down in Timmy's dad's easy chair and pulled out a pack of Lucky's, then lit one. Timmy saw the Zippo Santa used and noticed the initials KK on it.

(Authors note: *Kris Kringle, and if you don't know what I'm talking about, shame on you. Go watch Rankin and Bass' 'Santa Claus is Coming to Town,' then get back here, but I'm not waiting for you*).

Santa finished his milk and put the glass down, only he was a little tipsy now and the glass slid off the table. It smashed on the floor and Santa chuckled, not really caring. His cell phone rang and he pulled it out, opening it. "Go for big S."

He listened for a moment and said, "Look, Martha, we've been over this before. Now shut up and leave me alone. I'll be home when I'm home. And you can get your own damn cigarettes." He snapped the phone closed and let out a burp, then scratched his backside.

He shook his head to clear it and muttered something about "Damn elves not worth the food I feed them and it's a good thing they work for free," then went to the chimney opening. Getting down on his knees, and with a few more choice curses, he peered up into the shaft and yelled, "Are you idiots gonna toss down the rest of those presents or am I gonna have to bust some heads!"

Timmy couldn't believe what he was seeing and hearing, and he had to rub his eyes as if he was wiping away a mirage.

It was Santa, the *real* Santa, and though it was hard to believe, Timmy was discovering that yes, Santa Claus did exist.

And he was kind of a jerk.

SPECIAL DELIVERY

MARIAH DEITRICK

Abby bounced up and down on her parents' bed. "Santa Claus came! Get up!" she squealed.

"Coffee," Kelly muttered, rubbing her eyes and glancing at the clock. Six was way too early to even think about getting out of bed when work wasn't involved.

"I'll start the coffee, you keep her away from those presents," Sam said, climbing out of bed.

Abby was off the bed and down the stairs before Kelly had a chance to sit up.

Sam laughed. "We'd better hurry or she'll have the tree emptied before we get down there," he said and followed Abby, warning her to wait the entire way down the stairs.

Kelly wasn't a morning person. If it wasn't Christmas, she would have stayed in bed for a couple more hours. As it was, she had to force herself up and down the stairs with her eyes half open.

When she reached the living room, Abby was all ready shaking gifts. "I'm going to open this one first," Abby said, setting the largest box to the side.

Kelly barely noticed her daughter. Then a shaking gift caught her attention as it sat alone under the tree. "Sam!" she called for her husband. They'd talked about getting Abby a puppy for Christmas, but they'd both decided against it. Kelly wondered now if Sam had gone behind her back and had gotten one without telling her.

"It's almost done. I'll be there in a sec!"

The box shook more violently this time.

Abby squealed with delight. "I'm opening that one first." She hurried and plucked the present from under the tree.

"Hold on, hon," Kelly told Abby and stormed off to the kitchen. Sam getting a puppy after they'd decided it wasn't a good idea made her angry. She couldn't believe he'd do that; he had some explaining to do.

"All done," Sam said with a smile. He held out a cup of coffee to Kelly.

She didn't take it. "Did you get Abby a puppy?"

Confusion swept across Sam's face. "What? No. We talked about it. We agreed now was not the time."

She put her hands on her hips, not buying his story. The present *had* moved. "Well, one of the presents is moving. If it's not a puppy, what is it?"

Sam laughed. "It's probably just one of the toys we bought her. I guess we should have taken the batteries out." He held the cup out to her again.

She took it and mulled over his explanation while she drank. Coffee always cleared her head. "I guess it could be," she finally agreed.

"Come on!" Abby called. "I want to open presents!"

They both heard the sound of paper ripping and shook their heads as they hurried back to their daughter. Abby was sitting on the floor with a pile of snowmen wrapping paper beside her and a plain brown box in front of her.

The box wiggled and Abby giggled.

"Get it open," Kelly said. "Let's see what's making that box dance." She was just as curious as her daughter was.

Sam grabbed the camera and moved in close to get a good picture of Abby's surprised face. Grinning from ear to ear, Abby shredded the rest of the paper off the box and opened it. Her face paled as she stared into the box. Instead of delighted cheers of joy, as Kelly and Sam expected from their daughter, Abby screamed, shoved the box away from her, and ran to Kelly with tears streaming down her face.

"Shhh!" Kelly hushed her little girl as she eyed Sam suspiciously. She might not have remembered all the toys they'd bought Abby—some were wrapped months in advance—but she knew there was nothing that would make Abby cry.

When Abby had shoved the box, it had tipped over and Sam bent down to pick it up. He no more got a grip on the top edge of the box when he jumped back in surprise. "What the hell?"

"What is it?" Kelly asked.

"It seems someone made a mistake with our packages," Sam laughed and pulled a severed head out of the box by its blonde, blood-crusted hair. "Someone was going to play one hell of a prank this Christmas."

Kelly bent down to get a closer look at the box. It had a UPS tag on it with their address. They'd ordered some of Abby's gifts online, but neither of them had bothered to open the boxes before wrapping them. When she read the store's name, Kelly hurried to the phone. She was going to call and complain about this. Someone had made a huge mistake, and Christmas or not, they were going to pay for it. Her daughter was now without a present and they had a grotesque severed head in their living room.

"Who are you calling?" Sam asked.

"The store that package came from. I want this replaced… today."

He shook his head. "It's Christmas. They're not open."

Kelly ignored him and looked the number up anyway, then moved to the kitchen for more privacy. She didn't want Abby to over-hear her because Kelly was positive she wasn't going to worry about her words if she got someone on the line.

The phone rang twice before going to an automated voicemail that irritated her. Couldn't anyone answer their own phone anymore? She pressed one for English, two for customer service, five for the toy department, and three for problems with orders before she was told they were closed until the following business day.

"Damn it!" She slammed the phone down on the counter and pressed her face in her hands. She was angry with herself for not checking the box before wrapping it.

"Hey, Kelly, can you come out here?" Sam called.

She sighed, forced a smile on her face, and joined her family. In the living room, Abby was sobbing again as she stood on the couch, while Sam stared at an arm dragging itself across the carpet with its fingers. The look in his eyes was amusement, but Kelly was disgusted. Whoever did this was going to pay, she decided. She would have their job if it was the last thing she did.

"It's fascinating," Sam said. "It looks like there's a whole body in these boxes. I wonder where the remote is." He glanced down at the box the arm had crawled out of.

Fascinating wasn't the word Kelly would have chose. Disgusting or grotesque seemed to fit the situation much better. "Can you get those things out of here? Put them in the garage or something." She couldn't stand to look at them for another minute. Plus, she wanted to get back to Christmas with her little girl, who was still crying on the couch.

"Let's just stack them in the corner for now," he said.

Kelly handed Abby a present. "Why don't you open this one while Daddy and I get those other presents out of the way."

Abby pulled away, shaking her head. "I don't want to."

Sitting next to her, Kelly said, "I promise this is a good one," and smiled reassuringly.

Nervously, Abby took the package. "Nothing gross in there, right?" she asked.

"Nope."

Abby grinned and tore into the present while Kelly helped Sam stack the boxes in the corner. By the time they were done, Abby was already grabbing another present. "Can I open more?" she asked, putting her new building blocks next to her on the floor.

"If you don't open them, I will," Sam teased.

Now this is how their morning should have started out, Kelly thought as she sat on the couch next to Sam.

Abby dug into the rest of the presents under the tree, only briefly pausing to inspect the toy she'd just opened before diving into the next one. If present opening was an Olympic event, Kelly was sure Abby would have won. The six-year-old managed to open twenty-eight presents in record time. The living room was littered with scraps of wrapping paper from Abby tossing pieces over her shoulder as she yanked them off the packages.

"This baby eats and drinks," Sam was explaining to Abby while Kelly started picking up the mess.

"I love her!" Abby said, squeezing the baby in her arms.

Paying more attention to her baby girl than the paper she was picking up, Kelly didn't notice the hand poking out from under the couch until she stepped on it. "Shit!" she gasped, her eyes shooting to the boxes her and Sam had stacked in the corner. They had tipped over, and body parts were spilling out onto the floor.

"Okay, I want those things out of here right now," Kelly demanded. She didn't care if they were expensive or not. She kicked the hand to emphasis her dislike for it.

A fierce snarl, reminding her of a rabid dog, erupted from behind the couch. Sam and Kelly jumped; Abby screamed.

Sam pulled the couch out of the way to expose the severed head with its teeth bared. "That's strange," Sam muttered. "I guess we'll have to find the batteries."

"Oh, no! I want all those pieces outside in the garbage." Batteries or not, the dismantled corpse was too gross for her to allow in her house anymore. She didn't care what the store said. She wouldn't pay for it either. After all, it wasn't her mistake.

Sam bent down to grab the head by the hair like before when he'd taken it out of the box. This time, the head snapped its teeth at him, catching the tip of Sam's finger. "Damn it!" The head had drawn blood.

"Okay, this is ridiculous. I want that thing in the garbage." Kelly stalked over, set an empty box on its side, and kicked the head into it.

Another snarl escaped the severed head's lips and a hand shot out from under wrapping paper and grabbed Kelly's ankle. The shock of its cold, slimy touch made her flinch back, but the fingers around her ankle held tight.

"Get this thing off of me!" she shouted at Sam.

Sam pulled the fingers away one at a time. When he got to the pinky finger, it made a sickening snapping sound and broke off.

The head snarled again. Kelly finished shaking the hand off the rest of the way and kicked it away from her.

"Wow." Sam was inspecting the finger in his hand. "There are no wires or chips or anything. It looks real!"

Rolling her eyes, Kelly sighed. Leave it to her husband to be excited about a Halloween toy on Christmas. "Can you please get it out of here?" She jerked her head toward Abby who was crying again.

The smile on Sam's face faded when he watched the tears stream down his daughter's face. "Okay, I'm getting them out of here, Abby. You won't have to see them ever again," he promised.

"Thank you," Kelly said, relieved he was actually taking the things out of her house. She turned to Abby. "Let's get you some breakfast, hon. You'll need your energy if you want to play with all those toys later."

While Sam scooped up the first box in his arms, Kelly pulled Abby into hers. "What would you like for breakfast," she asked Abby.

"Ice cream," Abby said.

Kelly laughed. "Ice cream isn't breakfast. How 'bout some cereal with marshmallows?"

"Yes!" Abby shouted.

They went into the kitchen, and after setting Abby down on a chair at the table, Kelly reached for the cereal in the cabinet. She no more had it in her hand when Sam called out to her.

"Kelly, can you come here for a sec?"

"Just a minute!" she called back as she filled Abby's favorite bowl with cereal and milk. "I'll be right back, dear."

Abby nodded as she shoved a large spoonful of cereal into her mouth, pieces sticking to her lips.

Kelly patted her on the head and hurried to Sam in the living room. He was standing at the bay window, peeking out when she reached him.

"You have to see this," he said, waving her over.

"Why are the boxes still in here?" She pointed at the stack of boxes in the corner and the one he'd been carrying when she and Abby had gone into the kitchen by the front door.

He pointed out the window. "Something strange is going on."

Confused, Kelly pulled the curtain back and looked out at their neighborhood. It was in total chaos. Kelly couldn't believe what she was seeing. Old Mr. Vanhorn was running from his home, Mrs. Vanhorn chasing him with blood oozing from her mouth. The high school boy, Toby, from down the street, was chasing his dog. He growled louder than the dog did. Abby's friend, Molly, from next door, was running from her own mother, who then caught Molly by her hair and started chewing on her face.

Shuddering, Kelly let go of the curtain and it closed. She couldn't stand to watch anymore. "What the hell is going on out there? Should we call the cops?"

Sam shrugged. "I honestly have no idea." From his expression, Kelly could tell he was just as confused by what they'd seen as she was.

Nothing made sense. This was the worst Christmas ever. Not only had they gotten the wrong gifts for their daughter, but the entire neighborhood was acting crazy. Had everyone mixed up the holidays this year? It was Christmas, not Halloween.

"Why don't you start making sure all the doors and windows are locked and I'll call the police and see if they know what's going on," Kelly suggested, secretly hoping this was all some sort of prank put together by the neighborhood society.

Sam nodded and started by checking the bay window they'd been looking out.

Because the phone was in the kitchen, Kelly hurried in, told Abby she'd be right back, and called 9-1-1.

Thankfully, the police hadn't taken a day off and didn't have an annoying automated answering service. A woman answered right away.

Kelly waited through the woman's greeting of: "9-1-1, what is the nature of your emergency?" then dove into the situation she saw outside her window.

"Can you tell me if someone else has reported anything strange on Vine Street?" Kelly asked.

"Yes, ma'am. Officers are on their way. Actually, they should be there now. Can you look out your window and tell me if you see them?"

Kelly rushed to the window and glanced out. She didn't see any sign of the police, but more people were running around, cluttering the street. "No, I don't see them," she finally answered.

"Well, ma'am, they should be there any minute. Hold tight and I'll make sure they come and speak with you once they get the situation under control. But please stay in your home. Don't go outside until the officers say it's safe."

"Oh, I have no intentions of going outside, but thank you," Kelly said. Just knowing the police were coming was a huge relief.

After telling Kelly to have a nice day, the woman hung up and Kelly tossed the phone on the couch.

"What did they say?" Sam's voice behind her made her jump. "Sorry," he apologized.

"The police are on their way," she said. "They should be here any minute."

"Mommy!" Abby called from the kitchen. "Mommy! Mommy! Mommy!" Panic rose in her voice each time she shouted.

Kelly and Sam dashed for the kitchen.

Abby was hiding under the table with her head in her lap.

"What's wrong, sweetie?" Sam asked, crawling under after her.

Abby flung her arms around her dad and sobbed. "Molly was at the window. I thought she was hurt because she had blood on her face, but she growled at me like a doggy."

The image of Molly's mother biting her daughter's face flooded Kelly's mind. What in the hell was going on? Where was the police?

"Awe, Abby, don't you worry about it. Molly's just having a bad day like we are," Sam said, trying to get out from under the table with Abby clinging to him. He fumbled a little before he got to his feet.

Kelly eyed him. He was a good-sized man with muscles that rippled up and down his arms. She'd never seen him struggle under Abby's weight before. She was only forty-six pounds. But the closer she examined him, she saw that he was pale and sweaty. "Are you all right?" she asked him. Wouldn't it be just great if he got sick now? That would be the icing on their horrific Christmas Day.

"I'm fine. I'm just hot."

Although she was unconvinced, being over-heated was the only thing wrong with him, so Kelly let it go. "Let's check for the police. They should be here by now." She reached out to take Abby from Sam, but he shook his head and sauntered toward the living room as though trying to convince her he was fine.

Kelly followed.

"Looks like the cops finally made it," Sam said at the bay window, pointing out the squad car two houses down.

The car was empty, and the officers were nowhere in sight. The neighborhood was still in chaos like it had been the first time they'd looked out the window.

"Wonder where they are?" Kelly muttered, scanning the people running around.

Sam shrugged. "Must be in someone's house."

"There's Molly!" Abby shouted, pointing at her friend who was running down the street.

They all watched Molly race down the road. Kelly was trying to figure out where she was going when the girl didn't even pause at her house. Instead, she shifted until she was running straight at Kelly's house.

"What's she doing?" Kelly muttered as Molly grew closer and closer with no sign of slowing. Kelly had the urge to back up, but she couldn't take her eyes off the girl.

"Hi, Molly!" Abby shouted and waved.

Molly snarled and lunged at the window. She smacked head first into the glass, making Sam and Kelly jump back. The impact didn't even seem to bother the girl. She hopped back to her feet and continued to run into the window over and over again. Flesh and blood splattered the glass.

"Make her stop!" Abby cried and turned her head away.

Letting the curtain close, Kelly turned to Sam. "Did you check that every window is locked?"

"Yes, but I don't know how long that's going to hold if someone bigger smashes into the window, its only glass after all."

Molly smacked into the window again and the glass shuddered, emphasizing Sam's statement.

"We should call the police back and find out what's going on?" Kelly said, turning to get the phone off the couch where she's tossed it, only the couch was empty. The phone must have bounced off it, she thought and began searching the floor.

When she got to her hands and knees, she heard the annoying beep, beep, beep that meant the phone was off the hook somewhere. Reaching her hand under the couch, her fingertips brushed up against something cold and damp. She stretched farther to grab it.

The cold thing grabbed her back and held on tight.

"Sam!" she shouted, trying to yank her arm back, but each time she pulled, whatever had her pulled back. "Sam, help me!"

The couch slid, pushing Kelly back with it.

At first, she thought Sam had come to her rescue. That was before whatever had her let go, sending her flying backwards. On her back at Sam's feet, she watched as the severed head—now attached to a torso, arms and legs attached to that—lunged from behind the couch at them, knocking Sam and Abby to the ground.

Grabbing the first thing she could find, Kelly smashed her crystal candlestick holder into the back of its head while Sam punched it in the face.

"Get my gun!" Sam shouted when the thing didn't show any sign of stopping its attack.

Scooping Abby into her arms, Kelly dashed up the stairs. "Go to your room and shut the door until I come back for you," she told Abby, putting her down in front of her bedroom door. She waited for Abby to click the lock in place before going to her own bedroom to get the gun for Sam.

With shaky hands, Kelly loaded the small revolver Sam had stashed on the top shelf of their closet. The only time they'd ever used the gun was when they'd taken a training course so they could get the permit to own it. That had been two years ago.

She'd only managed to get three bullets in the revolver before she heard a window shatter downstairs. "Molly," she muttered.

In the mix of all the other chaos, she'd forgotten about her daughter's friend slamming into the window. She must have finally broken through.

Kelly's heart thundered in her chest as she raced down the stairs to help her husband. Her hands were so sweaty, and trembling so violently, that she feared the gun might slip right out of them.

When she reached the bottom of the stairs, she saw that Sam was pinned to the floor with four bloody people on top of him.

All eyes turned to her, leaving Sam bleeding on the floor. Kelly couldn't take her eyes off her husband. He was bleeding from large holes in his flesh where the people had torn the skin right off the bone.

Tears filled her eyes.

"Shoot!" Sam shouted.

The people were covered in gore, pieces of their faces and arms torn out. They looked more like monsters than her neighbors. One of them snarled and shifted closer to her.

Still shaking, Kelly aimed at the biggest one and fired, hitting it in the neck. The monster fell but it was still moving. Kelly moved on to the next two. Her aim was much better with them. The bullets shot right through their foreheads, splattering brains all over the Christmas tree and the wall behind them.

Kelly winced, not believing what she'd just done.

"Watch out!" Sam shouted as Molly leaped at Kelly.

As with the window, no matter how many times Kelly tossed the girl to the floor, she kept getting back up and diving at Kelly again.

"Kill her!" Sam demanded.

"I can't." Even if she had bullets left, killing a kid was not an option. She wouldn't do it. She couldn't do it. Kelly didn't care if the little girl had turned into some kind of monster or not, she wouldn't hurt her.

A window from the kitchen shattered as Kelly continued to fight with Molly.

"Here, take this." Sam tossed her the poker for the fireplace.

Two more monsters sauntered through the kitchen doorway. One turned toward the stairs, the other toward Sam.

With her heart in her throat, tears in her eyes, and a sickness in her stomach and mind, Kelly picked up the poker and jabbed it into Molly's left eye, five inches of metal sliding into the eye socket. The little girl's limp body thumped loudly to the floor, but Kelly didn't have time to fall apart like she wanted to. Sam and Abby were still in danger.

Unlike with Molly, Kelly didn't hesitate before plunging the poker into the back of the head of the monster attacking Sam. The thing dropped onto Sam.

Sam groaned and shoved it off.

With Kelly's help, Sam managed to get to his feet and the two of them ran up the stairs to help their daughter. Abby's cries echoed through the hallway as one of the creatures beat on the bedroom door in an effort to get at her.

More windows shattered downstairs.

Kelly stuck the thing threatening her little girl five times. The last one skewered its eye when it turned around and she plucked the orb right from its skull.

"Abby!" Kelly shouted. "It's safe to open the door now."

"Safe," Sam repeated.

Kelly shrugged. Okay, safe might not have been the right word, but she didn't want to upset Abby anymore than she already was.

"No." Sam shook his head. "The vault in the basement. We can use it like a panic room and wait this out."

The previous owners had built a walk-in vault in the basement that took up almost half of their cellar. Kelly never could understand why anyone would need a vault in their house. For years, Kelly had wanted it removed, but the cost wasn't in their budget. Now she was thankful that they hadn't been able to afford to have it removed.

"Abby, we need to get to the basement. Can you open the door?" Kelly was excited about the new plan. They'd wait out whatever was going on safely in the basement together, and she wouldn't have to kill anyone else. But she had to get Abby to open the door first.

"Mommy? Daddy? Is that really you?" Abby sobbed through the door.

"Yes, sweetie, it's us," Sam answered. "Can you open the door, please?"

The steps creaked behind them.

"Come on, Abby. We have to go now!" Kelly's voice was louder and harsher than she wanted it to be, but she was freaking out. More of those things were getting into the house. If they waited for much longer, they'd never survive. "Get more bullets," Kelly told Sam as she braced herself for what was coming up the stairs.

Abby slowly opened her bedroom door. Once she caught sight of Kelly, she threw herself into her mother's arms.

"Stay behind me," Kelly told her after giving Abby a huge hug.

The stairs creaked again. This time, a growl floated up the stairs with it. Sam was back with the gun fully-loaded before the creature reached the top of the stairs. He positioned himself between Kelly, Abby, and the monster with his finger on the trigger.

The instant the thing showed its ugly face, Sam put a hole in it.

"Let's go!" Sam said, leading the way, kicking the dead body down the stairs as they went. "Stay close and move fast."

Kelly shifted Abby so she clung around her neck in front of her instead of on her back, and squeezed as close to Sam as she could to keep Abby protected between them. "Should we take anything with us?" Kelly didn't like the idea of stopping, but they had no idea how long they'd be locked in the vault. If nothing else, they'd need food and water.

As though reading her mind, Sam said, "We'll stop in the kitchen on the way down to the basement for some food and water." His voice was no more than a whisper as he crept along with his eyes darting in every direction. He was on full alert.

With everything else running through her head, Kelly completely forgot about Molly's body on the living room floor until Abby screamed, "Molly! Mom you have to help her!"

Kelly didn't have the heart to tell Abby that Molly was beyond help.

Sam answered instead. "She's not Molly anymore, sweetie. That's not your friend."

Abby sobbed against Kelly. "It's okay, Abby. Everything's going to be fine." Kelly had to swallow past the lump in her throat to stop herself from breaking down. She had to stay strong for Abby.

Sam held up a hand for them to wait while he checked the kitchen. To Kelly, it seemed like it took him hours to sneak around the corner and wave her forward, though only seconds passed. She just wanted to get the supplies and get to the basement.

"We have to move fast," Sam said again. "Don't waste time rummaging through the cabinets. Grab the first things your hands touch."

Setting Abby on the floor, Kelly started filling her hands up with bottled water while Sam grabbed potato chips, a bag of apples, and a box of cookies. He passed the apples to Abby so he could keep one hand free to hold the gun.

Kelly paused and stared at the open basement door. "Someone's down there," she told Sam. She knew the door hadn't been open when she'd fed Abby her breakfast. They never kept it open for fear Abby might fall down the stairs.

Sam slid in front of Kelly and flipped the light switch. Nothing happened. The bulb must have blown and they'd never gotten around to replacing it. Nobody went down there very often. The vault took up too much room and the basement was poorly lit. Kelly made Sam turn the first floor bedroom—which was more like a closet—into a laundry room so she didn't have to go down there. Now, with the real possibility of one of the monsters, they were going down into the dark.

She shuddered. "Be careful, Sam" she finally muttered, then told Abby, "Hold on to me, hon." Abby gripped her shirt with her free hand and stayed right at Kelly's side as they all descended the creaky basement stairs.

Vicious growls from the darkness confirmed their fear. There was something in the basement and they couldn't see it.

"When I give the signal, I want you two to run as fast as you can to the vault," Sam whispered, his voice shaking.

Kelly tapped Sam's shoulder and whispered, "Hang on a second." Then she bent down. "Abby, I need you to get on my back and hang on as tight as you can." Fumbling with the bottles of water, Kelly took the bag of apples while Abby did as she was told and got on Kelly's back.

"Don't let go," Kelly said.

"Ready?" Sam asked.

A steady stream of growls erupted from the basement. They were too loud. Sam would never hear if Kelly answered him while the noise continued. So, instead of talking, Kelly pushed him forward to let him know she was ready to run when he gave the signal.

Just like a race, Sam fired the gun to get them going. They rushed down the stairs, Kelly heading for the vault while Sam shifted from side to side, ready to shoot at the first thing that moved.

Kelly moved as quickly as she could with the load she was carrying. Thankfully, the vault wasn't far from the bottom of the stairs. She could feel Abby's grip slipping from around her neck. "Hang on, baby," Kelly told her.

Abby nearly strangled her to keep from slipping.

"Keep going, I'm right behind you!" Sam yelled.

Kelly didn't risk a glance behind her. She could see the shadow of the vault door. It was open and inside was pitch black. No way could she make out anything inside that blackness. "Sam, you may want to check the vault before we go in." He had the gun after all.

"The tool bench to your right has a flashlight," he told her.

One by one, Kelly lobbed the water bottles into the vault, hoping it wouldn't scare something out at her, but she had to free up her hands to feel for the flashlight. God, she wished she could see more than shadows.

After tossing the bag of apples in, she put Abby on the floor, then grabbed hold of her with one hand and felt her way to the tool bench with the other.

More snarls erupted from all around them, making Kelly jump and Abby squeal.

"Hurry up!" Sam shouted and fired the gun. "I can see movement everywhere."

Kelly's trembling hand roamed over the bench, knocking things to the floor. "I can't find it. Are you sure it's down here?"

"I put it there last week when I came down to fix the blown fuse," he told her and fired the gun again.

Something clattered to the floor behind her, making the hair on her head stand on end. "Was that you?" God, she hoped it was Sam. Otherwise, her baby girl was closest to the danger. She didn't like that.

"No," Sam said. "You need to hurry." His voice was demanding, almost an order. Kelly had never heard him talk to her like that. He must really be scared, or he was seeing something she couldn't. Either way, she forced herself to move faster.

"Got it!" she shouted upon finally finding the flashlight. Without thinking, she flipped it on and lit the darkness around them—bad idea.

The basement was full of the monsters that had been chasing their neighbors around and had attacked Sam. They were everywhere she looked. Some crouched in the corners, others just standing and staring at them, all with bloody wounds and scowls on their faces.

Abby's screams kept up with the growling going on. The sound was almost painful to Kelly's ears.

"Run!" Sam shouted, firing the last of his bullets at the creatures that were now moving forward with violent expressions on their faces. There was no time to reload.

Kelly snatched Abby off the floor and aimed her flashlight into the vault. "It's clear!" she yelled. "Hurry!"

They both ran to the vault at the same time, fighting the grabbing hands the entire time The vault wasn't far, but far enough for them all to get clawed and snapped at.

Sam paused before closing the door.

"What are you doing? Shut it!" Kelly told him. She couldn't believe he was hesitating.

"We have to lock it so they can't get in, but we won't be able to get out either until someone comes for us," Sam said.

Hands pulled at the door. "You have to shut it. We'll get back out when someone comes," Kelly said. She couldn't believe he wouldn't close the door. Being locked in wasn't the worst thing in the world, but being eaten by one of those monsters, or having something happen to Abby was.

"All right," Sam agreed. He spun the enormous combination dial on the outside of the door. "Help me close this."

Snarls and growls echoed off the inside of the vault as the monsters wrapped their fingers around the thick steel door and pulled with all their might.

"Pull!" Kelly shouted, leaning backwards, putting all her weight into the effort to close the door.

The monsters were stronger. Sam and Kelly's feet slid across the floor as they tried to pull the vault door shut.

"This isn't working!" Sam shouted. The door opened farther and farther every second. If they couldn't close it soon, the creatures would get it completely open and Kelly, Sam and Abby would be trapped with nowhere to go.

"We have to get their hands off the door." Hanging on with one hand, Kelly pried fingers off one at a time. "Pull!" she shouted when she got a hand free.

The door inched closed a little more, so Kelly moved on to the next hand and Sam helped her. Together they pried fingers, pulled, and kicked at feet. Slowly and painfully, they finally got the door to close with a soft hiss.

Exhausted, Kelly and Sam collapsed to the floor, but the banging continued, though it was now muted. The monsters were still trying to get at them.

"Can they get in?" Abby asked.

Kelly searched for the flashlight and flicked it on. "No, Abby, they can't get in."

"How will someone get in to help us then?" she asked, tears in her eyes.

"We'll know if someone's out there to help us." It was Sam who answered. Kelly turned the light on him.

"Oh, God, Sam!" She hurried to his side, shining the light all over him. His clothes, what was left of them, were saturated with blood and wounds covered every inch of his open skin.

"I'm fine," he said. "Don't worry about me." He pulled more bullets out of his pocket and reloaded the revolver before stuffing it back in his pocket.

Ignoring him, Kelly continued to scrutinize his wounds, skin-color, and over all well-being. He didn't seem fine to her. "You're hurt bad," she muttered. "You need a doctor. We can't stay in here." Closing the door no longer seemed like such a good idea. A better plan would have been to get in their car and drive to the hospital and away from the house.

"We can't go back out there," Sam whispered so Abby wouldn't hear. "I'll be fine. Someone will come soon and help us." He smiled at Abby reassuringly.

"Can't we call the police?" Abby asked. "They'll come get us and help Daddy."

Sure, Kelly thought, if they would have remembered to bring the phone with them they could have called for help again. The vault was looking worse and worse by the minute. What good did it do to protect themselves from the creatures in their house if Sam died anyway? "Sorry, sweetie, we didn't bring the phone and we can't get out there to get it."

Abby sobbed. "Is Daddy going to die?"

"Shhh," Sam hushed her. "I'm not going to die. I'm fine." He scooted closer to her. "Why don't you rest. When you wake up, someone will be here to help us."

Kelly shot him a disapproving look. "*Maybe* someone will be here by then. It might take longer than that." She didn't want to give her daughter false hope. It could be days before anyone made it through the things roaming the streets to find survivors.

Abby yawned. "I can't sleep with them banging."

"They'll stop once they figure out they can't get in," Kelly said. "Try to ignore it and sleep." Although she wouldn't sleep herself, she knew her daughter needed a few hours of peace.

Reluctantly, Abby laid down in the corner and closed her eyes. Kelly waited until she was sure Abby was sleeping before she started talking with Sam about what to do next.

"We need a new plan in case nobody comes," she said.

"There's nothing we can do. We're trapped in here."

"Isn't there a way to pick the lock or something?" She knew nothing about safes, vaults, or picking locks, but she thought there had to be a way to open anything if you tried hard enough.

Sam coughed. "I need to rest. I don't feel very well. You should rest too and we can talk about this later." He shifted so he had more room to stretch out without disturbing Abby.

"No!" Kelly said sternly. "Abby can't hear us talk about this. We need to figure it out now." She felt bad for pushing Sam when he was injured, but she wouldn't allow Abby to know how serious the situation was after they'd reassured her everything was going to be okay and that they were safe.

Sam coughed again. This time, he doubled over as he tried to catch his breath. When he finally sat back up, she saw red around his lips.

"You're bleeding!" she shouted, more concerned than before. He was coughing up blood. He was hurt worse than she thought.

He wiped it off. "I just need to sleep, Kelly. I'm tired. Can we talk about all of this later?" He sounded exhausted. His words were starting to slur. "We have time to figure this out."

"Okay, you rest," she said. She could come up with something while Sam and Abby slept.

"Thank you," he whispered and slipped quickly into a snore.

He must be tired, she thought, letting her head fall back against the wall. Though they'd gotten up extra early, Kelly knew she wouldn't be sleeping. She had to come up with a way to save her family. Sleep wasn't an option when Sam wouldn't last long with internal bleeding. Getting in the vault and locking it had been the wrong move. Now they were stuck, and she didn't know if anyone was coming to help them. Sure, she'd called the police and saw the squad car, but the police were probably dead like Molly was.

Kelly sighed and moved to the door. She had to figure out how to open the vault from the inside. If there wasn't a way, then she had to accept the fact that they were all going to die in the vault. She wouldn't do that. Not yet.

With the flashlight held between her teeth, she examined all the gears and bolts and other metal items she didn't know the names of. "Damn it," she muttered. Well, at least the panel covering everything wasn't on and hadn't been for as long as she knew of. But everything looked like it needed some kind of tool or another to take it off. Why couldn't there just be a button to push? She could handle that.

She pulled and pushed on everything that moved, but nothing opened the door or sounded like she was moving the dial. She'd been working for a long time when Sam groaned behind her.

Kelly shone the light on him. He looked terrible. His face was white, beads of sweat rolled down his face, and he had dark purplish bruises under his eyes. "Sam, are you all right?"

He groaned but didn't talk.

"Sam, what's wrong?" She moved closer to him.

His eyes opened, his lips curled back over his teeth, and he snarled at her.

"Mom, what's wrong with Daddy?" Abby asked in a sleepy voice.

Before Kelly could answer, Sam leaped to his feet and lunged for Abby.

Abby screamed, as the monsters banged harder on the door, and Kelly grabbed Sam by his arm and yanked him off Abby. The gun clattered to the cement floor, as did the flashlight.

"Sam, what's wrong with you?" Kelly shouted at her husband, but he snarled and shoved her away from him. Sam was much stronger. Kelly flew back and knocked her head on the wall. Yellow dots flashed in her eyes and her head spun.

"Mommy?" Abby sobbed.

Kelly struggled to find the flashlight. "Abby, honey, come to me."

Sam snarled and lunged again, still going after Abby instead of her.

"Mommy!" Abby screamed as she tried to fight Sam off.

With tears in her eyes, Kelly knew what she had to do. Her hands shook as she reached for the gun, picked it up, and aimed it at her husband—only it wasn't her husband anymore before her. Sam had turned into one of the monsters they'd been fighting all day.

"Mommy, help!" Abby yelled, still thrashing under Sam.

Kelly reached out and pushed Sam to the floor. Her fear for her daughter made her strong enough to throw him without any problem. When he hit the floor, Kelly didn't hesitate. She fired the gun and Sam went limp.

Abby screamed without pause. "Daddy! Daddy! Mommy, what did you do?"

"Shhh," Kelly hushed her. "It wasn't Daddy anymore. He was one of those things."

"How?" Abby asked through sniffles, and Kelly thought that was a good question. She had no idea how it had happened.

"I don't know, but we need to worry about you now. Are you hurt?"

Blood ran down Abby's arm. "Daddy bit me." She held out her arm for Kelly to inspect it. "Will I be a monster now?"

"No," Kelly said quickly. "You won't be a like those things. You're fine." Tears welled in her eyes as she frantically wiped the blood off Abby's arm. Even considering Abby turning into one of those monsters broke her heart. They had to get out of the vault now. Abby needed help.

"Can we leave here?" Abby asked. "I don't like this place anymore." Her eyes were on Sam's bloody body.

Kelly flicked the flashlight off. "We'll get out soon, hon. I promise. Try to stay quiet while I go work on the lock some more."

"Daddy could have opened it," Abby said, wiping tears from her face.

Stroking her hair, Kelly said, "I know, baby." Though Kelly knew she should go to the lock and work harder, work on it until she got it open, she couldn't bring herself to move from her daughter's side. Not to mention, she'd have to sit by Sam's lifeless body. She just wasn't up for that yet. In truth, she wished this was all a horrible nightmare and that she would wake up to Abby bouncing on her bed, waking her up to open her presents like normal.

Kelly closed her eyes and let her head fall back against the wall. If only the horrible banging would stop, she might have been able to imagine she was somewhere else. Somewhere safe with her family, sipping hot chocolate, eating cookies, and playing with all the new toys Abby had gotten. As it was, the constant pounding kept her right there in the vault with her dead husband, her crying daughter, and the memories of all the horrors of the day. She needed a minute to let loose, to breakdown. Just sixty seconds of uncontrollable crying, whining, and rage. That's all she'd need to get her sanity back. After that, she could get back to work with a clear head and come up with a plan.

Since breaking down would upset Abby, she decided the best she could do was take her anger out on the lock. If she had to, she'd claw her way out. "Don't you worry, hon, Mommy is going to get us out of here," she told Abby. Thanks to the anger bubbling inside her, she actually thought she might be able to do it.

Abby grabbed her arm. "Don't leave me," she sniffled.

"I'm not leaving. I'm right here. You can talk to me the whole time."

"But I can't see you, it's dark," Abby said, and Kelly thought that was a good thing. If she could see Kelly, she'd be able to see Sam. Kelly didn't want her little girl to sit and stare at her father's dead body.

"How about if we talk while I work," Kelly suggested. "Tell me all the wonderful things you want to do when we get out of here."

Abby sniffled, but said, "I want to talk to Molly's Mommy and Daddy."

"That's a good idea. What else?" She didn't bother telling her Molly's parents were probably dead. The girl needed some hope.

"I want to see Granny and Papa. Do you think they're locked somewhere safe like us?"

"I'm positive they're safe. Papa is a very smart man. He'd make sure Granny and him were tucked away some place nice and safe."

"Good," Abby said, her voice perking up a bit. "Then we can stay with them. Our house is a mess."

Kelly couldn't help the laugh that escaped her lips. Only her little girl would think of the mess in their house instead of the invasion of monsters in it. "You're right. Those darn things made a huge mess. Granny and Papa would never allow us to stay in a messy house."

"Mommy, my tummy hurts," Abby said.

"You're probably hungry, honey. Why don't you snack on some chips?" Kelly flashed the light beam at the bag of chips so Abby could find them.

The bag crinkled as Abby snatched it off the floor and squeezed it until the top popped. That was something Sam taught her. Kelly hated it. The bag didn't always open at the top, which left a mess for her to clean up. But she smiled at her daughter and went back to working on the lock without a word, only the beam of the flashlight to see by. She tried not to think about the batteries dying and plunging her and Abby in darkness.

Her fingers pushed, pulled, and turned everything that would move again. There had to be a combination to the lock, she thought, and started over, turning, pushing, and pulling in a different direction. Each time she hit a dead end, she tried a different combination.

"Is it working?" Abby asked through a mouthful of chips.

"Not yet, but I'm close," Kelly lied. She knew she wasn't any closer to figuring it out now than the first time she'd tried. This was why she needed Sam's help. But he was dead and she was alone to figure it out. Not very easy when her anger fizzled and she no longer wanted to claw her way free, or believed she could.

The bag of chips crunched as Abby dug her hand in again. "I'm thirsty."

Kelly stopped in the middle of a combination and waved the light around until she found a bottle of water. "Right there, hon." She pointed at the corner a few feet away from Abby, who leaned over to get it. When she did, she hacked so violently that blood shot from her mouth and sprayed the wall and floor in front of her.

"Abby!" Kelly shouted, rushing to her daughter's side. She placed the back of her hand on Abby's forehead. "Oh my God, you're burning up." Her skin felt like a damp heating pad.

"My tummy hurts and I'm thirsty," Abby complained.

Kelly reached for the bottle of water, wiping the drops of blood off it with her shirt. She opened it and held it to Abby's mouth. She barely sipped when she coughed it back out along with another puddle of blood.

"Okay, we're getting out of here now," Kelly said. "I want you to stay right here and cover your head. I'm going to try and shoot the lock." She knew it was crazy. Hell, she didn't even know what part exactly was the lock, but she had to try something. Abby couldn't die in here.

She quickly opened the chamber on the revolver. Only three bullets were left. She had to make them count.

Taking aim with one hand and holding the flashlight with the other, she fired.

The bullet ricocheted off the vault door, making a spark, and clinking off something nearby. "Abby, are you all right?" She quickly turned the light on her daughter and gasped, the gun falling to the floor from a limp hand. Abby was slumped over with her head nearly in her lap. "Abby, talk to me." Kelly shook her, but she wouldn't wake or move.

Sprawling her out, Kelly quickly inspected her for blood from a wound before checking her breathing and pulse. She had none—no bullet wound either, but no pulse and no respiration. Abby was dead.

"No. No. No!" Kelly shouted, starting CPR. "You have to live," she told the small lifeless body as tears streamed down her face. "Live!" Kelly pressed on Abby's chest and blew air in her lungs until her arms went numb, but she wouldn't give up. Not even when her hands started to cramp and her breath came out in gasps would she stop trying.

The only thing that could force her to stop was the movement of her little girl under her hands. Kelly paused and watched her daughter's left arm twitch. "Abby?"

Abby's body convulsed for a second before going completely still again. Hands up and ready to start CPR again, Kelly nearly jumped when her daughter's eyes snapped open and she stared up at her with glossy eyes, reflecting the flashlight beam in her pale orbs.

"Abby!" Kelly yelled, relief washing through every inch of her body. She scooped Abby in her arms. "I was so worried about you." She pulled her away and started inspecting her again. "Tell me where it hurts, honey."

Abby groaned as Kelly pressed on the back of her head, but she didn't talk or cry. She just groaned like….just Sam had she realized. Slowly, she moved back to get a better look at her baby girl.

Deep purple circles shadowed Abby's glossy, lifeless eyes. Her face was completely colorless except the circles under her eyes. Kelly began to cry. Her little girl was gone. Kelly was staring at her, groaning, and moving, but she was dead. She was one of *them* now. As though Abby could read her mind, she bared her teeth and snarled. Blood still smeared her lips from the violent coughing fit.

Kelly scrambled away on her hands and feet in a crab walk till her back hit the vault door. "Abby, honey, I know you're scared, but I need you to listen to me." Her daughter had to still be in there. After all, it hadn't been that long since Sam had bitten her, if that was even the reason for her change. Kelly would reach her if it was the last thing she did. "Remember me? Mommy? I love you, Abby. You're going to be just fine, but I need you to lie down and rest for me."

Abby growled and stalked forward.

"Please, Abby. I can't hurt you. Please remember me," Kelly sobbed. Killing Molly was hard, but even considering doing it to Abby nearly crippled her.

Cocking her head to the side, Abby stared at her mother. Kelly thought she might actually be getting through to her. But then, just as Molly had thrown herself at the bay window over and over again, Abby threw herself the short distance at Kelly. Her teeth snapped as she tried to find a place to sink them.

Kelly fought her daughter, trying desperately not to hurt her, and finally pinned Abby's arms and legs to the floor and half sat on her. Staring her daughter in the eyes, Kelly said, "I love you, Abby. Please come back to me. Don't leave me like this. I'll get you help. We'll get out of here and go see Granny and Papa. We'll talk to Molly's parents." She knew it was hopeless, but she had to keep believing Abby would come back to her.

Abby snarled and continued to snap her teeth, whipping her head from side to side, trying to reach Kelly's arms that restrained her to the floor.

Body trembling, Kelly continued to reason with Abby, but her daughter's eyes were vacant. There was no reaching her. Kelly wouldn't let whatever evil spirit was inside take her daughter's body. She had to set it free so Abby could move on to be with Sam.

With trembling hands, she pushed Abby's hands together above her daughter's head so that she could pin them in one of hers while she found the revolver. A sick feeling rolled in her stomach as she searched for it. Somewhere deep inside her, Kelly hoped she'd never find it. She wished she wouldn't have to do what she was about to do once she found the gun, but most of all, she hoped she'd be able to do it quick and easily. With only two bullets left, she had to make sure she saved one for herself. She didn't want to live in a world without her husband and daughter, nor turn into a living dead creature.

Her fingertips finally grazed the cold, hard metal of the gun barrel, and she could no longer fight the sickness inside her for what she was about to do. Before she clamped her hand around it, she vomited violently on the floor. Abby took advantage of her momentary weakness and bucked, tossing Kelly off balance and onto her back.

Snarling, Abby leaped at her.

Kelly scrambled for the gun that had been within reach only seconds before. She found it a moment later and wrapped her fingers around the handle, one finger on the trigger.

Abby, moving as quickly as a cobra, taking a bite out of Kelly's neck and chewing on the warm flesh as blood squirted between her teeth.

"Abby!" Kelly shouted, tossing the little girl off her. "I'm so sorry," she muttered, and with tears rolling down her cheeks, she squeezed the trigger.

Abby's head snapped back from the impact, taking her body with it to the floor. Blood spilled out and pooled around her head, saturating her hair. Crawling, blinded by tears, Kelly reached for her little girl.

"I'm so sorry, Abby. Please forgive me. We'll be together soon, baby." She bent down, kissed her little girl on the forehead to the left of the small black hole, and laid her down next to Sam. She even placed one of Sam's arms around her baby girl so they could hold each other.

Then, without a second thought, Kelly stretched out next to Abby's lifeless body so she was lying down, held the gun to the side of her head, closed her eyes, and squeezed the trigger.

A YEAR WITHOUT A (ZOMBIE) SANTA CLAUS

ANTHONY GIANGREGORIO

"Vixen looks terrible," Santa Claus said as he stared at the small reindeer. He was wearing a red three-piece suit with a matching hat—he was in disguise. He hadn't wanted to leave the North Pole but when the elves Jingle and Jangle Bells had left to go to the cruel, real world with little Vixen, he had no choice. And looking at the small, sick reindeer, he knew his assumption was correct.

Vixen was lying inside a cage at the Southtown, USA Dog Pound.

"Is it the heat?" Jingle asked, his sidekick Jangle Bells—slightly taller but also slightly slower in intelligence—standing beside him with concern written all over his face. Both wore red outfits, and looked very out of place in the southern state that had had no snow in years.

"I suppose so," Santa said as he opened the cage door and picked up the small, shivering reindeer. He didn't notice the small bite mark on Vixen's right, rear leg. The bite had occurred shortly after Vixen had been captured by the dog catcher and taken to the pound. She had been in a cage with another dog and this dog had been diseased. It never should have happened, but the dog catcher wasn't the most caring man and he had wanted to go to lunch, so had simply tossed the little reindeer with socks on her head to cover her small ears and budding horns—so she looked like a dog…it was Jingle's idea—into the cage. Vixen had curled up in the corner but the dog had growled menacingly, and before Vixen could react, the dog had lunged and bit her on the leg. No doubt the dog would have probably killed Vixen if not for the dog catcher reconsidering his decision moments later and instead taking Vixen and putting her in her own cage.

But the damage was done; the bite had transferred the disease the dog had been carrying, whatever it was. Rabies, some kind of exotic disease, it was never known as no veterinarian examined the sick animal.

The dog had died an hour after biting Vixen and was carried to the back of the pound, where the incinerator was located. As the door had closed on the still carcass, and the flames began to lick out at the body, the dog's eyes had snapped open and it began to howl as the dead carcass began to reanimate.

But before so much as one howl could escape the fire pit, the flames consumed it and destroyed the abomination.

"Come on, girl, let's get you home," Santa said to Vixen as he cradled the small reindeer in his arms. Vixen's eyes were closed and her chest heaved slightly as she struggled to breathe. The socks had been removed from her head and the dog catcher was staring, amazed at the thought of a real live reindeer in his pound. He said as much but Santa only nodded. He wasn't here to get people to love Christmas, he was here to bring home his sick reindeer.

"You two boys are coming home, too," Santa said to Jingle and Jangle.

"But, Santa," Jangle said, "what about us finding out about the spirit of Christmas?"

"That doesn't matter any more, boys, we need to get Vixen home. Now, I called Maw and she's on her way to pick you both up, then we'll all fly home together."

"Mrs. C is coming here?" Jangle asked.

Santa nodded as he began to leave the pound, Jingle and Jangle right behind him. "That's right, and as soon as she arrives, off you go back home."

The dog catcher watched the curious group of people leaving: a rotund old man with a white beard, a reindeer, and two dwarves, all wearing red. Scratching his head, he got back to work.

Once outside, Santa and the elves walked around to the back of the building, where Blitzen was waiting for Santa. Blitzen had carried Santa from the North Pole and he didn't like the heat at all. He desperately wanted to go back home. When Blitzen saw Santa carrying Vixen, he began to shake his head, saddened that one of his kind was ill.

"Don't worry, Blitzen," Santa said. "Once we get home, we'll get Vixen better."

Blitzen only nodded in response, shifting a front hoof across the ground. They didn't have to wait long for Mrs. Claus, as Santa had called her before entering the dog pound after he'd met up with Jingle and Jangle.

She was in a small sleigh, only large enough for her ample frame and one adult passenger, or two elves, which were about the same width.

Dasher was attached to the sleigh and pulled Mrs. Claus through the air, and gently touched down before Santa and the elves. Santa walked over to his wife of many years and kissed her softly on the cheek.

"It's good to see you, Maw."

"And you as well, dear." Her eyes fell on Vixen and her face sank with worry. "Oh no, will you look at her. The poor thing, we need to get her home."

"I couldn't agree more," Santa said and turned to look down at Jingle and Jangle Bells. "You two get into the sleigh with Maw. We're leaving this place right now."

Jangle looked like he was going to protest but Jingle touched his shoulder and shook his head, telling his brother elf not to say a word. Jangle heeded the warning and simply climbed onto the sleigh, getting close to Mrs. Claus as Jingle also got in.

Santa nodded, glad his order was being followed without compromise, then he climbed onto Blitzen and the reindeer began to run before leaping into the air, flying high over the town. Mrs. Claus gave a light snicker and Dasher heeded her order and began to run, then leaped as well, taking the sleigh into the air. In seconds, the two flying objects quickly began to grow small in the sky. If any of the townspeople saw flying reindeers overhead, none admitted it later.

"Be careful now, boys," Mrs. Claus said. "We're flying into Snow Miser's territory."

"He almost got us last time we went through here with Vixen, Mrs. C," Jingle said as he peered over the side of the sleigh. He could see nothing but clouds, white and puffy.

"Ah, Maw," Santa said, flying beside her on Blitzen. "It's late in the day; I doubt he's keeping watch."

Suddenly, a blinding ray of freezing water and ice shot up out of the clouds and struck the back of the sleigh. It bucked terribly and Jangle would have fallen out if Jingle hadn't grabbed his brother elf and yanked him back on his seat.

"Oh dear, we're hit!" Mrs. Claus screamed as the sleigh began to go into a spin. Dasher let out a grunt and tried to keep the sleigh airborne but one of the struts had been hit and it was causing the sleigh to wobble like a toy top coming off the elf assembly line all warped. For the sleigh needed to be aerodynamic to help keep it aloft. Try as he might, he wasn't able to accomplish this task and he and the sleigh began to tailspin into the clouds.

"Maw!" Santa yelled and directed Blitzen to follow the falling sleigh. The clouds surrounded them all as Santa tried desperately to catch his falling wife, but she was moving too fast. He feared the worst when suddenly, a giant mound of snow appeared through the clouds, and the sleigh, Mrs. Claus and the two elves, along with Dasher, all landed heavily but safely in the powdery substance, disappearing from sight as they sank into the mound.

Santa steered Blitzen over the mound of snow and landed on its outer edge, Vixen still cradled in his arms. The small reindeer was sleeping. As for his wife and the elves, there was no sign.

"Maw! Maw! Where are you? Are you all right?" He wondered what he could do to help. Trying to dig her out seemed foolhardy and though he was Santa Claus, he wasn't a god. He might be immortal but his Christmas magic only went so far.

He was still pondering all this and thinking he should head back to the North Pole for help when the snow began to shake and shimmer near him. A second later, the two elves stepped out of the snow, followed by Dasher and then, finally, to Santa's relief, Mrs. Claus.

"Oh, thank the Maker," Santa said and went to his wife, hugging her. "I was so worried; I didn't know what to do."

"I'm fine, dear," Mrs. Claus said. "We all are. This pile is as soft as a cloud and as fluffy as new-fallen snow. We were able to simply walk through it, as if it was nothing more than a thick cloud."

"What a ride," Jingle said. "My heart was in my throat. I had to swallow it back down."

Jangle only nodded.

Jingle then turned around and went back into the snow mound, coming out backwards a second later. He was dragging the sleigh. "Hey, give me a hand, you lazy elf," he said to Jangle. "This thing is heavy." Jangle went and helped and the two elves continued to drag the sleigh free of the snow, a lot of huffing and puffing the result. When they finally had it clear, everyone took a good look at it.

"Oh dear, that won't be flying anytime soon," Mrs. Claus said as she examined the sleigh.

"What I want to know is what happened," Santa added.

"I think I can shed some light on that one, fatso," a voice said from behind them. The group all turned as one to see none other than Snow Miser coming towards them, an entourage of his two foot tall minions that were identical to him in every way—right down to their scarves and attire, only much smaller—right behind him.

"Snow Miser," Mrs. Claus said, her mouth falling open. "It was you who brought my sleigh down."

"Of course it was, madam, who else would it be?" He sidled over to her and put an arm around her ample shoulders. She cringed but held her ground. "So tell me, my little icicle," he said, "when are you gonna leave old fatso over there and come and live with me?"

She brushed off the arm from her shoulder as if it was the most detestable thing that she had ever come in contact with her. "Never, and I've told you that before."

"Oh come, come, Mrs. C, I can give you so much more than this old fart ever could."

"I'm standing right here, you know," Santa said, staring at Snow Miser with what looked like anger—though Santa was supposed to be always jolly, even he had his breaking point—and Snow Miser was it.

Next to his brother Heat Miser, Snow Miser was the worst, though the two siblings fought terribly. Snow Miser wanted snow and his brother Heat Miser always wanted it hot.

"Yes, I know, tubby," Snow Miser quipped. "And I don't care." He clapped his hands and the little entourage of Snow Misers jumped to attention. "You guys take Mrs. Claus' sleigh and get it fixed up for her." The little ones did as they were told. Snow Miser turned back to Mrs. Claus with a wide smile that resembled a fox after it had gotten inside the hen house. "And you, Mrs. C, will stay for the night till your sleigh is fixed. You'll be my honored guest."

"What about us?" Santa asked, not liking being left out of the conversation. He was Santa Claus after all and he was being treated like a second-rate citizen by Snow Miser.

"Huh?" Snow Miser said, as if just noticing Santa was there for the first time. He waved his hand at Santa and the elves. "Yes, yes, I suppose you can stay, too."

Snow Miser walked over to Santa and stared him down. "You're lucky I'm in a good mood, fatso, or else I'd ship you home in a block of ice." As he said this, he was poking Santa with his right index finger, each word followed by a jab into Santa's chest.

Vixen woke up and saw the hand over her head and couldn't resist. She didn't understand why, but for some reason she was craving flesh, and even Snow Miser's cold flesh would do in a pinch. Before anyone could stop her, Vixen lunged up in Santa's arms and sank her sharp teeth into Snow Miser's right wrist.

"Yow!" Snow Miser yelled and yanked his arm back, a good-sized chunk of flesh now gone from his wrist. Vixen chewed thoughtfully as she stared at Snow Miser.

"What the blue blazes is wrong with that animal, fatso?" He was cradling his arm. "Put that thing in a muzzle!"

Santa was as shocked as Snow Miser but he had to admit that when he considered it, he really wasn't too upset. He did pull Vixen back from Snow Miser, and when she tried to bite Santa, too, he had to adjust her so her neck was under his arm, her head sticking out so that if someone was standing behind Santa, they would see his back and Vixen's head protruding from between his arm and body.

Snow Miser was examining the wound, frowning. It was bleeding slowly, but as soon as the blood seeped from the wound, it froze up and dropped to the ground as red ice crystals.

"Stupid reindeer," Snow Miser mumbled. "I oughtta make hamburgers out of you."

Mrs. Claus walked over to Snow Miser and held out her hand. In her other one was a handkerchief. "Here, Snowy, let me see that," she said, her voice one of a caring mother.

Snow Miser melted when she said it and he held out his hand like a small child, his lower lip quivering. "It really stings," he said, his voice high-pitched.

Mrs. Claus examined it and nodded to herself, then wrapped it up with the handkerchief, tucking in the loose end under a fold. "There, all better. It's just a small cut, you'll be fine. Though you need to make sure you clean it good."

"I will, Mrs. C, thank you," Snow Miser said, then he flashed Santa Claus an evil stare. "I want that animal on a leash from here on out. You got me, fatso?"

Santa sighed, too tired to want to duel with Snow Miser. "Yes, I understand."

Snow Miser clasped his hands, then winced and regretted it. "Minions, take Mrs. Claus to a room for the night, and the others as well."

The little versions of Snow Miser all nodded and ran over to Mrs. Claus and the elves, taking them by the hand and leading them away.

Santa stood alone as everyone was moving away and he cleared his throat and said, "Uh, what about me?"

Snow Miser turned and glanced back at Santa. "Oh, sorry, tubby, I forgot about you. It's so easy to do. I swear, you're as memorable as a cup of water in the ocean. Follow me; I have a *special* room for you."

Santa didn't like the sound of that but he said nothing. With Vixen fighting him as she struggled to get free, Santa followed the others, while behind him, more of the Snow Miser's minions got to work dragging the sleigh away to get it fixed and also to get Blitzen and Dasher fed and stabled.

Santa looked around his room, frowning as the second airplane in as many minutes flew by. Snow Miser had put him in a room at the very end of his airborne complex and it seems it was right on the fly-by route of a local airline.

So much for getting any rest, Santa thought with a deep frown.

He placed Vixen in a corner of the room, on a wadded-up blanket and patted her head gently. This time she didn't try to bite him. "Hang in there, girl, we'll be home soon." Santa stared at the reindeer as she curled up and went to sleep. He didn't understand the way Vixen was acting. Now that they were long gone from Southtown, the heat had abated and she should have been recovering. And the biting of Snow Miser was even more unusual. Vixen had never showed a bad bone in her body, and was the gentlest of creatures, so the biting was very unlike her. But Santa couldn't find too much fault in her for doing it. Hell, he had wanted to take a bite out of Snow Miser on more than one occasion over the years. Snow Miser was always hitting on Martha and though he hated to admit it, Santa was jealous.

He let his eyes play over the room, taking in the modest furnishings, all made out of ice. Well, the host was called Snow Miser after all, a magical entity who could harness the power of snow and at the snap of a finger could make it snow anywhere in the world—or never snow there if that was the choice.

There was a fireplace in the corner and a roaring fire was already going, but heat didn't affect the ice furniture—magic again.

Santa slid out of his suit and put it on a hanger, then slid into bed, exhausted. His cold wasn't much better and every bone in his body ached.

He expected the bed to be warm and comfortable, for despite being made of ice, magic should have made it cozy and snug, but the bed was freezing. He frowned so deeply it was a miracle his mouth remained on his face. Snow Miser had taken the magic from the bed so Santa would have a terrible night's rest. But Santa had some magic of his own and it wasn't long before the bed was the way a bed should be, warm and snuggly.

Of course, the planes flying by couldn't be helped, but Santa was so doggone tired that he barely heard the next one as he drifted off into a heavy sleep, snoring loudly.

Curled up near his bed, Vixen's chest rose and fell, rose and fell, until finally in the middle of the night, she stopped breathing. As the reindeer succumbed to the virus sweeping through her frail body, her bladder and bowels voided in death, seeping into the blanket. The room shook as another airplane soared by.

While Santa, Mrs. Claus, and the elves lay sleeping, Snow Miser was tossing and turning in his massive ice bed, carved from a giant block of ice; he seemed lost in the large bed.

His face was creased in pain as something amazing began to happen to him. Vixen's wound had festered and now, the virus was doing its best to take over his frigid body.

But Snow Miser wasn't human, he was magical, and the virus mutated because of this, still taking over Snow Miser's body but leaving his intellect intact. As he sweated ice cubes and shivered as if he was cold, the virus filled every cell, every nerve ending, until Snow Miser was no more, and instead, an undead entity took his place.

The next morning, Snow Miser's eyes snapped open and he got up and went to the ice mirror near his bed. Gazing at the gaunt face looking back at him, he saw he was paler than he'd ever been—and that was saying something! He flexed his hands, feeling how different they felt, how *he* felt.

Then he realized something. He wasn't breathing. Normally, when he exhaled, his breath came out looking like steam—though he was the master of snow, he was still a living creature.

But now...

He breathed out onto the mirror but no condensation crystallized. He touched his chest, feeling for his heartbeat but the cold cube within wasn't beating. Of course he still didn't know what was wrong with him and may have stayed that way for quite a while if not for the door to his bedroom opening. In marched his small entourage of a half dozen of his minions. Each was carrying a piece of his breakfast, whether it was a glass of juice or a dish of food, while another brought his cloths and another the newspaper of a town in the north he enjoyed reading about. Whenever he made it snow—the town, which was a ski resort—praised him to no end.

"Ah, it's time for breakfast," he said as the minions set up a table at the far end of the room and laid out the food, newspaper, and other items. But as he sat down, Snow Miser realized he *was* hungry, but not for the food on the table. His eyes went to the closest minion, and as he studied the little fella's small neck, he felt his stomach rumble with a craving he'd never had before.

Before any of his entourage knew what was happening, Snow Miser lunged for the closest one, grabbed him, and pulled the little guy to his mouth, taking a good-sized chunk of cold flesh from his neck.

Blood squirted out of the gaping neck wound to freeze as it hit the floor. Snow Miser dropped the little version of himself to the floor as he chewed happily. The rest of the group stared in shock at their brother, not quite understanding what was happening.

Snow Miser stood up, crossed the room and slammed the bedroom door closed.

"That was just a light snack, boys, now it's time for the real meal," he laughed.

The group of mini-versions of Snow Miser all swallowed as one, as they stared up at their master.

Then Snow Miser ran at the next one in line, his teeth shredding flesh, his hands tearing at tiny skin.

The killing began in earnest.

Santa was dreaming.

He was in the stable back at the North Pole and for some reason he had fallen down and was lying on the hay-covered ground. A reindeer was on his chest and it was sniffing him. He could feel its breath on his face and hear the huffing of its rasping lungs as each intake of air was exhaled. Only the breath wasn't warm, it was cold—ice cold.

He crinkled his nose at the odor of feces and the smell of bad meat. It reminded him of the time Martha had left thawing meat in the back of the refrigerator for far too long after forgetting about it.

The meat had become rancid, turning green. That was the odor that tickled his nostrils now.

Suddenly, the dream wasn't a dream but was real as he felt something nibble the tip of his nose. But before whatever had a grip on him could do more than press on his nose, his eyes snapped open and he found himself looking into the dead eyes of Vixen.

The reindeer was on his chest, her teeth clamped on his nose, and from the pressure Santa felt, she was about to snap her jaws closed and take his nose clean off. Acting fast, he shoved his hands between her upper and lower jaws and spread his arms apart, separating her teeth from his nose. It wasn't easy, because he was lying down and had no leverage, but he only needed to move her teeth a fraction of an inch. As he did it, the move was enough and his nose was free a moment later. Santa turned his face away as he pulled his hands out of her mouth, her teeth snapping closed with a loud *clacking* sound.

"Vixen, what in blazes is wrong with you!" Santa yelled and sat up, pushing the reindeer off him. Vixen fell off Santa and rolled to the foot of the bed, but then jumped up to face him. Her rear haunches were pointed up, her head low to the bed, her teeth showing as she growled from deep within her throat. Her eyes creased and Santa knew she was going to attack him.

Simultaneously, as Vixen jumped at Santa's face again, Santa reached around and grabbed his pillow, swinging it around to use as a shield. Vixen's teeth sank into the pillow and began to tear at it, fluffy feathers filling the air to rain down on the floor like snow.

Santa fought with the small reindeer, in shock at the viciousness and strength the small doe was showing. He wondered if it was due to her being sick, as he fought to keep her at bay. She was nothing but snapping teeth and raking hooves.

Santa managed to get off the bed, and as Vixen swung her head wildly to the side to toss away the deflated pillow in her mouth, Santa reached for the blanket on the bed and threw it over Vixen just before she tried to charge him again. Wrapped in the blanket, the doe began to hiss and growl. Santa moved in fast, grabbing the ends of the blanket and pulling them together so that all four corners were in his hands. Then taking the empty pillow in one of his hands while the other held onto the corners of the blanket, he used the torn material like a rope and tied the ends of the blanket so that he had a makeshift sack. Within the blanket, Vixen howled and growled as she tried to get free.

Santa took a step back and stared at the sack on the bed containing the once gentle reindeer. Within the blanket, Vixen gnashed her teeth as she tried to escape her cloth prison.

Seeing that the reindeer was trapped for the moment, Santa quickly dressed, and with a slam of the bedroom door, left the room. He needed to find Martha, and fast.

Mrs. Claus was pulled from sleep by what she thought were elves pounding on wood as they made toys for Christmas. But as she slowly opened her eyes, she realized someone was at her door.

Getting out of bed, she padded across the floor of ice and opened the door…and promptly fell back when Santa Claus came barreling in, slamming the door after he was inside.

"Maw, it's terrible. Something's happened to Vixen. She tried to attack me, bite me even."

Mrs. Claus was still groggy from sleep and she blinked at her long-time husband, while trying to wake up and take in what he was saying. "What are you talking about, dear?" she asked as she went back to her bed and sat on the edge. The room was cold and she wanted to get back into her warm and snugly ice bed, in which the magic was working correctly and had kept her quite comfortable while she slept.

Santa told the story about Vixen, and when he finished, he stared at his wife, who was looking at him as if he was crazy.

"Well, don't just sit there, Maw, we need to do something? Vixen's gone crazy!"

There was a knock on the door and Mrs. Claus looked to Santa and then the door. "Oh my, it's Grand Central Station in here." She got up and went to the door, opening it to see Jingle and Jangle looking up at her, both with bleary eyes.

"Mrs. C, are you all right?" Jingle asked.

"Yeah," Jangle added. "We were both woken up when we heard yelling coming from your room."

"Oh, Jingle, Jangle, it's good you're here. Come inside. Santa has told me something awful." The elves quickly shuffled into the room. "Okay, dear," Mrs. Claus said to Santa once the elves were inside. "Tell me one more time with the boys here."

Santa did as he was told, his arms waving in the air before him as he became animated, reliving the experience one more time. When he was through, he felt exhausted and sat on the edge of the bed to rest.

"Oh no, Vixen sounds like she's really sick," Jingle said to Mrs. Claus. "What do we do, Mrs. C?"

"Well, dear," she said to Jingle as she considered Santa's story. "We need to get her back to the North Pole where Dr. Crackle can have a look at her." Crackle was the North Pole veterinarian and he took care of all the reindeer. "But first we should go see Snow Miser and tell him what's happening. Maybe he can do something to help."

Santa was so frazzled that he didn't even flinch at the mention of Snow Miser's name. If the cold blowhard could help, Santa was all for it and he said as much. "That's a good idea, Maw, let's go see him. Maybe he can do something to help the poor little girl."

"Just let me get dressed and then we'll go," Mrs. Claus said. "I won't be but a minute." She gathered her clothes and went into the bathroom, returning a few minutes later, dressed. "There, all set. I'm sure Snowy will be able to help us," she said with confidence as the group of four filed out of the bedroom. "I mean, he may be a big ham, but he is the Snow Miser after all."

The Grand Hall where Snow Miser received his guests was empty when Santa and the others arrived. Like the rest of Snow Miser's castle, the large room was made of ice, including the throne located in the middle of the room.

Santa was about to ask Mrs. Claus what she thought they should do next when a door at the far end of the room slammed open and Snow Miser appeared in the doorway.

Only he didn't look the way Santa had seen him the day before. While always pale, now Snow Miser was even whiter. His eyes had sunk into his head, the face gaunt and hollow. Cracks in the frozen skin could be seen and some of his ice-hair had fallen out.

But that was nothing compared to his state of attire. His clothing was covered in what looked like frozen ketchup, but as Snow Miser walked closer, Santa saw he was carrying something in his right hand, and was chewing on it as if it was a turkey leg.

When Snow Miser was only ten feet away, Santa's eyes went wide upon the realization that Snow Miser was gnawing on a small arm—the same size as one of his little minions.

"Ah, fatso, and the elves, and Mrs. C, all here in one place," Snow Miser said. "Excellent. This saves time so I don't have to chase all of you down in your rooms."

"You don't look too well," Santa said. "What's wrong with you? And why in the blazes are you eating an arm?"

Snow Miser smiled, his blood-stained teeth showing through his thin lips. "Ah, and there's the rub, fatso," he said. "It seems something has happened to me since last night." He held up his arm to show off his wounded wrist to Santa and the others. "I think this is the culprit. Your reindeer is sick and whatever it has, it's given it to me when it bit me. But that's okay, because you know why? I like what I've become." He turned his head and called out to his minions. "Come on in, boys, show the Clauses your new look." More than two dozen minions entered the Grand Hall, but they were all zombies now, the scalps on their heads sitting there like top hats, frozen blood seeping from under their pale pates. Their throats had all been torn out, more frozen blood on their small suits, their attire matching Zombie Miser perfectly.

They gathered around Snow Miser, a deep hunger in their dead eyes as they eyed the group of four, licking their lips at the warm flesh standing only a few feet before them.

"Snowy," Mrs. Claus said. "What's the meaning of this? We need your help."

Snow Miser laughed. "Ah, my sweet little icicle, I think I shall save you for last. But please, don't call me Snowy or even Snow Miser anymore. For you see, since last night, I've taken on a new title."

"And that is?" Santa asked.

"Call me Zombie Miser," he said and turned to his minions, while yelling out, "Hit it, boys!"

Music began to play from hidden speakers as Zombie Miser began to dance, his minions all right beside him.

[Zombie Miser]
I'm Mr. Zombie Miser,

I'm Mister Death.
I'm Mister Walking Corpse,
I am Mister No Breath.
People call me Zombie Miser!
Whatever I bite,
Begins to rot in my mouth!
I'm too dead!

[Chorus—Minions: The little Zombie Misers. While dancing, they would take off the top of their skulls as if they were hats.]
He's Mister Zombie Miser.
He's Mister Death.

[Zombie Miser]
Yes I am!

[Chorus—Minions]
He's Mister Walking Corpse,
He is Mister No Breath!

[Zombie Miser]
People call me Zombie Miser
Whatever I bite,
Begins to rot in my mouth!
I'm too dead!

[Chorus—Minions]
He's too dead!

[Zombie Miser]
I never want to see a day.
That's not filled with dying folk.

I'd rather have 'em dead and rotting,
One, two, three, a million!

[Chorus—Minions]
He's Mister Zombie Miser,
He's Mister Death.

[Snow Miser]
That's me!

[Chorus]
He's Mister Zombie Miser,
He is Mister No breath!

[Zombie Miser]
People call me Zombie Miser
Whatever I bite,
Begins to rot in my mouth!
…too dead!

[Minions]
Too dead!

"Huh, that's catchy," Santa said. "Tell me, is that part of being a zombie? Breaking out into song for no justifiable reason?"

"Hey, fatso, I'm a Miser. I can do whatever I want. If I want to take off all my clothes and run around naked, I can."

"Oh, please don't do that, this is a family show after all," Mrs. Claus said and winced, the image of a naked and skinny Miser haunting her mind.

"So, Zombie Miser, if that's your name now. Why the dance number?" Santa asked.

Zombie Miser shrugged. "Oh, it was just to lull you all into a false sense of security." He looked at his minions. "Go 'head, boys, get 'em. It's time for breakfast."

As one, the minions hissed and moaned, then charged Santa and his wife, as well as Jingle and Jangle, the hunger in their eyes apparent to all who stood with mouths hanging agape in horror.

Santa looked at his wife and sighed. "I swear, Maw, I should have just stayed in bed back at the North Pole." Then he raised his hands, curled them into fists, and prepared for a battle with the undead minions.

At first, Jingle and Jangle cowered behind Mrs. Claus, but when she yelled at them to fight or else they would all die, the two elves gathered what courage they could find and joined the battle.

Mrs. Claus hadn't said much since arriving in the Grand Hall but there was no need. What she was seeing with her eyes was enough for her to accept it as real. And after taking into account what Santa had told her about Vixen...well, she wasn't a stupid woman and never wasted time arguing what her own eyes told her. Besides, she lived in a world where magic was common. If a fat man in a red suit could deliver Christmas presents to the entire world in one night by using flying reindeer that towed a large, red, open sleigh, then zombies didn't seem that farfetched.

She retreated a few feet and picked up an ice chair, then smashed it onto the ice floor. The chair shattered into a dozen pieces and she grabbed a broken leg. The ice was cold in her hand but the leg was now nothing but a giant icicle with a sharp tip. She shoved it out in front of her as the minions charged, yelling at Jingle and Jangle to get pieces of the chair as well to use as weapons.

Santa went for a different tactic.

After four minions ran at him, Santa punched and kicked them away. The little people rolled across the floor like bowling balls only to get up at the end of their travel, turn, and race back at Santa to continue the fight.

Santa Claus spotted an old sack lying in a corner of the room and he spun around on his heels and dashed for it, the four zombie minions following close behind. Off to the side, Zombie Miser laughed and clapped as he danced a jig.

Santa ran right into the wall as he slid on the ice floor, then scooped up the sack and held it before him with a smile. "Now, it's my turn," he said with a sparkle in his eye.

Every Christmas, Santa used magic to get all the presents to each home of good little boys and girls. He did this by having a bottomless sack of toys. Now, though he used a large red sack with embroidery on it, in reality, any old sack would do. Even a lunch bag would work in a pinch, though he could only take out toys as big as the sack opening. The sack in his hands now had a good-sized opening, and with a wave of his free hand, he plunged it into the sack and began fishing around, while the other hand held the sack by its opening.

Just as the minions reached him, Santa pulled out a hockey stick, and with a laugh that made his belly shake like a bowl full of jelly, he began whacking at the minions, taking off heads and legs with each blow.

As soon as he finished off his tiny attackers, he reached into the sack and began rummaging for more goodies. Pulling out a handful of candy canes, he yelled to Jingle and Jangle and threw the candy canes at the two elves. "Use them like daggers!" he instructed.

Jingle caught three of them and Jangle caught two, the elves spinning the candy canes around so that the hooks were pointed at them, then they began stabbing at the zombie minions with the bottom tips as the minions tried to bite the elves.

Jangle closed his eyes and lunged forward with a candy cane as if it was a sword. Though quite by accident, his aim was true and the tip of the candy cane slid into the left eye of a minion as the little zombie charged at the elf. Jangle cringed as he felt the tip of the candy cane slide into the eye socket, grating on bone as a pinkish fluid oozed out around the candy cane. When Jangle withdrew the weapon, the minion's eyeball was still stuck to the tip, the impaled orb looking like a mushroom on a kebab stick. But the candy cane had penetrated into the brain as well and the zombie minion dropped to the floor, dead for good.

Jangle turned and promptly threw up all over his red outfit.

Mrs. Claus was an Amazon woman in all but attire. She swung the icicle she'd taken from the broken chair back and forth, taking down minions one at a time. She plunged the icicle into the chest of the closest small zombie, the tip bursting out of the little guy's back, covered in red. But the minion still clawed at Mrs. Claus, sliding its body down the icicle so it could get at her. Using her foot, she kicked it off and then stabbed downward into its head, killing it when the icicle impaled the brain.

Heaving heavily, she spun around to see who was in need of dying next.

Santa had pulled out some ornaments and he threw them onto the floor, where the minions stepped on them, crushing them beneath their feet. The sharp shards impaled their slipper-like footwear and the flesh within but the minions felt no pain and just kept coming. Frowning when that didn't work, Santa reached into the sack and pulled out a BB gun. Cocking the weapon, he began firing at the zombie minions' faces, more than one BB penetrating an eye and the brain behind it, taking out the small zombies before they knew what was happening.

Jingle punched and kicked his attackers, using the candy cane he held as a dagger, just like Santa had told him. He plunged the tip again and again into minions until their chest cavities were gaping open, their insides dripping out to splash onto the frozen floor. Then Jingle would finally deal the killing blow, stabbing the candy cane in either an eye or an ear hole. One time, when the angle was bad, he jammed the candy cane up a minion's nose, sliding it into the nasal canal, then he twisted and felt the weapon slip into the brain cavity. When the small body went limp, Jingle knew he'd hit paydirt.

The battle was furious, Santa and Mrs. Claus stomping on bodies and snapping necks to sever spinal cords, a pile of small bodies surrounding them.

Santa pulled out firecrackers, set them alight, and jammed them into open mouths when the minions tried to snap at him with their teeth. Exploding, the firecrackers were like small grenades, blowing off heads and leaving tottering, headless bodies that would sometimes keep walking before finally falling over.

And then the battle was over, only Zombie Miser remaining.

"You haven't won anything, fatso!" Zombie Miser screamed from the far end of the room as he prepared to make his escape through a back door. "As long as I'm alive, I can infect anyone I please. In a matter of hours, I can have an army of undead at my disposal!"

"Well, we can't have that now, can we," Santa said and reached into the sack and pulled out a genuine tomahawk, the edge of the axe head razor sharp. Dropping the sack, Santa weighed the tomahawk in his hand to get the feel of it, then with the expertise only magic could deliver, he pulled back his arm and threw the tomahawk at Zombie Miser. The steel weapon zipped through the air, the light dancing off the polished metal sheen.

Zombie Miser was just turning to flee when the tomahawk struck him on the back of the head. The axe end of the weapon embedded itself into his skull with a meaty *thwack*, practically splitting his face in half. He slumped to the floor, gray brain matter seeping out of the jagged wound to freeze as it touched the floor of ice.

"Well, I'll be," Mrs. Claus said, impressed, her hands on her hips. "I didn't know you could do that."

Santa shrugged. "Maw, there's a lot you don't know about me. Even after all these years I still have a few tricks up my sleeve." He gave her a wink and she smiled.

"Can we please leave here now, Mrs. C," Jingle asked as he stood in a pile of gore. Jangle nodded, too, wanting to leave this charnel house behind him.

"That is an excellent idea, boys," she said. "Let's get to Dasher and Blitzen and fly away from here. There's four of us, Santa and I can ride a reindeer each with one of you boys on each of our laps."

She went to Santa and kissed him on the cheek, ignoring the frozen blood splatter there. they were all covered in blood and gore. With one last look at the carnage, she and Santa turned and walked out of the Grand Hall, the two elves following close behind.

"I tell you, Santa," Mrs. Claus said as they were leaving. "I'm not looking forward to explaining all this to Snow Miser's brother Heat Miser."

"One issue at a time, Maw, one issue at a time," Santa said as they walked down the hallway that led to the stable, where the two reindeer were being kept.

Soon, the group of four was flying to the North Pole, with Santa on Blitzen and Mrs. Claus on Dasher, an elf perched on each of their laps.

"So, dear," Mrs. Claus said to Santa. "Are you going out this Christmas Eve to deliver presents?"

"Yes I am," Santa replied. "After what we've been through, I've shaken off my melancholy."

"Good, then at last something good has come from this terrible experience," she said as they flew off into the horizon.

Back at Zombie Miser's ice castle, all was quiet, the zombies destroyed for good.

But as time went by, there came a sound. It was faint but slowly grew louder.

In the bedroom Santa Claus had slept in, Vixen finally managed to chew through the blanket keeping her prisoner. In his haste to leave, Santa had forgotten about Vixen.

Once free of the blanket, her head snapped back and forth as she looked for Santa, but seeing that the room was empty, she began to look for a way out. That came soon enough when her eyes fell upon the only window in the room.

Without pause, she leapt off the bed and through the window, glass crashing around her. One jagged shard of glass embedded itself in her front leg, but she ignored it, feeling no pain.

Though a zombie, she still had the power of flight, and she turned and flew away from the castle, back down to earth, which was only now awakening from a long night.

As she flew over Southtown, USA, she could see people already about, some going for a morning walk, some getting the newspaper, while others were on their way to work.

Picking a target, she soared down and attacked a hapless man, her teeth sinking into warm flesh before the man knew what was happening. As soon as she finish chewing on the man, a woman appeared from around the corner at the end of the street. Leaping into the air, Vixen flew at the woman, taking her down to the ground by running into her chest. Standing on the woman, Vixen's head snapped down and she tore out the woman's throat. Chewing happily, her eyes lit on another pedestrian and soon she was feeding on that unlucky soul.

And so it began, as each time Vixen took down a victim, said victim rose from the dead to join in the slaughter. By the end of the day, Southtown would be a home for the living dead, and the remaining humans would be cowering for their lives and then it would spread across the globe.

It's wasn't over yet. In fact, it was only the beginning… of *An Undead Christmas*.

THE FEAST OF STEPHEN

R P. STEEVES

As Christmas gifts go, a single Hershey's Kiss was not the most exciting present one could imagine. Though if it was indeed the last Hershey's Kiss on Earth, Wendell Ross thought it was better than nothing.

Of course, he wished he could give her more. For her birthday, for example, when they were on the run, he had managed to scrounge and scavenge enough supplies to make her a 'Favorites Feast.' It consisted of graham crackers, a box of frozen waffles hijacked from a mini-mart that—to his astonishment—actually had power, some bacon-flavored candy and a jar of applesauce. His goal had been to procure samples of her favorite foods, but he'd been forced to make due with what he could locate. All the bacon he'd found, for example, had been rotten, but he was pretty proud of the creative substitute he'd jacked from the jeans pocket of a former computer nerd—after he'd crushed its undead skull with a hammer.

But despite his efforts, it was far from perfect. How was he supposed to know that someone who counted apples among her five favorite foods wouldn't like applesauce?

Still, she'd been impressed, even if the crackers were stale and the waffles inedible. She'd laughed and said that she'd have no choice but to L'Eggo those Eggos.

Before the world ended, Wendell had loved her corny jokes, but after six months on the road with her—the last month spent cooped up in this tiny cabin with nothing to do but read the same two books and play endless games of cards—the habit had lost a bit of its luster.

Wendell hoped she would be *very* impressed by the Hershey Kiss—her number one favorite food, she'd told him once, in another life. He had risked life and limb to rescue it from the Easter basket of a tiny, hate-filled four-foot monster in a flowery bonnet; the very first zombie he'd killed when all of this had started in the spring, and he'd held onto it throughout their journey, waiting for the perfect moment to present it to her.

They had come a long way since that Easter Sunday. Wendell wasn't normally one to dwell on irony, but the fact that the world had descended into endless, living death around the time of year when Pagans, Christians and Scientists alike celebrated rebirth and renewal in springtime rituals had struck him as bitterly tragic.

Paige Masters had found the whole matter hilarious when seen through the lens of her black-as-night worldview. Her sense of humor had been a big part of the reason Wendell had latched onto her when things started to go south. It was so much like his that he figured she'd make a good companion for the rest of their lives, however long that might be.

But frankly, he was starting to think she was getting sick of him. She would frequently groan at jokes she'd once found funny, and she always called him out when he repeated a story he'd already spun on more than one occasion. Early on, she never would have done so; she'd hung on his every word, calling him her 'hero.' These days, lives were a lot like a marriage, an old, tired one, but stripped of the ceremony and legal standing, just a two-person partnership against the world.

Still, he was going to do everything in his power to make his sure his common-law-by-way-of-zombie-apocalypse wife had the best damn Christmas ever.

That is, if their calendar was even remotely correct.

It was, to the best of his estimation, Christmas Day, the twenty-fifth of December. Or, perhaps, it was the twenty-sixth of December, also known as the Feast of Stephen, or the Second Day of Christmas, or around these parts, Boxing Day.

Either way, he was going to make it special.

He couldn't exactly decorate their tiny hilltop cabin located on the outskirts of New Brunswick, Canada. Their supplies were limited to say the least, and besides, it's not like he had much time to himself, anyhow. The 'cabin' was little more than a single room with a fireplace, a few rugs and lots and lots of weapons.

The two of them had vowed to stick together for safety's sake. They'd both seen plenty of horror movies and knew what happened to people who wandered off on their own. And now that the whole world had mutated into a living horror movie, they'd learned the harsh truth. Those films that had guided the fantasies and nightmares of their youth were now the catechism for surviving in this brave new world.

Many of their original traveling companions had learned this lesson the hard way, and the fact that Wendell and Paige had even survived to see December was a bit of a Christmas miracle.

On Memorial Day, they had finally fled their small, parochial Connecticut town. By Labor Day, the size of their ragtag group had been slashed in half, and their attempt to seek solace in the nation's capital had been a disaster. While the plague ravaged the east coast, the closer they got to the designated 'safe zones,' the larger were the hordes of undead they faced, and the more their group was eaten, bitten, scratched and blown to smithereens.

Around Halloween, they decided to turn north, hoping beyond hope that there was some succor to be found in the frozen tundra. In fact, one of the brighter—though likely insane—members of the group had observed that the zombies didn't react well to colder temperatures. So they pinned their last, desperate hope to finding a cold climate, one where snow and ice could slow down the creatures, perhaps even stopping them in their tracks, freezing their locomotion and eliminating them as a threat. Trading comfort and warmth for safety was the new paradigm, it seemed.

By Thanksgiving in America, they had arrived here. Their final surviving companion, Willie Steeves, had directed them toward the province of New Brunswick, specifically to the town of Hillsborough, where his family had property. He had died, though, before they reached their destination. His death had been caused by—of all things—an infected leg wound. Steeves had been a pediatrician in his previous life, but again, Wendell took no pleasure in the irony. These days, nothing terrible was unexpected. No tragedy, and no negative outcome was a surprise anymore. In a world where *every* outcome was negative, where fiction was reality and horror was daily life, irony had rusted away.

But Wendell and Paige had survived, and by the first of December—or thereabouts—they had arrived at the cabin.

And now Wendell was determined to celebrate life amid the cold wasteland.

But then they saw smoke. A few gray streaks in the sky that had the potential to change everything.

Since they'd lost Willie, it was just the two of them, alone together against the world. For nearly a month they hadn't seen another soul, living or unliving. And they had been vigilant about keeping watch, even to the point where their sleep cycles suffered, no doubt contributing to their increased tension.

There had been no lightning strikes in the past twenty-four hours, so the smoke meant that someone—or something—was nearby. Could it be a mindless undead creature, somehow keeping mobile in the bone-chilling cold, wreaking havoc at a gas station or other combustible target?

Neither had heard an explosion, so that meant it was more likely that the smoke was a sign that another person, another human being, was making tracks on their virgin snow. But could this person be a boon, a new ally with talents and resources they could use? Or would this newcomer be like poor, doomed Marv, the former SWAT team member who'd suffered unknowable trauma in the early days of the outbreak, and whose mind had finally crumbled under the stress, until the day that Wendell had been forced to plunge a screwdriver into his left eye.

After very little deliberation, Wendell and Paige decide to venture out into the wilderness. For the first time in weeks, they would leave the comfort of their log-lined womb.

"Are you sure we should both go?" Paige asked as she loaded bullets one by one with a sure, practiced hand into her .38, her voice raspy from disuse. Wendell merely glared in reply, as he often did.

It was, from a man who was little more than a collection of quirks and peccadilloes, one of his more annoying, condescending habits. "I mean, what if this is a ruse, a distraction to get us out of here so some gang can loot our home?" she said.

Our home. Wendell shuddered involuntarily. He'd been in love with this woman for so long — long before the world ended — and though it had taken the destruction of the human race to bring him to her attention, the idea that the two of them had built something together, something she had willingly referred to as *their home,* sent shudders of pleasure down his spine.

The scathing tone of the comment was lost to him. "If they plan to ambush us, they'd want us to split up. You know as well as I do that being alone is a death sentence these days. We need to stick together. Agreed?"

She gave a single curt nod.

Wendell saw something in her eyes, as if her fantasy of separating from him had sunk as fast as the human government under a tide of undead bodies. But like it or not, he was right, of course.

"Grab your handgun, then," she said simply. "Let's get this over with."

They walked single file to hide their numbers, just like Sand People from *Star Wars*, except they were traversing the planet Hoth instead of Tattooine, and they weren't hunting Wampas, but rather stalking the living in the world of the dead.

Wendell and Paige made a beeline toward the smoke, rising as it was in the twilight, wishing to spend no more time away from their shelter than necessary. Though they hadn't yet seen a zombie lumbering through the cold, snowy terrain they'd inhabited the past few weeks, they knew they must remain ever vigilant, lest they fall prey to an ambush—inhuman or otherwise.

The irony of the situation—the fact that they were about to ambush the creator of the smoke—was not lost on them. They simply didn't care. There was little they cared about anymore.

They came to the top of the ridge and looked down on the valley below. Squinting in the dusky light, they could see a single set of tracks through the snow. Wendell could make out individual footprints. This sight gave him a small twinge of relief. He'd half expected to see matching troughs cutting their way through the pristine white, indicative of the lazy, damaged gait of the mindless undead.

As his mind tried to grasp the potential implications of a newcomer, a fresh human personality added to the precarious partnership in which he found himself, he felt a jab in his ribcage. Startled from his reverie, he followed Paige's slender finger as she pointed.

A figure was emerging from the forest, swaddled in cold-weather clothing, a bundle of sticks in his—or her—hands. The figure looked up—perhaps hearing Wendell's tiny gasp, or maybe sensing the heat of actual human beings, a rarity in this frightening new world.

The figure dropped the sticks and ran for cover.

Wendell turned to Paige, seeking her wisdom. But that wisdom had perhaps vacated the premises like the souls of the dead fleeing the broken earth. Paige was sprinting down the hill after the newcomer, her arms pumping with fervor.

"Stop!" Paige shouted, her voice raspy and hoarse from disuse. "Wait!"

Cursing her impulsivity—the first lesson they had learned on their harsh journey was never to make more noise than absolutely necessary—Wendell followed her down the slope and toward the great unknown.

The cold, bitter wind whipped at Wendell's face as he tore down the hill in the growing darkness. He still wasn't accustomed to true blackness, something that was completely unknown in the urban universe. The night enveloped him, cloaking him against his crippling fear yet blinding him to the danger that lurked in every shadow.

Branches tore at his flesh, marking his face with red straps of pain. The frosty air cut through his lungs, atrophied after so many weeks cooped up in the cabin, and the cold chilled his bones. Up ahead, he heard voices rising up through the night.

He almost ran into the women who stood, embracing in a small clearing. Both were crying, but not the tears of the modern age, the cries and wails of loss and death. These were something else: tears of release and disbelief, of connection and hope, discovery and relief.

"What's going on?" Wendell asked, panting with exertion and wracked with confusion.

"I thought I was alone," the newcomer said. The voice was female. She was small and slight, and Wendell could hardly believe he'd thought she could have been a man when he'd seen her from a distance. Her voice was high and shrill, and caught in her throat. "I never thought, I mean, here you are…" She trailed off, heaved one sob and looked at the pair before her. Her eyes glistened, tears threatening to crystallize in the icy night.

A million questions rolled through Wendell's mind in that moment, like a rolodex on speed, rifling through all the Ws and an H: Who was she? Where was she from? When did she arrive? What had she been doing these many months? Why was she here? And how had she survived? These were the tools he'd used in his previous life as a journalist, covering high-society events and business meetings, meaningless human intercourse that had once seemed so vital in the long-dead world. "What's your name?" was all he could manage before his brain shut down.

"My name is Agnes, and I… "

Her words seem to hang in the air for an instant, formed in frost like a word balloon in an old-time comic book…until the night was shattered by screams and moans, blood and horror.

In retrospect, it was easy to rationalize their carelessness. After all, each had found something they'd thought gone from their lives—hope. But in truth, they *had* let down their guard. Perhaps it was due to the false assurance that the cold would protect them from the undead, or maybe they simply had lost their minds, letting their training fall aside in a rush of adrenaline and excitement, tears and distraction. But their guard was down and the zombies were upon them, faster and fiercer than Wendell had remembered.

At first it was impossible to tell how many of the creatures were in the swarm. All he could make out was a rush of arms and legs, chomping maws and fetid odors.

One of the zombies crashed into Wendell, dropping him to the ground like a sack of meat. The wind fled from Wendell's lungs as his back smashed against the turf, and his gun tumbled from his hand as he instinctively thrust his arms forward to keep the zombie at bay. The zombie snapped its teeth, a primal instinct to consume and transform fueling its lunges, the odor of death, decay and putrescence spewing from its mouth. Wendell had seen so many of his companions killed just like this, with feverish bites subsuming their life essences and transforming them past death to the horror beyond.

It took all of his strength to keep the teeth at bay. Wendell pressed his palms against the shoulders of the monster as it chomped and lunged. His elbows shook from the strain; his formerly compact muscles, honed from months on the road, now slightly atrophied from weeks of disuse.

Then, he could hold no longer, and the panic of imminent death breathed down upon him.

He let go.

The creature's momentum carried it forward, and its torso slamming against Wendell's, its bony ribcage smashing into his own; the zombie's forehead smashed down against Wendell's nose, sending a red blossom of pain cascading through his vision. This raised Wendell's ire, and before the slow-moving creature could recover from the shock of collision, Wendell rolled to the left, turning the tables on it.

He pounded his fists, smashing the jaw of the creature again and again, dislodging bone from tattered flesh, as the zombie let out a low, warbling moan.

As the former journalist screamed and raged, pulping the skull with his bare fists, he felt a pair of hands grab him and pull him backwards. He stumbled to his feet, smashing an elbow back in rage and fear.

"Ow!" was *not* the response he expected to hear. Then he felt a hand grasp his wrist, tugging him once more. He followed the pull, stumbling into the woods, his vision finally clearing. He saw that the newcomer, Agnes, was leading him away to places unknown.

They ran, without direction or purpose, for as long as their legs could manage, and perhaps a bit longer than that. It had been weeks since Wendell had felt the sheer terror of imminent death at the hands and teeth of the zombies, but the adrenaline rush had been lurking below the surface the entire time, waiting to ignite his fight or flight response—though he had no fight response. His *only* instinct was to flee. Perhaps it was the reason he'd survived this long.

After a time, Wendell and Agnes simultaneously dropped into the snow, as if their bodies were secretly communicating their exhaustion and coordinating their collapse. They heaved the frigid air into their screaming lungs for a few moments, neither speaking to, nor looking at each other, their eyes locked on the white turf beneath their feet.

Then, after a bit, they spoke at the same time.

"Who are you?"

"Where are you based?"

Wendell smiled in spite of himself. It was a gesture that felt odd, as if the muscles associated with the expression atrophied from lack of use. "You go first," he said, trying to sound as gracious as possible.

She nodded, handing him his gun, which he'd thought lost forever. He shrugged as graciously as possible and tucked it into his waistband.

"I'm Agnes," she said, "Agnes Stephens. I've come a long way. Everyone I know is dead."

"Everyone that everyone knows is dead, Agnes," he found himself saying. It was far harsher than he needed—or wanted—to be, and he immediately regretted it. "My name's Wendell Ross, and if you trust me, you can follow me to my cabin." *Our cabin*, he mentally corrected himself. Then an icy stab of panic slashed into his gut. For the first time in months, he didn't know where Paige was. He didn't even know if she was alive.

That thought sent true fear through him. It was an even greater terror than he had felt moments earlier when he'd faced down the attack of the walking dead. He'd always been more concerned with Paige's safety than his own. He'd never felt that about any-one before.

But he didn't have time to consider the implications of his feel-ings, as he felt a tug at his sweater. He looked at Agnes and for an instant, his mind's eye superimposed Paige's face atop hers. Perhaps it was because he had spent so much time with that face, imagining it in lonely nights when they had worked together, and then staring at it as she drifted to sleep during their time on the run. He'd vowed to protect her always, but perhaps he'd failed.

Agnes was, in many ways, similarly built. She, too, was small in stature but not meek in frame. Beneath her hobo-like assortment of mismatched clothes, she was lean and wiry, her body hardened by the harshness of survival.

Her hair was also dark like Paige's, her eyes light, but her face was not as rounded. It was harsh, and a scowl darkened it even more than dirt and scars. Wendell idly wondered what had hap-pened to her in the past few months, what her story was. But there was no time for pleasantries.

"The fire was a stupid mistake, you know," he said bluntly.

She frowned. Her pout sent a stirring sensation through him, something he hadn't felt in weeks. "I caught a squirrel," she said. "I haven't had meat in ages. I just…I couldn't bring myself to eat its flesh raw."

As she gazed at him with her ice blue eyes on that cold winter's night, something inside Wendell melted. "Then come with me. We have plenty of food to spare."

The trip wasn't an easy one. Wendell had lost his bearings as they'd fled from the zombies, but fortunately, Agnes had a well-honed set of survival skills. She declined to say more about herself: where she'd come from, why she was here, or how she'd survived so long, but she did have a keen knowledge of the outdoors, something Wendell, despite his time on the run, had never developed.

She knew from which direction Wendell and Paige had come, and using nothing more than the stars, she was able to turn in the right direction. At Wendell's urging, they opted to take a circuitous route back. He didn't want to run into any lurkers who might be in their path.

Even then, the paranoia was palpable. With every step, Wendell felt the urge to hold his breath, to stare down at the ground to make sure his feet didn't snap a twig hidden in the snow, and at the same time look forward, darting his eyes back and forth to see if he could spot any lurking zombies.

He couldn't understand how they'd been ambushed before. In his experience, the zombies had always been slow moving and somewhat dimwitted. It was the only reason he'd survived for so long.

But from what Agnes had told him—though she was reticent to speak as they walked, which was perhaps, for the best, considering their need for stealth, the majority of creatures she'd encountered in recent weeks had...*evolved*. The thought was terrifying, and as they moved through the night, it began to consume him.

So when they came upon a small horde of the creatures, blocking the only path through the forest to the hilltop, he was ready — or as ready as he could be.

He drew his gun and aimed.

It's just a video game, he thought, and as he started putting bullets through the skulls of the shambling things before him, his mind cast back to a Christmas morning, long ago, in a different life, when he was but a boy. He'd received a video game system from his stepfather, and in an attempt to subsume his adolescent pain in a haze of *Left 4 Dead*, he'd obliterated hordes of zombies, picturing the face of his own father superimposed over the pixilated visages of the digital monsters. In a simpler world, killing monsters was a form of entertainment.

But now, somehow, that happy day from his childhood had been twisted into this horrific existence, where shooting creatures through the skull was not a matter of emotional release but rather one of survival.

Then, as he was lost in thought, slaughtering creature after creature in the icy Canadian woods, he was taken unawares, tackled from the side and once more dropped to the turf, a zombie's teeth snapping at his neck.

Wendell rolled down the hill, the zombie chomping at him. He knew that if he could get his arms free, it would only be a matter of placing the gun against the thing's temple and pulling the trigger. The splatter of brain would mist through the night air, and the danger would be over.

Except, it seemed, that Wendell had fallen into a trap—an ambush.

He tumbled downward and rolled to a stop at the feet of another group of zombies. They moaned and wailed, and as the initial creature clambered off of him, Wendell rose to his feet.

He was hopelessly outnumbered, and he realized as his mind suddenly snapped into hypernatural clarity, that he was out of bullets.

Wendell turned to run, but his feet slipped on the snow and the creatures nipped at his heels. He could sense them just behind him, moving in unison. He imagined their arms outstretched, reaching for him. He could almost feel their fingertips brushing against his collar.

Were they toying with him?

He would never know.

Gunshots rang out in the night and he heard explosions, a series of bursting wet cantaloupe sounds he'd come to know so well. He tried to count the shots and recall how many creatures had been in the pack.

He turned around.

Agnes was running, skidding down the hillside, sliding in the blood and brain matter, her hand tightly gripping an automatic pistol.

She ran straight toward Wendell, who stood, shaking, staring down at the carnage before him, the death beyond life that could have been his fate if it hadn't been for the sharp-shooting of this veritable stranger. She threw her arms around him and held him tight.

Among the many drawbacks of this northern latitude was the seemingly endless night. It was just a few days after the winter solstice, and this was one of the longest nights of the year. Wendell had set out shortly after sundown with Paige and now, so many hours later, he was returning to his makeshift home with a far different companion.

He had hoped to see lights in the windows as he approached, imagining that Paige had somehow survived the original assault and managed to return to the cabin unscathed. Perhaps she would even have a treat ready for them, a can of yams or pumpkin pie filling. At that moment, he thought of the Hershey's Kiss in his pocket. A few hours ago, he'd been ready to present it to Paige, and now he feared it was little more than a crush of powder in a dull foil wrapper.

No lights greeted him and Agnes as they drew near the cabin, and if the windows had been lit, perhaps Wendell would have been more prepared for the ambush that awaited him.

Instead, the gun barrel that was pressed to his temple the moment he opened the door came as a complete surprise.

"Merry Christmas, bitch," came a gravelly voice in the darkness.

While the thugs who had beat him silly sang *Let it Snow* and drenched themselves in the last remaining booze in the cabin—and perhaps all of the world—the only sound that echoed in Wendell's mind was the taunting voice of Paige, repeating the same words, over and over again. "I told you so. I told you so. I told you..."

If she had really been present, he would have told her she was right. Indeed, she was always right.

And if she had really been present, she wouldn't have tolerated the three hairy, thuggish men who had taken the cabin, alongside the smiling, cackling Agnes, belting out an off-key rendition of *Walking in a Winter Wonderland*.

"You don't have a whole lotta food here, boy," spat the largest, hairiest of the men. "The four of us've been dodgin' them zombies for a spell now. We ain't had nuthin' good ta eat fer weeks now." He stepped toward Wendell, his words drenched in a fetid mixture of decay and alcohol, a combination perhaps even more stomach-churning than the breath of the undead. The man took his

Bowie knife and pressed it against Wendell's Adam's apple, twisting the point until it drew blood. "You know, it's been awhile since I've tasted some real meat, and you've got a bit of that on you," he hissed. "Maybe you'd be a tasty treat for us. Makes more sense than throwing you to them." He jerked a thumb toward the outside world, and as he did so, Wendell imagined that he would rather be consumed by mindless undead monsters than this true horror of a human being.

Thankfully, it wouldn't come to that.

Suddenly, as if Wendell had jumped from a clichéd horror movie to a cheesy action flick, the front door of the cabin burst open, and with two quick shots, the two smaller, nameless thugs dropped to the floor, roses of blood gushing from fatal wounds in their foreheads.

"Paige!" Wendell cried out before taking a pistol butt to the head. He dropped to the floor and felt the cold metal barrel pressed once more to the rear of his skull. But he was able to look up and gaze into a pair of warm green eyes.

"I was lost, Wendell," Paige said, her weapon trained on the large man whose gun was one twitch away from ending Wendell's life. "But I found your tracks. I followed you back here."

Wendell said nothing in return. He merely choked back a sob. He was happy she was alive, but he couldn't help but feel a pang of guilt. She shouldn't have followed him. She should have fled, escaped into the woods. Alone in a world of zombies, she would have had at least a chance to live until the New Year. Now, she was sure to die here in the cabin alongside Wendell.

"Now you can watch yer boyfriend die," the man snarled, and Agnes let out a hoarse laugh.

"He died long ago," Paige spat in return. "But I found some of his friends."

With the grace of a ballerina that Wendell had never seen from before, Paige stepped aside and a pair of zombies came shambling into the cabin.

Wendell felt the gun barrel move away from his head and heard a flurry of gunshots.

He closed his eyes, waiting for death to take him... but it didn't.

After what seemed an eternity, he opened his eyes.

Inches away were the clear, green eyes of Paige. Relief flooded his body.

"What?" She stepped back as Wendell looked around. The cabin was littered with corpses—the two zombies were dead, their heads obliterated. So, too, were the thugs who had tried to usurp their little castle. They were dead, bleeding out on the floor.

"How did you do it?" he asked.

Paige smiled, and the room, full of carnage as it was, lit up. He had missed that smile. He thought he'd never see it again. "Something is happening with the zombies. They almost...understood me. At the very least, they're open to suggestion."

Wendell couldn't process the implications of this development. All he could do was fall back on his sole coping mechanism—humor. "It's a Christmas miracle!"

For the first time in a long while, Paige laughed. "A real Christmas miracle would be cleaning up this mess," she said, pouting.

"We'll do it together," Wendell replied, and they both smiled. Perhaps all they needed to bring them closer together was a simple act of betrayal and carnage.

"Good, because I didn't get you a present." She shrugged and smiled.

Wendell reached into his pocket, and the second Christmas miracle appeared; the Hershey's Kiss was still in pristine condition. He offered it to her with a sheepish grin. She took it from his hand and marveled at it. Paige looked at him, her wide green eyes filled with a mix of surprise, happiness and—perhaps—love. She stood on her tiptoes.

"Thank you for the Kiss," she said. "I have one for you, too." She planted a small peck on his nose.

It was the best Christmas gift he'd ever received.

HIGH DESERT HORROR

MICHAEL D. GRIFFITHS

The campsite was about as good as we could hope for under the circumstances, especially when considering how quickly we had fled Phoenix. I'd always heard that if any trouble went down, the big cities would be the worst places to be. In theory, I agreed, but I never truly thought I would ever live to the see the day that I'd have to worry about such things.

The zombie plague changed all that.

Changed everything.

In the end, only three of us made it. More were invited, and in some cases, begged to join us, before the cell phones went dead. Our friends and loved ones knew where we were going. We'd given them directions, but so far no one else had shown up. I hoped they were okay, but as the days passed, we grew more worried.

With me were my wife, Maureen, and my old school buddy, Kent. Maureen and I had been married for six years. She was a petite beauty with a cascading mane of lustrous chestnut hair. Kent was a bit older than me, but that hadn't faded his head of thick blonde hair and robust Nordic beard.

Me, I'm taller than most. I'm a…well, I guess I used to be a bartender. Not really the type of profession that did much to prepare me for this crap, other than breaking up a few fights once in a while. Oh yeah, my name is Lyle.

We made it out of The Valley as fast as we could. Others thought that the National Guard would contain the situation, but all they seemed to be doing was shutting down the roads and keeping people trapped within the undead, feeding frenzy the city had quickly become. As we fled, we saw many people hitting grocery stores in a last ditch chance to gather supplies before the apocalypse closed its cold hands around them. It was eerie, almost as if the zombies had anticipated this move, for I saw them circling the supermarkets in the hundreds. No one would be getting out of those places alive.

After gathering every bit of food we could find from both our houses, we headed out to a remote spot on the eastern face of the Four Peaks mountain range. It wasn't too far from the city and not particularly defendable, but it had the one essential anyone trying to survive in the desert needed—water.

We made it there without mishap, only seeing one lone RV along the road. The last quarter mile was pretty rough going, but I hoped that this would help deter others, because I had no illusions about the friendliness of the other people still breathing. They were just as likely to shoot me for my food, or even beautiful Maureen, as give us any aid.

As darkness fell that first night, we could still hear the sounds of gunfire in the distance. It was the last dying gasp of civilization, but even that wouldn't last long.

Days went by, and despite our best intensions, our meager food supply slowly dwindled. Kent and I set ourselves to making whatever traps we could, mostly deadfalls, but so far we had experienced only minimal success.

On our sixth day out, Kent and I went to check our traps. One of our deadfalls had been triggered, but more times than not, this didn't mean we'd had any luck. Leaning over, Kent had pulled up the head-sized boulder.

"Hey, we got one!"

"Sweet, what is it?" I asked.

"You won't believe this, it's a quail."

I laughed. "Who would have…?" My voice trailed off as we each heard the garbled echo of an approaching vehicle. "Shit, Maureen's down there alone!" We sprinted down the rocky hill, but even as we went, I wasn't sure what I'd be able to do against a hostile force with my sharpened staff and a few throwing knives.

Reaching the campsite, I found Maureen crouching behind a boulder. She wore a pained expression and was clutching her walking stick in a fierce grip.

Kent moved a few yards down the rugged dirt road, while I checked on my wife. "Hey wait," he called out. "I think that might be Mark's truck!"

Good fortune had again smiled on us for it was Mark and his family. Although, as soon as they exited the vehicle, we could tell something was wrong. At once, we realized that both his wife and daughter were missing.

Only his three sons, Travis, who was eighteen, and the young boys, Rich and Josh, were in the truck with him. The absence of his wife made the greetings subdued, but once he caught his breath, we drew Mark aside while his sons set up their giant tent.

"Tell me what happened," Kent demanded more forcefully than I liked.

Mark sighed, steeling himself. "You were lucky to have escaped when you did. We kept hoping things would get better, that Phoenix could be saved. Now, I realize how stupid we were. If only we'd left with you…"

For a moment, just the sounds of the insects could be heard.

"I'm sorry," I managed to get out.

"Thanks," he said, while quickly drawing an arm across his eyes. "I…I decided to make a run to the warehouse, where I worked, to gather more supplies. I took Travis with me. I couldn't believe how quickly everything had turned to shit. All the stores were looted, controlled by gangs, or swarmed with those fucking undead bastards. While I was gone, June's friend, Marci, showed up at our house. I never got the whole story from the kids, but I think her husband tried to get food for them and got bit. When he turned, he must've bitten Marci because when Travis and I returned to the house, she was…" He hesitated, taking on a look of horror. "Oh God!"

"You don't have to tell us now," Maureen said softly.

"No, no. I want to because once I do, I never want to speak of it again!" A deep inhale shook his wide frame. "Marci killed June and my daughter. The only reason the boys survived was they were able to lock themselves in the bathroom, while the thing Marci became was busy eating…"

"You don't have to go on," I said, putting my hand on his shoulder.

He panted for a moment. "I know. I know. After killing that bitch I grabbed my boys and headed out here. The barricades had been overrun, but somehow I made it past the hordes. Phoenix is gone, man, just gone. The only good news is that we gathered a bunch of supplies. It should help us last for a while." He looked up at us, his eyes rimmed with red. "Because I can tell you one thing: I intend to kill every last fucking walking corpse I can. I don't care if I have to bash their heads in with a rock, but besides keeping what's left of my family safe, I'm dedicating my life to putting down every undead bastard I can get my hands on!"

The days blurred into a stream of weeks. Soon, we were living off the land as best we could. It was really only Mark's hunting rifle that saved us, for he was able to bag a deer every week or so. We always tried to hunt on the other side on the main ridge so the sound of gunfire wouldn't bring anything down upon our camp. Even with that help, rations were scarce and we slowly grew thin, then gaunt, and before long, I wondered how different we looked from the zombies we were hiding from.

Not long after that, the first zombie showed up. Little Rich spotted him first, but despite only being four, he was smart enough to start screaming at once. The shambling form looked like it had once been a clerk of some kind due its uniform, although the front of his turquoise shirt was now stained with streaks of matted gore.

Mark was about to shoot it, but I quickly shouted, "No wait! Don't waste the ammo. Besides, gunshots can be heard for miles, it could bring dozens more down on us."

He blanched and ensured his kids were behind him. Kent had my back, but I was the one that picked up an axe and buried it in the center of the thing's skull. It went down surprisingly easy and I was a bit proud of myself.

If only everything had remained so simple.

Then they started coming in twos and threes. One time, a half dozen wandered into our camp in the middle of the night. Only the strategic use of keeping the roaring fire at our backs kept anyone from being bit. After that, we kept a watch.

We started rigging trip wires with old beer cans that we filled with pebbles. This usually gave as a little more warning. And of course we made weapons.

By then, we each had at least ten sharpened staffs leaning against every tree in camp. We had developed a special technique, which we called the 'Trip and Trap.' When they came at us, we wouldn't try to kill them. First we would do our best to knock them off their feet. The uneven ground and loose rocks helped us a lot here. Once they were down we'd just keep stabbing them in the face until we scored a lucky hit to the eye or just broke through the skull.

This style of fighting was even easier when more than one of us could gang up on a zombie, because then one person could be 'bait' and the other could easily knock a zombie over from behind.

Despite our adversity and general lack of food, morale began to grow better. We'd killed almost forty zombies by then and none of us had been bitten. Things were going pretty good until winter set in.

I know what some of you northerners are going to say. Poor desert folk, what a tough winter that must have been. However, when you're living in a tent, things become rough pretty damn quick. It was snowing by Thanksgiving, for we were nearly a mile above sea level. Not only was food becoming scarcer, but finding firewood was also a problem. We gathered it along the sides of a little stream, but what once might have taken one man an hour to do, now took four of us several hours each due to the snow. We also dreaded leaving the kids with less of us there as we trekked further and further upstream to search for wood.

We weren't too far from Christmas when our youngest member, Josh, became ill. We hoped it was just a normal cold, but it clung to him. Then an icy sleet hit our camp and it was all we could do just to keep the fire going. Everything became hopelessly soaked and Josh grew even sicker.

My soggy sleeping bag chased me out of my tent early one morning and I joined Kent hovering over the fire with the faint hope that our sodden clothes might somehow dry. Gray clouds owned the sky and dumped more snow upon us. The entire camp was covered in two inches of wet slush and I have to admit that I was feeling pretty low.

Mark slipped on the way out of his tent, which brought forth a fury of cursing.

He stumbled over to us like he was ready to start throwing punches and we quickly moved to make room for him around our struggling fire.

"Rich is sick, too."

"Oh shit," I said.

"Well, kids are tough. I'm sure they'll get better," Kent said.

"Bullshit! No one's going to get better out here in this crap. Maybe I should just take them back to Phoenix and try our chances there," Mark said.

"What? You wouldn't last a day," I said.

"Maybe, but they might not last another day out here," Mark said. "I have to do something. They need medicine. They're just little kids." He covered his face with a dirty hand and tried not to let us hear him sobbing.

For a moment, only the crackling of the smoky fire could be heard. Then I said, "There was a little town I passed through, not too far to the north. I'm sure their general store has some basic meds. It'll be dangerous, but there could be food, too, maybe even ammo, and who knows what else."

"I'm not so sure," Kent began. "Even a small town could have hundreds of those walkers in it."

"It isn't really the zombies I'd be worried about," I said. "A place like that might have held out against the plague and I doubt they'd be too keen on us stealing from them."

"Yeah, well, if they held out, there might not be much left to steal," Kent added.

"I don't care," Mark was quick to say. "It's a chance. Any supplies we can get will help. My kids aren't going to get better eating a few pieces of venison a day. Who knows, maybe if there are people, we could join them. If there aren't, maybe we could move there. Either way, I'm going to check it out. Who's coming?"

"I think just the three of us should go, then Travis and Maureen can take care of the kids and keep them safe," I said.

"I agree," Kent said. "I'll tell Travis and you had better talk to your wife," he told me. "I'm sure she won't be thrilled."

Our tent had become a wet nightmare, as each day, despite all our tarps, the condensation reached further into our bedrolls until we only had a three foot circle of dryness in the center of our sad home.

"I really wish you wouldn't go."

I held Maureen's hand as we talked. "Come on, baby. You know I have to. I can't leave those guys go alone."

"Then I want to go with you."

"No. Someone has to stay here and protect the kids. Besides, you're the closest thing to a medic we have."

We were kneeling, facing each other, and I gave her a tight hug. It didn't help things when she started to cry. "Why did this have to happen? Why does everything have to be so hard?" she sobbed.

"If this works out okay, then things could get easier. We could get all sorts of supplies."

"But there's still a city full of walking corpses just on the other side of the mountains. Everything we worked for our whole lives, our dreams. It's all gone."

"We can have new dreams," I said. "Maybe we can move into that town or something, set ourselves up like kings." I tried to smile. She didn't return the favor.

"I just wish you wouldn't go, Lyle."

"If they're going, I have to."

She sighed. "I know, but please just hold me a little longer first."

* * *

Mark's monster-sized truck was our choice for transportation, and we slammed over the dirt without incident. Once we made it to Route 160, the paved road felt like an undeserved luxury. Pumpkin Center was about thirty miles away.

It didn't take us long, and we rode in silence until Kent said, "Does it strike anyone else as funny that we're doing this on Christmas Eve? Not to make light of things, but getting medicine for children, this is almost like some sort of Christmas story but with zombies."

"I thought it was the twenty-third," I said.

"Nope," Kent countered. "I've been keeping careful track. To-morrow's Christmas."

Mark's voice was stern. "I don't see how it makes any difference, unless the people still there are kissing under the mistletoe. One thing's for sure, the zombies won't give a shit what day it is."

We fell into silence again, and as I listened to the truck glide over the pavement, I reviewed our meager weapons situation. Mark had his rifle, but refused to tell us how many rounds he had left. He also had a pistol, but that had been left with his eldest, Travis. Kent carried an old revolver which had seen better days, and his machete.

By traditional standards, I was the most poorly armed. I had a few throwing knives, which I practiced with daily, but besides that there was only my wood axe and a heavy club I'd been working on. I might hold up all right against a few zombies, but angry human survivors with guns could leave me seriously screwed.

Before we even reached the outskirts of the town, a row of parked cars stretched across the road. Mark decelerated.

"Slow down. Don't even park near it," I said. "We should sneak up there."

"Are you nuts?" Mark replied. "The shorter we travel on foot the better."

"I have to agree with Lyle," Kent broke in. "We don't know what we're facing. I don't see zombies up there, but even that could be a bad sign."

In the end, we talked him into parking and the only zombies we found were dead ones. A lot of dead ones.

"There must be fifty of the fuckers out here," Mark said.

"Points in favor of there being survivors, I'd say." Kent rubbed his beard as he searched for any movement on the wall of abandoned cars.

Crouching down near one of the corpses, I said, "I'm not so sure. It's hard to tell with people that are already rotting, but these wounds look like they're at least a week old, probably older. I don't see any fresh bodies around. They could have lost after putting up a good fight."

"Yeah, it isn't like the zombies can't just walk around this wall of cars."

"But wouldn't there be more zombies milling about?" Kent asked.

"Let's just do this," I said. As one, we moved around the left side of the short, abandoned wall of vehicles.

There was no movement between the houses, but we were still on the edge of the small town. I read a sign. "Population twelve hundred. Not too many, or an insane amount, depends on how you look at it I guess."

"But where is everyone?" Mark asked in a low voice as we continued forward, seeking cover where we could. The town was mostly modular homes, each claiming their square of sparse desert sand. More than one had Christmas decorations on it. I thought back to my old neighborhood. There were always those few who put up their decorations in early November or even earlier, wanting to get a jump on the Christmas holiday. Evidently, there had been those people here, too. Plastic Santas, reindeer, snowmen and elves, littered the lawns and rooftops, some having fallen over in neglect and faded in the harsh sun. It was an eerie sight.

It was almost a relief when we spotted a pair of zombies. They lumbered towards us groaning. "No guns," I said while advancing. "Trip and trap."

That was when shots rang out.

We dove for cover, with the zombies drawing nearer. The groaning had attracted more undead and I could make out a second wave of at least a dozen gathering.

"Shit, what now?" I asked and then winced when a thorn from the Palo Verde I had leaned behind found my neck.

"I'm not sure they were shooting at us," Kent said. When we asked him why, he went on to say, "There were three shots, which can mean help, and I didn't see the impact of bullets anywhere around us."

"Well, anyone that has bullets to waste like that, I might be inclined to help, especially if they have medication with them."

"Are you sure of that?" I gasped, as I finally made out where the shots might have come from. About an eighth of a mile away there was a fortified general store with several figures waving from the roof. But what shocked me more was the three hundred zombies that surrounded the store, and more importantly, the fifty walkers that had broken off from the mob and were heading our way.

"Hey, guys, look!" Kent yelled, pointing east out across the lake that bordered the town. On the water, three giant speedboats were racing toward shore.

"What the hell?" I said. Beyond the racing boats, some kind of flotilla had been created in the middle of Roosevelt Lake. "It's like a small town out there."

"More like a big one," Kent said.

"What did we get ourselves in the middle of?" Mark asked, as the first zombies drew near.

"Save your bullets," I said, while I base-balled half a zombie's head off with my axe. The others followed me.

Kent pointed to a few cactus-covered gullies to the north. "If we could attack them and then lead the walkers into the canyon, the *wait-a-minute brush* will slow them down and then we can circle around back to the store."

"But there'll still be over two hundred around the store!" I yelled while smashing in another face as our group weaved through the growing horde of undead.

"That's why we have to get them all to follow us," Kent said.

Thirty minutes later, the three of us were lighting small fires and shouting. Our plan had pros and cons. It was working well enough as far as attracting the dead to us, but they were so spaced out, that we were forced to fight the closer ones while we waited for the others to make it into the canyon. Still, we had position. I broke out with my lighter club, and when any zombie reached the top of the steep hill we were perched on, I pushed them ass-over-elbow back the way they'd come. This rarely killed them, but usually I knocked two or three more over with the first falling body.

"The people on the boats were holding back for some reason," Mark said, as he lit another creosote bush on fire. The bright flames also helped keep the growing horde of zombies at bay.

"Why aren't they coming to help us or the people at the store?" Kent asked.

"It could be because they're enemies." I said. "I think we'd better move, guys. Even with these fires they'll overrun us soon."

Kent smiled. "Time to play a little fox and the hare. Let's go!"

We rushed away just as they came over the lip of the hill, scores of them. Almost at once we had put a dozen yards between us and the shambling mob of walkers. We then ducked under the clinging thorns, and the zombies stumbled straight through, getting caught up by both their clothes and their rotting flesh.

We led them on a merry chase, and as we went, Kent began to sing. "Over the river and through the cactus, to grandmother's store we go. The heroes know the way to lead the sickening zombies through the grasping catclaws."

"Hey, look," Mark said, while pointing at the General Store. One of the doors had opened and a good percentage of the lingering zombies began to pour into the building. "I'll never be able to get any medicine now!"

"Wait, check it out," I said. "The survivors are using boards to cross over to that roof covering the pumps. I bet they're going to try to reach those vehicles that are parked there."

Shots rang out.

"What the hell!" Kent yelled. "The people from the boats are shooting at them. This is insane."

"I say we help the people in the store," I said.

"Lyle, you don't even have a gun," Mark reprimanded.

"But they do." I said, pointing as the first people that had gained the roof over the pumps began to shoot back at the people rushing from the boats. Their shooting caused another problem, for it was drawing some of the walkers back out of the store.

Meanwhile, an all out firefight had erupted between the men on the roof and the boatmen. The latter were using what cover they could and slowly advanced on the General Store, while our little group was coming down from the foothills on the opposite side.

"Mark, find some cover up here and use that rifle to even the odds. Kent watch his back," I said.

"What do you think you're going to do, Lyle?" Kent nearly screamed.

"I'm gonna try to talk to our new friends."

At least thirty zombies were clustering below the people on the gas pump roof, and they were too busy fighting the boatmen to think about killing the zombies below. We had to hurry; besides the boatmen and the thirty zombies, over two hundred more walkers would be pouring out of the foothills before too long.

I swung my axe at the back of a zombie's skull, feeling bone give way to metal. I was fighting two-handed and my club pushed one back and it lost its footing, knocking two more over with it. I killed two more before they noticed me.

"Hey, hey there!" I shouted up to the people on the roof. "Who are you people? And who are those guys in the boats?"

An older, grizzled face peered over the western lip of the roof. His face was quickly followed by three others who were all certainly children.

"Who are we?" the old man shouted down at me. "Why, we live here! Those bastards in the boats are just a bunch of upper class bastards from Phoenix that think, since they ran out of their caviar, that they should be able to steal what little we got. Last I heard, they were waiting for us and the zombies to kill each other, then they were gonna come in and kill whatever was still moving and steal all we've worked for."

"We just need some medicine for some sick kids," I called up to him as my arms swung my weapons in manic arcs in order to keep the walkers at bay.

"We got plenty of medicine along with our best gear in our cars. If you help us get out of here, we'd be happy to help your kids." He shouted something to the men with guns and then returned his attention to me. "Try to shut the door to the store if you can, that'll keep the rest of them in there and then we'll have less to fight."

Looking across the decayed faces of the ten zombies that were now focused on me and stood between me and the door, I figured that this would be no simple task.

I tried to do it anyway.

Almost at once, I realized the error of my ways, and soon the walking dead had surrounded me on every side. My axe took down one after another, but then got stuck in the neck of a zombie. Before I could pull it free, hands were grabbing it out of my fingers. With a curse, I let it go. Then grabbing my club, two-handed, I laid into them as quickly as I could. Hands were clawing and pulling at me from every direction.

I probably wouldn't have made it if Kent and Mark hadn't run around the corner of the store just then. Kent rushed up to a zombie, then shot it in the back of the head at point blank range. Mark hung back a little and made each shot count. With their help, I was able to make it to the gas station's door and I slammed it closed. The zombies were all over me, clawing and looking to take a bite of me, but at least a good forty or fifty were locked inside the building now.

I swung out with my club, just trying to keep them back. Kent was attempting to work his way to me, while Mark was doing everything he could, but I had been there too long. They were all over me. Teeth clamped down on my arm, but I tore my leather clad limb away from the attack before teeth found my skin. I was off balance, and then a giant whale of a zombie got before me.

There was no way I could keep the big bastard at bay with just my club and axe.

That's when my face was suddenly sprayed with gore and I heard a hoot from the old man on the pump roof. "I got 'em! I got the bastard!" The old man held a rifle and had helped me by blasting the head off the closest zombies to me.

Between the gore, snapping teeth, and gunfire smoke, it was hard for me to see what the boatmen might have been doing, but I did see the men on the roof tossing ropes over the side and climbing down to their vehicles below. One of them was shot during his descent and he fell from the rope with a scream to land heavily on the ground. As soon as he landed, the walkers were on him. His screams were mercifully short.

Just when I was starting to think that we had some handle on the zombies lingering outside of the store, Mark came sprinting forward. "We have to go now!" After seeing the look on my face, he added, "The first zombies are making it out of the canyon. There'll be a hundred of them on us in less than a minute."

"Shit, we need to get out of here!" I screamed, while I whacked my club onto a zombie's skull, caving it in, blood and brain matter spewing out to splat wetly on the dusty ground.

"No shit," the old man said from above. He was lowering child after child into the back of a Suburban with its roof taken off. Many of the zombies were going for the vehicles and my friends and I did what we could to keep them at bay.

I heard Mark scream in anger and I quickly asked, "What is it?"

"I'm out of ammo."

The vehicles were pulling away and I leaped on the sideboard of the Suburban, yelling, "Around this way! Our truck is on the other side of that wall!"

The boatmen were still firing at us, but once we had the zombies off our back, our return fire kept them behind their shelters.

"Looks like the zombies are heading their way now," Kent pointed out.

"The cowards," the old man said. "They thought they'd have easy pickings on all that was ours, just waiting for us to die instead of helping. Well, we showed them. They're probably too scared to even check on the store now. Filthy backstabbers."

I just held on while trying to take in how many people had survived and figured we had twenty.

"So where you taking us, sonny?"

It was a bittersweet reunion with Mark and his family. The survivors had the medicine that could save Mark's children, but it turned out that Mark had been bitten. He only lasted three more days. Old man Mitch and the other survivors were more than happy to move into the campsite with us. Though we had our problems and issues, having them along sure made a lot of things easier and certainly safer. Soon, log walls and deadfalls surrounded our growing camp. Tarps draped over larger kitchen areas as well. We had already made a few raids into the little town to get more supplies. Whenever this happened, the men on the boats always watched us.

One day they might come for us, but that day wouldn't be today. And as I looked around at the big New Year's feast we had prepared for ourselves, and the Christmas tree we'd put up in the center of the camp, decorated with whatever we could find, for the first time since the plague began, I let a small sliver of hope enter my tired heart.

The kids were all counting down to the New Year, and as it drew closer with each passing minute, I put my arm around Maureen and pulled her in for a big kiss.

CHRISTMAS OF THE ZOMBIE GNOMES

KELLY M. HUDSON

Some things are just too ridiculous to be believed, and I don't expect anyone to believe me when I tell them my story, but every word of it is true, regardless of what you might think.

First off, my name is Tommy Kotter, and I'm a nobody. I'm so much of a nobody that when you read my name you were probably like, "Hmm, don't know him." Yeah, well, while that may be true, I used to be known and loved. I had parents and they did care for me, but they died when I was five, right before Christmas, and it was horribly tragic, as you can guess.

That Christmas, after I lost my folks, I wrote a letter to Santa. In it, I told him I wanted to come work for him at the North Pole. It was dumb and cute, yes, the kind of thing only a child would believe in. Well, wouldn't you know it? That next Christmas, I was woken up at three in the morning to hear reindeer tromping on the roof of my foster parents' house. My window popped open and in flew Santa Claus!

I know, I know. But it's the truth.

Now, don't think that my life was so wonderful after that. Santa took me in, all right, but he learned pretty quickly that I was fairly useless. Yeah, I'm a nice guy and I can get along with just about anyone, but as far as skills, I don't have many. I went to the school Mrs. Claus taught and did okay enough to graduate, but when it came to specialized skills, I had none. They tried me at computers and I promptly shorted one out. They put me to work on some machinery repair, and wouldn't you know it? The car I tried to fix came out worse than when I got my hands on it. I worked the library, but they still use the Dewey Decimal System, and that's beyond me.

On and on it went, until I'm pretty sure Santa was wondering just why he took on a kid like me for. Eventually, and I remember the day as clear as the one when my parents died, Santa called me into his office.

"I have no use for you, my son," he said. He was facing out the window and it was quite a view. The entire North Pole stretched out before him, the snow gleaming and glittering like a field of diamonds in the sunlight.

"Please, sir," I begged. "I'll do whatever you need. I have nowhere else to go."

I was eighteen when we had this meeting. I'm twenty now.

"There's no place for you here," he said. He still wouldn't face me. He wore his usual red flannel long underwear with a green shirt over it. He only dressed up when we had our special Friday dinners and for the Big Night.

Santa sighed, his conscience heavy.

"We can't put you to work making toys. The elves and their union, you know. And as far as everything else, you're... well... there's no nice way to put this."

"I'm useless," I said.

Santa sighed again. I could tell he didn't want to do this but he really didn't seem to have any other options. Santa wasn't a communist. You had to work to earn your keep, and he already had plenty of dumb guys just like me to shovel snow and feed his reindeer and keep their stalls clean.

"I don't want to say that about you," he said. "You surely do have some talent. We just haven't discovered it yet, and frankly, we're running out of time."

I didn't know what to say. My heart was heavy in my chest. Since I was a kid, all I wanted to do after my folks died, was to live here—and I did. I lived the dream. But it seemed the dream had turned to a nightmare and now I was going to get kicked out.

I shuddered. I couldn't even conceive of facing the outside world.

"I can give you another year," he said. "In that time, we must discover your hidden talent. If not, then you'll have to go." He turned at last to face me, tears glistening in the corners of his eyes. "The Man Upstairs," he said. "He makes the rules. I'm but His humble servant, and you know about earning your keep."

I did, and told him as much.

"Thank you for the extra year," I said.

Santa smiled a sad smile.

"I'm going to send you someplace special, in the hope that maybe there you can find your place."

My stomach dropped. I knew where he spoke of and I hoped beyond hope that it wasn't where he was sending me.

"The Island," he said.

I knew then my fate would be unkind.

It wasn't really an island. It had been, at one time, but they'd since moved the location, bringing it closer to Santa Land. It was actually a peninsula now even though everyone still referred to it as The Island.

The Peninsula of Misfit Toys just doesn't have the same ring, you know.

I was welcomed with open arms by the current leader of the Island, a tall elf known as Turner the Tan. He was named right, because unlike the other elves—that were so pale you could almost lose sight of them in a good snow fall—Turner was as bronze as an Olympic medal. He was bigger than most of the elves, too, as he stood nearly to my waist.

For comparison's sake, I'm six feet tall, gangly, weigh next to nothing, have long feet I constantly trip over, have a big nose and bug eyes, and acne that just won't go away. I'm a classic nerd while Turner, with his tan, rippling muscles, and chiseled good looks, was nothing like a classic elf.

He'd taken over when King Moonracer had been promoted by Santa. Turner ran a tight ship. He put the misfit toys to work, which mostly consisted of trying to repair returned toys that had a chance of being something whole again. The Misfit Toys who lived on the Island were all too far gone or too old to ever be anything more than what they were.

I fit right in.

My job was sweeping up every night and taking out the garbage and basically keeping things clean. I did it well enough that after my first year, Santa didn't send me packing. But still, I found no special skill, no trade that would move me up in the ranks of Santa Land or even The Island.

I have to say, though, that my fears of getting stuck there with the undesirables were stupid. I really grew to like the people I worked with. A lot of us were there: broken or malfunctioning toys and people like me who didn't fit in anywhere. The Island had its own hierarchy and we took orders from managers, just like the other places in Santa Land, only our managers were pretty nice, for the most part. No one took themselves too seriously because we all knew, deep down, we were where we were because it was either our last chance or we had nowhere else to go.

One of these good toys was my main manager, Peter. He was a big old stuffed white elephant with pink polka dots all over his body, and almost as tall as me. At first glance, you couldn't see what was wrong with him. But when you paid attention, you started to notice the polka dots weren't evenly distributed and they weren't even dots, really. Some of them were squares and others were oblong. It was like an elf had gotten really drunk on Santa Beer one night and started stitching away, stuffing in that magic dust that brought all the toys to life. Where the magic dust came from was Santa's trade secret, and only he and the elves knew anything about it. Peter's problem was those that couldn't be fixed, and that's why he lived and worked on The Island. Most of toys that came through we could repair, but the ones that couldn't be repaired but still had that crimson, magic dust Santa had given them, became one of us.

Peter was a regular kind of guy and he sure didn't have to be. He was a hero, of sorts. It's an old story; some say a legend, about how Peter and some other Misfit Toys saved Christmas with Rudolph's help. I never bothered to ask him about it so I never learned the truth. I didn't care very much, anyway. He was good to me and that was what mattered.

"Yes, sir," Peter said. He lit a cigarette and took a big puff on it. Peter loved to smoke. He loved it so much that the white cotton between his toes had long since stained yellow. "It was a rough one today, buddy, but we made it through."

"You made it through," I said. "I'm still working."

I was sweeping up what was left of the mess in the Main Hall. The Island had four buildings, all connected by one long hallway. The biggest was the Main Hall, where all the work went on. The second largest was the dorms, where we slept. There was also the cafeteria and the library. The cafeteria had a gymnasium built in and the library had a rec room where we could play games or watch TV. It was a pretty nice set up. We received three meals a day plus a snack at night, so none of us went hungry.

Peter laughed, sucking down some smoke. He let it plume from his mouth as he smiled, his long trunk stirring the cigarette smoke as he exhaled. "Well, I tell you, every year, I think the Big Day can't be any bigger, and then more humans like you get squirted out and I'll be damned if we don't have even more work to do. Things are getting too complicated for old timers like me. Plus, now there's all those new-fangled video games and electronics. Shit."

Peter liked to swear, too, even though it was frowned upon. He looked over at me with those big black button eyes of his and shook his head. "It's getting so a regular toy can't even get any shelf space with all the gadgets. Whatever happened to kids using their imaginations?"

I shrugged. I didn't have much of an imagination, myself. I liked toys when I was a kid but when I got older, well, life kind of took over. I didn't have time to play around anymore.

"Ah, what do you know? You're just another loser like the rest of us," he said. He coughed, spat a wad of cotton phlegm into the garbage can next to him, and hummed to himself.

"I don't think we're losers," I said. "But we're not winners, either."

Peter grinned and snorted smoke from his fluffy trunk.

"Now you got that right," he said. "I hear the Big Man is going to build a new annex onto Santa Land. This one's going to be totally dedicated to all the electronics. I guess it had to happen one day, but if you ask me, that shit is going to take over our entire operation. Within ten years, mark my words, all the stuff we're doing now will be obsolete and they'll have machines in here doing the work. You know what happens then, right?"

I did. Toys that couldn't get along, that had attitude problems or were deranged or had become useless, were sent to the edge of the peninsula, out where the water flowed when it wasn't frozen over. We called it Alcatraz. That's where the bad toys went to be locked up or put down. When I say put down, I mean, The Furnace.

"Don't worry about it," I said. "It's never gonna happen."

"Don't worry about it?" Peter said, spinning his button eyes. "You don't have to. The Big Man will just send you back to the World." He shivered. "That would be worse, though. Worse than Alcatraz."

Tina strolled in then, and let me tell you, Tina was a real pain. She was one of those Raggedy Ann dolls gone all wrong. Her hair, despite all the dying, kept turning yellow. It refused to stay red. She was missing half the teeth in her mouth, and even though they'd tried for years to give her bridges and false teeth, they never stuck. She talked out of the right side of her mouth so you wouldn't notice, but everyone knew. On top of all this, she thought she was the sexiest thing on the planet. If you didn't treat her right, she gave you hell, and then she got her current boyfriend, Turner the Tan, to really give you grief. She was a whole lot of trouble rolled into a small, cotton body.

"What are you boys doing?" she asked. Her voice was very nasal, like one of those drunk Jersey girls on TV.

"Shooting the shit," Peter said. He gave her a sideways glance and looked away, his big head wreathed in smoke. There was a rumor they used to be an item, but once Turner came along, things changed. Again, I don't know. I kept out of that kind of thing.

"Give me a smoke," she said. Peter grunted and slid a cigarette out of the pack he kept in his pocket. She took it, lit hers from the end of his, and sucked down half of it before exhaling. She saw me staring and curled her nose at me. "What are you looking at?"

"I thought Turner didn't like it when you smoked?" I said.

"He doesn't own me. He doesn't own any of this," she said, gesturing to her petite body.

"Who'd want to?" I said. I went back to sweeping. Peter barked a laugh that echoed in the empty room. It was so loud it got the attention of Cozmo, the little green wind-up rocket that could never fire. Cozmo was on the other side of the other room, emptying some garbage cans. He had little legs and arms that jutted out, making it hard for him to walk, but he got by. His biggest flaws were his inability to actually launch and a pair of giant buckteeth that made him speak like the biggest hillbilly you'd ever seen.

"What're y'all doing in here?" he asked. His torso was the body of the rocket and he had a winch on his back that, when cranked, was supposed to shoot sparks out of his butt and send him flying. He was about four feet tall.

"Nothing!" Tina shouted. She liked to shout.

"Y'all don't have to be rude," Cozmo said, drifting over. When he saw Peter and Tina smoking, his little eyes grew big. "You all ain't supposed to be smokin' in here."

"I'm the boss," Peter said.

"And I'm sleeping with his boss," Tina said. "I think we'll be okay."

Cozmo grinned. "Hell then, give me one of those smokes." He waddled over and stuck out a small hand. Peter placed a cigarette in it and Cozmo flipped it up to his mouth. Peter flicked his lighter and Cozmo was smoking with the best of them, until he saw me looking at him funny.

"What? You don't think a rocket can smoke? You think it's dangerous?" he asked.

"Uh, yeah. What if you explode?" I said.

"Explode!" Cozmo spat. "Hell, I ain't ever gonna explode. Why do you think I'm in here with you all? It ain't cause of my good looks."

Turned strolled in. Peter and Tina ditched their cigarettes so fast it was almost like they'd never been smoking at all. Cozmo was slow, and completely busted. He was shooting a stream of smoke from his mouth when he saw Turner and froze.

"Aw, hell," Cozmo said.

"What have I told you about smoking in here?" Turner said. "We have designated spots for smoking. This isn't one of them."

Tina slid next to Turner, purring against him like a cat. "I tried to tell him, honey," she said.

"If that don't beat all," Cozmo said, scratching his cheek as he ground out the butt beneath his foot. He shook his pointed head with disgust.

"We don't have time for this," Turner said. "I just received an emergency shipment and I need you boys to get out there and haul it in."

"Come on, boss," Peter said. "I'm off work."

"Me, too," Cozmo said.

I shrugged. I was stuck. "What is it?" I asked.

Turner smiled at me. "There was a fire at one of our auxiliary factories down in Haiti," he said.

So it was one of those things. Santa and the elves couldn't possibly keep up with all the demand, so they hired out to factories in poorer countries. Now, I hear that those people get paid good wages, but I wouldn't be surprised if corners were cut. Everyone is looking for the easy buck, you know.

"They had this big order of lawn ornaments ready to ship," Turner continued. "Well, they were burned up to the point that they need some repairs and they should be good to go. So we get them in here, get them set up, and we have an emergency shift later tonight."

Emergency shift was where we did extra work. It was supposed to be fun, with festive music playing and we all got to eat marshmallow s'mores and drink hot cocoa. It usually turned out okay, but it still made most of us grumpy.

"Let me get this straight," I said. "If we get the ornaments in here, we won't have to do the emergency shift?" I smiled and wiggled my eyebrows at Cozmo and Peter. They grinned in return, admiring my bartering skills.

Turner rubbed his chin, thinking it over. Finally he smiled and nodded.

"All right!" I said. "Let's get this done!"

It took almost an hour to get all the boxes in and another half hour to empty them. They were all full of—get this—garden gnomes. You know the kind: they were all about two feet tall with conical red hats, little blue shirts, red pants, black shoes, and each had the same exact face full of gray whiskers, beady blue eyes, and pursed red lips.

Their bodies were made of thin aluminum and they had fully-articulated limbs. They were all burned in some fashion. Some had melted faces, others arms and legs. Some were just greasy with smoke and others had melted hats. They were almost all fairly useless.

They would work, sure. You could wind them up and set them loose in a garden and they'd wobble around, but they weren't pretty. Our job was to clean them up and get the jammed gears working.

Correction: their job. Ours was almost finished. Once we had them on the work tables, we were done. Peter and Cozmo and I exchanged looks, smiled with satisfaction, and headed back to the dorms. We did stop at the kitchen along the way and snatch up a few s'mores and a mug of hot chocolate on our way out.

Everyone else, either roused from their sleep or already up, were in the kitchen, mumbling and shooting us glares of contempt. We smiled like we'd won the lottery, made a big deal of getting to go to bed while they worked, and escaped before the mob turned against us.

"Good work," Peter said, munching on a s'more.

"Hell yes, son," Cozmo added.

I grinned and we were off.

I woke three hours later to the screams.

At first, I thought I was just dreaming, even after I'd woken up, but after a few more seconds passed, I realized it was real and happening very close to me.

You have to understand something. I've never heard a real scream in my life. Living in Santa Land, there's not much misery and suffering, and when it does happen, it's kept under wraps. I've seen scary movies and heard people screaming in them, but to hear it for real was something I'll never forget. The shrieks rattled my teeth and shook my nerves. I sat up in bed, quivering, pulling the covers up to my neck. I didn't know what to do I was so stunned.

Peter burst in, slamming my door open. I screamed. I'd never done that before in my life, either. Blind panic hit me and I shoved my body back against the headboard, trying to get away.

"Tommy!" Peter yelled. I couldn't process what was happening. I knew it was Peter and I knew he wasn't attacking me, but I also couldn't make that work with my fear. I clawed at the wall behind me like there was some way I could crawl up it and get away.

Peter ran across the room, his bulk moving faster than you would think, and he slapped me across the face. That did the trick. I grabbed my cheek where he struck me and winced. "Why'd you do that?"

"To snap you out of it. Something's going on in the Main Hall," he said.

He grabbed my shoulders and hauled me out of bed. I could smell the cigarette smoke on his paws, so thick I almost gagged. I was clad in my pajamas so I had to take a couple of extra seconds to climb into my jeans and slip into my favorite flannel shirt.

"What's happening?" I asked while getting dressed.

"I don't know," Peter said, constantly glancing down the hallway. "I've never heard anything like this. Even when Shaggy was loose."

Shaggy was the Abominable Snowman and he was part of that legendary tale I'd referred to earlier. He'd been a resident here for a long time, before he became too wild for everyone. I'd heard hushed tales about what had happened to him, but I never knew for sure.

I was dressed and ready to go.

"We're going to run off and get help, right?" I said, hopeful Peter wouldn't want to play hero. He shook his head and took off. I could do nothing else but follow.

We'd made it to the entrance of the Main Hall when the smell hit us, foul and intense.

If you've never smelled the mixture of the torn innards of toys and the leaking of the magic dust that animates them, you're lucky. It's a queasy combination of burning oil, cabbage, and leaking natural gas. It hung in the air, filling my lungs with its stench, making me gag and stagger to the side. I leaned against the wall, and tried desperately not to vomit. When I was finally able to lift my head and see what was going on, I wished I hadn't.

Carnage. Ripped and torn toy parts were everywhere. A wheel lay to the right, an arm to the left, and between them yards and yards of stuffing, hissing magic dust—which is what the dust did when it made contact with the air; it hissed—eyeballs, teeth, and a few severed heads, still alive and screaming at the top of their lungs.

Running amidst all the death and destruction were over two dozen of the gnomes that we'd been issued to repair. They were all snarling, metal teeth snapping together, as they attacked those still alive and those dying, slurping up the magic dust and guzzling the leftover body parts, be they plastic, wood, or metal.

It was a chorus of sounds and smells too rich and powerful to stand. There were the screams, of course, and the howls of the suffering and dying. But there was also the crunch of metal gnome teeth and the shredding of softer materials. There was the hissing of the magic dust and the sucking of the metal tongues that ate it up. The odors were like I described, but now that I was in the room, there were others. The stink of fear and panic, and sweat, and under all that was another scent, the stench of the gnomes themselves. They wore a burnt perfume of decay and rust, along with something else, a reek I couldn't hang a name on.

"Zombies," Peter murmured. I heard what he said but it really didn't register beyond the sound of it. "Dear God."

I clutched the wall next to me. In those few seconds since we'd entered the room, we hadn't been noticed, but that was a thing of the past now, because even as I tried to figure out what Peter meant by what he said, one of the zombie gnomes looked up from the doll he was chewing on, spat out the button eye he'd just bitten from its face, and shrieked.

All the other zombie gnomes looked up at us as one.

"Oh, shit," Peter said. "Run!"

Somehow, I listened. Somehow, my legs, which had been wobbling and threatening to bail on me at the first opportunity, found strength and reacted. I sprinted from the room, hot on Peter's heels, before the closest zombie gnome could get me. Fortunately, I thought to spin around and slam the door closed behind me.

They crashed into the wood, a clatter of metal and anger, the wall the door was in shaking from their impact. I knew it was just a matter of time before they either smashed through or figured out how to turn the doorknob, and our survival rested on the flimsiest of chances. I sprinted along with Peter, both of us hollering as we ran.

Peter found a door to our left and threw it open, intending to hide in there. He stopped two feet into the room and I had to skid to keep from running into him. He was staring at something just out of my sight, and when my eyes fell upon the same image, I stared as blankly as he did.

Tina was on her knees between Turner's legs, her head bobbing up and down. Turner had his eyes closed and his head back, groaning. How they didn't hear the commotion out there or our loud arrival, I'll never know.

Strangely, they heard Peter clear his throat. Tina spun around with a popping sound and Turner gaped as he tried to haul his pants back up.

"What are you two doing?" Tina shouted.

"Uh, don't you hear all that screaming?" Peter said.

She tilted her head and listened. "Oh, my, God."

"We have to get out of here," I said.

"What is that?" Turner said.

"Zombie gnomes," I said, still not sure what it meant. But it made a certain sort of sense.

Down the hall, the wooden door gave and we heard the zombie gnomes pour through, screaming towards us.

"Run!" Peter yelled.

They hauled ass, caught up with the two of us as we made for the exit, and passed us by. As we ran, more toys who'd not been in the shop for one reason or another came out of their rooms to see what all the fuss was about.

First out was Toby, a small blue train with wheels that were square instead of round. He told me once they tried to replace his wheels but the pain was too much. He was fated to be a Misfit, he said, and was happy to be here.

He wasn't so happy when two zombie gnomes fell on him. One bit his right eye out even as it grabbed his smoke stack and ripped it free from his body. Magic dust filled the air with its bright red brilliance, hissing like a rabid snake. Toby wheeled to the side, his whistle tooting, as the other zombie jumped in front of him, grabbed his grille, and tore it off. Toby's mouth, which was underneath the grille, opened and screamed as the same zombie dipped its head and rammed its pointed metal hat down Toby's throat. The zombie crawled inside Toby and didn't stop until it had clawed its way out of his caboose. Toby's square wheels stopped spinning as he sat down, steam whispering from his side vents.

Second was Dora, a jack-in-the-box. She had a busted spring that served as her backbone and the reason she was never repaired was because they feared that if they went in, she could be paralyzed forever. She didn't accept her fate as well as some of the others and was almost always quiet. She was the saddest jack-in-the-box I'd ever seen. She never spoke and kept to herself.

Her bouncing head peered from the room as a zombie gnome spied her. It grabbed her by the sides of her ping-pong ball head and yanked. She screamed as her body followed; the long coil, twisted upon itself, and her main part, the box she could never leave. The zombie gnawed on her spiral column, metal scraping metal, until her spine snapped and came free. The box shot backwards, slamming against the wall. Four zombie gnomes ran inside it, hands like talons ripping and teeth like alligators chomping.

The zombie who'd bitten off her long neck grabbed the small end of it and whipped it around, shattering her head against the wall. The ping-pong ball burst and the floor and wall were showered with red magic dust. The zombie dove into it, sucking down the hissing sand and rolling in the refuse of Dora's skull.

The next toys out were a tiny battalion of green, plastic army soldiers. Peter called them Bob's Brigade because their leader, Sgt. Bob, was the only one of them who could speak. They stood six inches tall and were all misshapen in some way. Some held rifles that had no triggers melded to arms with no hands. Others were missing limbs or had other maladies. None could be repaired and even if it were possible for them to be fixed, not a one of them would have done so. They were like brothers and did everything together, so the idea of one of them leaving without the others was worse than death for them.

"Attack!" Sgt. Bob yelled, and his battalion did as ordered. There were fifteen in all, and if they'd been properly armed or prepared, they might have stood a chance. As it was, they went down quicker than the others.

Zombie gnome after zombie gnome swept over them, grabbing a soldier and shoving them down their throats. Metal teeth gnawed on squirming, plastic men who had no mouths to scream. They were plowed over in seconds, leaving only Sgt. Bob. He stood at attention, shot a salute to his fallen brothers, and was promptly bitten in two by a zombie with a melted face.

That left only us.

How or why these things lived, I couldn't say. Maybe they were bewitched, maybe since they were from Haiti it had to do with some kind of voodoo, or maybe whatever had burned them had also brought them back to life. What I did know was that they loved to feast on the magic dust that made every toy live, and the more they ate, the stronger they seemed to become.

We made it to the doors at the end of the hallway and burst through them into the gym. Four more toys were huddled in the far corner, too frightened to move. I recognized them immediately. Amongst them was Cozmo, and the other three were Andy, a green plane that was missing his tail, Becky, a fire truck that was painted purple with splotches of yellow, and Boris, a shark with legs who had no eyes.

"Oh, dear Lord!" Becky shouted. She zoomed around in circles, her little siren whirring and her ladders going up and down.

Andy sputtered and coughed a cloud of black dust. When he saw us, he took off across the floor, trying to catch wind and fly. He would rise and crash to the side, as he always did. His eyes bugged out from inside the cockpit, wild and crazed.

Boris stood where he was, pressed against the wall, his mouth snapping open and shut. Boris hardly spoke.

Cozmo ran over to us.

"What in the hell is all that racket?" he demanded.

Behind us, across the gym, the doors we'd come through burst open and in poured the zombie gnomes.

"Oh, heavens!" Becky shouted.

"Run!" Peter yelled.

We followed behind Peter as he brought us to the doors that led outside. All but Boris, who instead charged the zombies, going straight for the sound of their bustling.

"Boris!" Andy called to him.

"I'm a shark!" Boris cried out. "I'm a predator!"

He ran right into their midst, his big mouth chomping left and right.

He took the head off one zombie and the arm from another before they converged on him, their fingers and mouths tearing chunks from his plastic hide.

His magic dust drained from the wounds but he pressed on, thrashing and biting. He tore the face from one undead gnome and knocked four more over with his efforts.

"Well, I'll be damned," Cozmo said, taking a moment to glance over his shoulder and check out what was happening.

The last I saw of Boris was his tail whipping in the air as the full might of the zombie gnomes pressed down on him. We slipped outside into the cold.

The night air was clear but the sky wasn't. It was filled with dark clouds, obscuring the stars and reflecting the manufactured lights of our headquarters down onto the snow. We were able to see quite well, which was a lucky break.

Just then, a loud alarm clanged from inside the building. Someone had tripped the emergency chimes. Joy rushed into my heart as I realized that soon, Santa and his forces would sweep in and save us. When I turned my grin towards Peter, his frown froze my happiness in my chest.

"Shit," Peter whispered.

"What?" I said. We were still running, headed towards Peppermint Lane; the road that led from our peninsula over to Santa Land. "They'll be coming to get us!"

"No," Peter said. He choked up and shook his head as he slowed down.

"What're you talking about, buddy?" Cozmo asked.

We all stopped to catch our breath. We were a good three hundred yards from the building and the zombie gnomes had yet to show themselves.

"That alarm isn't to bring help," Turner said. He pressed his lips together, as if to keep the next words from coming out of his mouth. "That alarm warns Santa Land to close its borders. Nothing will get in or out because the Christmas Field will dome up over and around it."

The Christmas Field. It was the device Santa used to keep prying eyes from spying on our activities. Many were the times foreign nations marched on us to take over, but they could never find us because Santa's magic foiled their technology. It covered the entire area except for the peninsula, which was left to fend for itself if outsiders came. We were evacuated, of course, and led to safety, but sometimes we came back to a burned-down home. It had happened once since I'd been assigned with the Misfits and now it seemed it was happening again, only this time, we were left out—literally—in the cold.

As that horrible realization fell over us, the doors to the gym opened and the zombie gnomes poured out, teeth gnashing, sprinting straight for us.

We ran again. What else could we do? These creatures wanted us; they were after the magic dust from the toys and the blood from me and Turner. But there was no place to go. They'd already swept through the main building and we couldn't go to Santa Land because it had been cut off from us. We were on our own and desperate. The problem was: desperate people usually don't make good decisions.

I followed Peter, who was leading us away from the building, towards the water. We were about two hundred yards from the shore, and if we kept going in that direction, we were going to be pinned in.

I hollered out for Peter, but the wind whipped and whirled, even this far from the water, and took my words away. I had no choice but to catch up.

So I ran, harder than I ever had in my life. I was towards the back, with Cozmo and Becky. Andy was just ahead of us, and the poor little guy kept building up speed in order to try and take off, but every time he clattered back to the hard-packed snow, defeated. Becky's siren wailed and Cozmo was quiet, his breath sending giant white plumes of desperation into the air. I passed Turner and Tina and caught up with Peter, who, despite his size, age, and cigarette smoking, was ahead of us all.

"We can't go that way!" I shouted. He slowed down, looked up ahead, and back behind. I saw the light of realization dawn in his eyes.

"Oh, shit," he said.

Charging up on us, closing the gap faster than we could keep it filled, were the zombies. I'd guess there were still two dozen of them and they scampered across the snow like they were born to it. They were of a single mind and purpose and feared nothing.

"We're screwed," Peter said. He was puffing so hard I thought he'd have a heart attack, but he was right. There was really no-where to go. If we ran to the right or left, we'd still get caught by the little monsters.

Then Peter did something extraordinary. He shoved me and Turner aside and strode out towards the zombie gnomes.

"You guys keep running!" he yelled. "I'll hold them back!"

"No!" Cozmo cried. He and the others had finally caught up. "You can't! It's suicide."

Peter nodded, his expression grim. "I know, but I can't run another yard. I'm done. And I'm damned tired of running," he said. "You guys go. You'll think of something. Just get out of here."

"We can't!" Tina cried. "We won't leave you!" Turner looked at her kind of funny, like he didn't like that she was so concerned, but he let it go. I locked eyes with Peter and saw he was right. Our only chance was for someone to run interference and he was just the man—excuse me, toy—for it.

"You take care of them," he said to me. "You guys go on. Run for it."

He turned his big back to us and strode out after the zombies.

"He's right," I said. "Let's go."

I ran to the left, away from Santa Land and further into the white wastes. The others followed, reluctant at first, but catching up quickly.

I risked one last look back at my friend Peter. He reached into his pocket, lit a cigarette, took a deep drag, and exhaled.

"I always knew one day these things would kill me," he said. Then he let loose a loud blast from his trunk and he charged the evil little bastards with all he had. I turned away and kept running. I glanced back once more when I heard his screams, and although I was fairly far from him, I could see that he'd trampled four or five of them, smashed a couple more, and had his paws on two others by the time they got him down. They tore into his fur, ripping out his stuffing, his magic dust spraying out in great gouts of glittering crimson. He writhed and screamed, the cigarette still in his mouth, still smoking.

I looked away, a tear in my eye.

That's when the idea came to me when I saw Alcatraz looming in the distance. We had a chance.

"There!" I shouted, pointing ahead.

Turner caught up with me and saw what I meant. "There's nothing in there," he said.

"I thought it was a prison," I said.

Turner shook his head. "Not anymore," he said. "They burned all the defectives and nothing's left. Nothing but..." Then the light dawned in his eyes, too. "You can't be serious," he said.

I grinned from ear to ear.

* * *

We reached the entrance just as the zombie gnomes had tired of Peter's carcass and turned towards us again. Turner was searching through his tights, looking for the keys. He was the only one of us that would have a set.

"Got it!" Turner said. He stuck the key in and turned the lock. It creaked and groaned and the door popped open. "I'm not really sure where it is. Peter was the one who came in once a day and looked in on things."

Peter. Damn. He was lying out there, dead, beyond repair, lost forever. He was my friend and he was gone.

"Let us in!" Becky cried. She zoomed through us, nearly running my foot over. Her siren was whooping and wailing. Once inside, the sound of it echoed off the walls, chiming loud and irritating.

The others followed until it was just me and Cozmo outside. He was staring back at what was left of Peter.

"It just ain't right," he said. "He was a good fella."

"Come on in," I said and closed the door.

Alcatraz itself was pretty easy to navigate. The front doors led to a long corridor that opened into a larger room. There were four jail cells on each side except for the one facing where I stood. That wall held a door that led to the furnace: the final stop for the bad and deranged toys. All the cells were empty except for one.

"You can't be serious," Tina said.

I shrugged. "If they get in here, we don't have a choice."

"They ain't getting' in. They can't," Cozmo said. "This place is a jail."

"Jails were built to keep people in," Andy said. "Not out."

As if on cue, the front doors rattled with the assembled might of the zombies. Behind us, the only prisoner stirred from his sleep and grumbled.

"You're going to have to be the one," I said to Cozmo. "He knows you."

"Hell, son, he barely knows me, and that was a long time ago, before he went crazy," Cozmo stated.

The front doors buckled. The gnomes would be through soon.

"Okay," I said to Andy. "Plan B. Go get her ready."

Andy glared at me, clearly not happy about being bossed around.

"Go!" I yelled.

He whirred away, Turner going with him. After he opened the door, Turner tossed the keys to me. Our eyes locked and he nodded. Tina followed him. Becky buzzed around our feet, fretting and crying, as the front doors finally gave way and the zombie gnomes burst through.

We ran to the cell door and I stuck the key in. Cozmo looked at me and I smiled, then he looked inside the cell.

"All right, buddy," he said. "We need your help. These things are gonna eat us all unless you can do somethin' about it."

The large creature moaned and barked, then pressed against the bars, sensing freedom and smelling the onrushing zombies. Cozmo stepped behind me, joining Becky. I turned the key and yanked the door open, steering clear of the opening to the cell.

The Abominable Snowman roared out of his captivity, filed with savage anger and crazed insanity. He bounded forward, like a great ape on the attack. He slammed into the onrushing zombie gnomes, knocking them to and fro. Five flew to the right, slamming into closed cells. Four flew to the left, smacking against the wall. Seven were caught under his large feet and trampled. The others stopped their dash and backed up to assess the situation.

Hollow, metallic ringing filled the room where the zombies had been knocked around. They hit where they landed and bounced a few feet, their faces and bodies becoming dented from the blows. Then they rose to their feet, formidable in their undead state.

We ran for the door to the furnace. The corridor was only about twenty yards long and dead-ended at the giant iron doors that opened into the pit. It was there that Andy and Turner were twisting knobs and pushing buttons, both cursing. I could barely hear them over the din of the battle just behind me, but I could tell they weren't having any lucky getting the fires lit.

I turned to see how Abominable was fairing as Becky drove over to join the others. Cozmo was with me, standing and staring. What I saw, I would take to my grave. The Abominable Snowman was stomping two zombie gnomes flat, his giant feet crunching their aluminum bodies beneath him. Yellow pus squirted from the gnomes' ears, eyes, noses, and mouths as his feet came down—again and again. The zombies he was crushing were dying for a second time, and their high-pitched screams echoed off the walls. Then they were crushed, and stopped moving altogether.

Abominable snatched up two of the zombies biting at his legs and bashed their heads together. The metal popped and more yellow pus gushed from the stumps of their necks. He threw them to the floor and raised his fists to pummel two more at his feet. He smashed their heads through their bodies until they clanked to the floor. Yellow pus burst from between their shoulders and splashed into the air.

The Abominable Snowman himself was tall and wide, but he was gaunt, the years of imprisonment having taken their toll. He was still strong and powerful, though, and he was wreaking havoc on the zombies. His matted fur was thick with the pus of those he'd killed and as he whirled around, destroying one after another, a wild fire burned in his eyes. Abominable was in his element. He was free to do what he did best, and he was having the time of his life.

A hand tugged on my arm and I spun around. It was Tina, standing next to me, tears in her eyes.

"They got the gas on, but the pilot won't light," she said. "They don't know what to do."

Neither did I. If any of us had a match, maybe that would work, but no one had anything like that. All thoughts were erased from my mind, though, when Abominable screamed behind me.

"God a'mighty," Cozmo gasped.

Three of the zombie gnomes had gotten past Abominable's rabid actions and climbed up his fur. Two were clawing his eyes out and a third was boring its pointed red hat into Abominable's neck. He reached up and yanked them off but it was too late. That tiny moment gave the other gnomes the window they needed. Of the dozen or so left, all but three of them ran up Abominable's body, ripping and gouging. Great tufts of hair and chunks of flesh flew around. Blood plumed from the wounds, pouring over the floor and painting the area a deep red. The Abominable Snowman stumbled backwards, slipped in his own blood, and fell hard onto his back. The zombies quickly swarmed over him, moving in for the kill.

Abominable let out one last, great war cry, managed to sit up, and slapped his hands together. He crunched two zombies between his palms. Their heads exploded in geysers of yellow pus and flew across the room, but by then, it was much too late.

The gnomes carved his chest open and exposed his ribs in a matter of seconds. It was like watching piranha at work, how quick they were. Abominable laid back down, a long moan escaping his lips. Then he closed his eyes, and the great Abominable Snowman died.

I barely had a second to take this in before the zombies turned their greedy eyes to me and the others. I had time to shove Tina and Cozmo behind one of the doors we were standing next to and I dove in after them. I pulled the door to the wall and we were hidden for the moment. Metal clanged against it as the zombie gnomes charged into the corridor, heading straight for Turner and Andy. Tina opened her mouth to scream, but I clamped my hand over it, muffling the sound so it was lost in the advance of the zombies.

Seconds later, Turner and Andy were screaming, being torn apart by the gnomes. I shielded Tina's view with my body, but I couldn't silence their cries. I saw it all. I watched as they jabbed and poked, ripped and pulled, until the flesh was peeled from Turner's face and his legs were broken in a dozen places. He sank beneath the gnomes' assault, long-dead by the time his torso hit the floor. Andy tried to fly away but that was a joke. Black smoke puffed from his tail and he spun over to the right, slamming into the wall. The zombies plucked his wings and began chewing on his wheels before he even had a chance to turn back around. His magic dust sloshed to the floor, mixing with Turner's blood, hissing and popping.

As for me, Tina and Cozmo—we were trapped. There was no way out of this other than throwing the door open and running for it. But run where? The zombies would catch up before we got very far, and no place seemed safe from them. It was in that moment of sheer panic that a crazy idea came to me. I reached out and put my hand on Cozmo and met his eyes. "You think you can fire up, just one time?" I asked. He stared at me, awareness of what I was planning dawning on his face. He knew it was suicide, but to his credit, the old toy didn't even blink at the thought.

"I can sure try," he said.

Tina was shaking, her mind fried. I gently took her arm into my hand and led her to the door. I pushed it open and we slipped around, followed by Cozmo. Even though we tried hard to be quiet, the gnomes still heard us. As one, their heads lifted, stained with blood and magic dust, strips of fur and flesh and bits of toy parts stuck to their bodies. They stared at us, another meal there for the taking.

"Stand back, y'all," Cozmo said. "A real toy is about to step up."

I grabbed the crank at his side and whirled it around. I spun it until it was as tight as it would go. Cozmo grunted and wheezed, but all the straining accomplished was a loud fart that banged from his butt and filled the air with a noxious cloud. The zombie gnomes left their feast and took a step towards us.

"You can do it," I said.

Cozmo grunted again, wheezed, and let out another fart. This one wasn't as loud, but it smelled infinitely worse.

"I'd rather those things eat me than smell another one of your damned farts, you hillbilly idiot," I said. I hoped to anger him and get him going. It worked.

"I ain't no idiot!" Cozmo hollered. He faced the zombies, his eyes red, his green body turning blue from the effort.

"Take this, you undead toys from hell!" he yelled.

Fire sparked from his rump and he launched into the air. He flew towards the zombies and crashed into them, shoving the whole lot into the furnace.

"Oh, hell yeah!" Cozmo yelled.

The sparks from his butt ignited the gas in the furnace and he exploded. Fire blew down the corridor as I shoved Tina outside and leapt after her. It was hot, like standing next to the sun, and then the fireball rolled back and was gone.

It took me a few moments to get my bearings, but when I did, I peered down the corridor.

All the zombie gnomes had been engulfed in the flames and were melting, one by one, turning into a quagmire of cheap metal and pools of hissing, yellow pus.

They were all dead.

So there it is. My story. It doesn't have a happy ending, because how could it? So many toys and lives were destroyed; it was impossible to celebrate the victory.

Tina eventually was put in charge of the new batch of misfit toys and she drove them hard as they worked to fix mistakes the elves had made. I see her every now and then, and when I do, she avoids my eyes.

I guess I remind her of that horrible, terrible day, and I can't say that I blame her for never wanting to see me again. She eventually met a nice stuffed panda bear named Billy and I hear they moved in with each other.

As for me, I finally found my purpose. Santa awarded me the Rudolph Nose Medal of Valor and I'm proud to say that I'm only one of five to have ever received the honor.

He appointed me the Protector of Santa Land, and every day I go out on patrol, checking the borders. I even have a small, elite group of elves as my foot soldiers.

I'll never forget that day. Whenever I pass by Alcatraz, I think of my buddies Cozmo and Peter, and the sacrifices they made. They were the true heroes that day.

I was just lucky to live through it.

BRAINS FOR BREAKFAST

JULIE R. KENDRICK

The eyeball rolled across the floor and stopped at the zombie's feet. He picked it up by the optic nerve and dangled it in front of his face. A green eye. Mmmm, he thought, I prefer blue but green will do. He stuck out his tongue and gently laid the eye on the tip, rolling his tongue around the underside. He made a disgusted face.

Urggh, stale, he thought and threw the eye into the bin with the other unwanted body parts. Christmas was crap. No one was roaming the streets and carelessly wandering into his grasp. No nice juicy brains to suck on. He lumbered off up the street, casually rummaging through the odd trash can and finding the odd eye to keep his hunger at bay just a little longer. Yes, Christmas really was crap if you were a zombie.

Santa was pissed, really utterly pissed off. He looked at his long list and sighed. Naughty and nice, yeah right. Should be *dead* and *undead* more like it. His job was getting harder each year as the zombie population on Earth grew.

A rattle at the door turned his attention to the elf coming in with his favorite hot chocolate drink.

"Hey, Santa, how's it going?" The elf put the tray with the milky drink down on an ornate table made from candy canes. Santa looked at the elf. Kester was one of the oldest still here in The Grotto, and had been with him for about forty-five years. Taller than most elves, he commanded respect from the workers but still maintained his fun, child-like manner which made him so easy to work for. Santa was glad that with all the changes over the years, Kester was still exactly the same as when he'd first arrived. Unfortunately, that was pretty much the only thing that hadn't changed in recent years.

"Do you really want to know?" Santa sighed.

Kester inclined his head, indicating that he did indeed want to know.

"My list of naughty and nice is ridiculously long in favor of naughty this year," Santa said. "The zombie epidemic is out of control. Any hopes we had of the humans taking back the world is useless. I predict that this time next year we'll have only a few hundred thousand humans left to cater for."

Kester sat down next to Santa, a sad look on his cherubic face. "It's the elves you're really worried about isn't it?"

Santa met his friend's eyes and nodded. "They already do so much and I know they're aware of the problem, but I really hate to ask them."

"They are prepared, Santa. They know that the spirit of Christmas is alive and well here and they'll do what they can to make your life easier. Even if it means they give up their lives earlier."

They sat in companionable silence while Santa drank his hot chocolate. After a few minutes, Kester rose and took the tray. When he reached the door, he turned and looked sadly at Santa and said, "We know you'll make the right decision."

"That's completely the *wrong* decision!" Kester exploded. "I can't believe you seriously think that canceling Christmas altogether is the answer."

"What other choice do I have?" Santa stomped back and forth across his office agitatedly, his big bushy beard swaying back and forth.

"You can do what we talked about. You have to tell the elves that they must help."

"Oh okay," Santa said. "I can see how that conversation is going to go. '*Hey, elves, thanks for all your help over the last few years, but I need more brains for the zombies. If you don't mind lying down while I scalp you and remove your brains to make up the numbers, I'd be terribly grateful.*' I can see them all rushing to help." Sarcasm was not readily used in The Grotto but it was not lost on Kester.

"You underestimate them, Santa. They'll do whatever is necessary to fulfill their Christmas destiny, even if it means giving up their brain. But you must ask and soon. It'll take a while to organize everything."

Santa said nothing, only looked at Kester with a serious face, completely unnatural to the jolly man depicted across the world.

Five years ago when the living dead began to take over the world, Santa wasn't even sure that the zombies celebrated Christmas; surely they didn't have any religious beliefs? However, on Christmas Eve, as he flew across the skies dropping off his presents to the nice children on his list, he noticed through the windows of the houses of the undead, little zombie children pinning up ripped stockings on broken-down fireplaces.

Somewhat confused, Santa turned to Kester sitting next to him in the sleigh and asked, "What on earth could the zombie kids want for Christmas? From what I can see, they don't play with anything; they just wander around, sucking people's brains out."

Kester thought for a moment or two. "That must be what they want then," he said.

"Brains? I can't give them brains. Where would I get them from for a start?" Santa landed the sleigh on the roof of a 'nice' family and popped down the chimney with their gifts, leaving Kester behind, deep in thought.

"I don't know," he said on Santa's return, handing him a Kleenex to wipe the milk from the jolly man's top lip. "Maybe we just don't give them anything and see what they do in the morning."

Santa agreed, but the next morning both he and Kester realized what a huge mistake it had been. They'd watched through their telescope at the zombie house they'd passed the night before, and when the kids had looked in their empty stockings, they went ballistic, smashing up the already badly-damaged house before going straight to the house next door and eating the brains of the kids who were happily opening their new presents. It was a huge mess. Parents were screaming, blood and brains became splattered all over the room. New presents got trampled-on as the zombies grappled with the mother and father, trying to bite them and turn them into more of their population. Privately, Santa thought he was partly responsible for the massive rise in the zombie population that year due to the amount of attacks there had been across the world on Christmas morning alone.

"So, where do we get them?" Santa asked Kester after watching more brains becoming breakfast.

"Buffalettis?" Kester asked tentatively.

"Buffalettis!" Santa repeated. "Do you want to go get them?"

"Errr, no, not really. But I can't think of any other option and there are plenty of dead ones around."

Buffalettis were a cross between a buffalo and a yeti that roamed around the North Pole near The Grotto. They were pretty useless creatures, slow and lumbering with no actual purpose. They didn't hunt for food; they just ate any dead creatures they came across. However, they were huge and their mere size kept people, elves and other creatures away.

Buffalettis had a relatively short life span, only surviving for a year or so due to the fact that they would slowly starve to death when they couldn't find any more dead things to eat. That meant that there were buffaletti corpses in abundance throughout the year. But they rotted so quickly it was like watching them melt into the ground, so any brain harvesting would have to be swift. Zombies hadn't made their way in to the North Pole yet. It was too cold for them. Buffalettis hadn't made their way out of the North Pole either, but that was because they were too dim to realize there was more world out there to roam. This meant that there would be a new source of brains for the zombies and maybe they would leave the normal population of Earth alone. At least for one day out of the year.

For the rest of that year, Buffaletti brain harvesting became just as important as toy making. Santa had assembled a band of the quickest and fittest elves to run up to a recently-deceased buffaletti, slice open the top of its head, and grab its brain. It sounded a lot easier than it actually was. Although the beast's head was huge, its brain was pretty tiny and set deep into its cranium. The little elves—wearing yellow, protective hard hats—had to crawl into the cavity and form a chain down to the brain. Once it had been detached from the spinal cord, the elves would throw the brain into a waiting basket. Sometimes, the elves found the brain difficult to remove; other parts of the buffaletti would remain attached to the brain when it was finally removed.

The eyes for instance, quite often popped out, still dangling from the veins and nerves connecting the whole gory caboodle together. But the elves never once complained. Day after day they came back to The Grotto, heaving baskets full of brains, their tiny elf clothes and faces covered with blood and other viscous fluids. They bathed, went to bed, and the next day did the same thing— throughout the entire year.

Christmas Eve eventually arrived and Santa and Kester loaded up the sleigh with the toys in one sack and the brains in another.

They successfully dropped off the presents at the relevant houses, and once back at The Grotto, they duly watched the Christmas morning festivities: the human kids racing around with their new toys, the zombie kids devouring their new brains.

Santa and Kester high-fived and celebrated with the elves a successful Christmas.

Four years later, and Santa had to decide how he would tell the elves that the buffaletti were almost extinct due to their very successful harvesting expeditions, and that now the elves themselves were going to have to be the new donors.

He could ask Kester to do it and he knew the elf would, but it wasn't really his place. Santa knew he couldn't just cop out like that. He had debated whether to send a letter to each elf or to just announce it over the intercom system, but he knew that was a coward's way out. No, he needed to deal with the situation properly.

He decided to call a full staff meeting. Santa knew that there would be outrage and many of his faithful workers would turn against him, but it was something he was going to have to accept, unless he could think of another way.

Santa had wracked his brains for weeks trying to think of a way to spare the elves that had been the backbone of Christmas for hundreds of years. It was the first time in centuries that he'd had sleepless nights and he wished that the myth of Mrs. Claus existed. Contrary to the stories that parents tell their children, there was no Mrs. Claus. Still, Santa longed to have female company, and although Kester was his confidant, there was no substitute for a loving hug and comfortable breast on which to rest his troubled head.

The meeting was set for the first of August, so there would be plenty of time for harvesting and preserving before Christmas Eve.

Santa had paced in his bedroom the previous night, reading and rereading his speech. He hadn't even read it to Kester, wanting to assume all the responsibility himself. There was no point in the elves turning against Kester, too, so they had agreed that the head elf was to act as surprised as the others at the terrible news.

The great hall fell silent as Santa took his place on the platform that had been erected for him. There was an atmosphere of expectation and nervousness. As he looked out at the little faces turned towards him eagerly, always anxious to please, he felt a sick twist in his stomach. Catching Kester's eye, the head elf nodded almost imperceptibly.

Santa took a deep breath and plunged right in. "My loyal workers and friends, I have some important information to tell you today, and no doubt you'll not like it, and it will change things forever here at the North Pole." The elves looked at one another with questions in their eyes but soon turned back to their leader expectantly.

"As you know, the zombie population on Earth has grown to magnificent proportions, so much so that five years ago we had to start including them in our Christmas preparations. I firstly want to thank you for your dedication and hard work in the harvesting of the buffaletti brains over the past years. It's been vital to the success of the holiday festivities ever since. But you'll also be aware that the buffaletti are now almost extinct and that means we will run out of brains before the end of the year." Santa paused so that the little workers could take in the gravity of what he was saying, but all he saw were hundreds of small, eager faces staring back at him. Not a hint of what was to come was visible in their expressions. This was going to be harder than he thought. He took a couple of deep breaths before continuing. "I've given this very serious thought and if there was any other way, I would go with that, but unfortunately I'm going to have to ask all of you to make a huge sacrifice, the biggest sacrifice you'll ever have to make. I'm sorry but there's no other way. You're going to have to..."

"Excuse me, Santa," a small voice rang out in the great hall.

The elves looked around to see who had called out right as Santa was getting to the point.

"Santa, I have something to tell you." The voice belonged to a worker who was slowly pushing through the crowd to get to the front. His cheeks were red with embarrassment, as he could feel all eyes on him.

Santa waited patiently for the elf to get to the front, not at all in a hurry to impart his bad news. He saw it was an elf of about eighty years old called Banjo. "Yes, Banjo, what it is it that you have to tell me?"

Banjo crawled up onto the stage so that his voice could be picked up by the microphones and said, "I've worked out a way to provide brains to the zombies in the future. It'll work, I'm sure of it."

Santa looked at the little man and hoped that what he said next would be the solution.

"Marshmallow," Banjo announced.

"Marshmallow?" Santa tried not to let the disappointment show in his voice. The elf had obviously realized how dire the situation was and was clutching at straws like himself. He decided it was only fair to hear Banjo out.

"Yes, we can make pink marshmallow brains to give to the zombies at Christmas." Banjo flashed a big wide smiled that showed off a lot of very white, straight teeth.

There was murmuring in the crowd and someone shouted out, "The zombies won't be fooled with pink marshmallow. They may be dead but they're not stupid."

The chattering grew louder and there were a few shouts of: "Don't be silly Banjo!" and "Let Santa finish now!"

But Banjo wasn't to be put off. He turned to Santa and said, "Not just white marshmallow. We would have to cover it in blood in order for it to appeal to the zombies. So my idea is that throughout the year, all the elves should donate some blood at least two or three times, then on Christmas Eve, we dip the large marshmallows in the blood before delivery. The zombies will smell the blood and see what looks like a brain that they won't even realize it's marshmallow."

The murmuring started up again but this time there was an air of excitement in the room. Santa said nothing, only stroking his beard in contemplation. It could work, it could actually work, Santa thought. He caught Kester's eye and saw that the head elf was nodding vigorously. "Mmmm, well, Banjo, I see that you've given this as much thought as I have. I'm very impressed with your loyalty and I think you may be right. It is a much better idea than mine, so I'm going to put you in charge of production." Santa smiled down on the crowd, relieved that no one would be giving up their brains this year.

"Santa, what was your idea?" Dusty, a large rotund elf, asked.

Santa spluttered and coughed and tried to bluster his way out of revealing what he had almost asked the elves to do.

"Now, now, we don't need to worry about that," Santa said. "Banjo's hit the nail on the head so to speak and we must make this work. So get to it everyone, chop-chop, ho ho ho."

Marshmallow production was in full swing from that afternoon on, and by the beginning of December it was calculated that there would be more than enough brains to go around. Elves had also been busy donating blood, and a room had been set aside especially for this. Another room was used to store the blood.

On Christmas Eve, Santa and Kester loaded up the sleigh, taking care to store the vat of blood in a secure position. It wouldn't do to spill it and waste all their hard work. The plan was to land on the roof of homes as usual and if it was a zombie residence, then Santa would grab a marshmallow brain and dip it into the blood. He would then put it immediately into a plastic bag and drop it down the chimney into the waiting stocking. Nothing could really go wrong, but it didn't stop everyone from feeling nervous as they waved Santa, Kester and the reindeer off.

The first few houses were still human homes so the presents were dropped off without incident. When the sleigh landed on the first zombie roof, Santa dipped his hand into the sack of marshmallow brains, selected two, and pulled them free. They stuck together a little bit and had to be pried apart, but Kester said it made them look more authentic if they weren't totally intact.

The brains were dunked into the vat of blood and quickly bagged, then Kester tied them up and tossed them down the chimney and into the waiting stockings. They'd decided a few years ago not to go down the chimneys of zombie homes after a very close shave at one house where Santa had landed on one of the undead, which had been sleeping by the hearth. The zombie had, of course, woken up and tried to make Santa's brain its present for that year. Luckily, Kester had pulled Santa back up onto the roof before he lost his scalp.

By 5.30 Christmas morning, the delivery was complete. Once the sleigh and the reindeer were settled, everyone sat down to watch the festivities on the big screen in the great hall. Humans were always awake first and opened their presents with gusto, screaming with delight at their toys and games. As the dawn broke, the zombies rose and lumbered to their stockings. Santa and the elves watched with baited breath as one by one the zombies withdrew their brand-new marshmallow brain, dripping with elf blood. They looked at it quizzically, sniffed, licked, and then, much to Santa's relief and the elves' delight, began to devour the pink, squishy brains. A huge cheer went up in the great hall and some of the elves hoisted Banjo onto their shoulders and started parading him around, singing 'For he's a jolly good fellow.'

"Oh no, this isn't good." Santa shook his head, still watching the action around the globe on the big screen. Slowly, the elves stopped cheering and singing and turned back to see what was wrong.

The zombies had wandered out of their houses, brains in hands, and were knocking on their neighbors' front doors.

"No, this is not supposed to happen. Zombies and humans keep to themselves on Christmas Day. There should be no hunting and eating of humans today," Santa said. "I guess the marshmallow brains weren't enough for them."

Santa and the elves could only watch in horror as the families opened their front doors to be confronted by the zombies from their neighborhood. Helplessly, the inhabitants of The Grotto saw the looks of shock and horror on the human faces and waited to see the undead people rip the heads from the humans' necks, tear open their scalps, and devour their brains.

But amazingly, this didn't happen. Santa watched in stunned silence as the zombies held out the marshmallow brains to the humans, then waited.

"Oh, my bushy beard," Santa said. "They want to share."

Tentatively, the humans took the brains, recognizing that they were made of marshmallow, and pretended to take a bite. The zombies looked happily on and then shuffled into the humans' houses.

The tableau before Santa was unbelievable. He was watching history being made. Zombies and humans, spending Christmas together, sharing brains and toys, and not a beheading or scalping in sight. He breathed a huge sigh of relief. Oh, he knew it was only for one day and that tomorrow the rules would be back in place:

zombies would hunt humans and rip them to pieces, and humans would defend themselves by spearing the undead through their heads or shooting them with flaming arrows.

He also knew that next year and the years that would follow, there would be a greater population of the undead, but he'd worry about that next year.

Now it was time to drink his hot chocolate and start searching internet dating sites. Maybe this year would be the year that he found the future Mrs. Claus.

THE TOMTIN

MARC SHEMMANS

Something had eaten everything except a beak, a pair of web-footed legs, and some white feathers. Lucy was thankful that she was the first to discover the remains.

She was in the kitchen-garden, a big walled area of neat vegetable plots and graveled paths. She kicked the feathers about so they wouldn't be noticed, gathered up the beak and legs, and hurriedly buried them. Afterwards, she made her way back into the kitchen.

She knew it was the tomtin that had eaten it. Her Alsatian, Tom, was too well-trained to chase poultry, and the farm cats had long ago learned they were no match for the flock of geese, ducks, chickens and turkeys that strutted about the farmyard. Lucy had always known about the tomtin. Many people thought it was an old horror story about creatures that had lived in the Black Forest many centuries ago. But she knew they really existed and came here to Bucks Cross every December.

Myth had it that the tomtin were vicious *little people*—pretty much like gnomes or elves—and were said to roam the area committing terrible atrocities and vicious crimes against humanity during the harsh winter months. Myth had it that they were dead children—children that had been murdered due to being sinners. The tomtin were said to dress in the color red—however, some people believed they didn't dress in red but were just covered in the blood of their victims. They were led by a man called Nacht Ruprecht, who rode on a black sled drawn by eight black dogs. He guided the tomtin through small towns in December and they broke into children's homes that had been bad all year. The tomtin pulled them out of their beds and beat them with sharp sticks, while Ruprecht pelted them with hard coal. When the children were unconscious, Ruprecht would behead them and the tomtin would lick the blood from the fatal wound.

Lucy knew that Ruprecht was where the Santa Claus story had originated but understandably the negative associations had been wiped out. After all, what child wants to know that Santa Claus was born from a murderer who went around killing children?

Lucy also knew that every December in Bucks Cross, for as long as she could remember, there had been murders. Only last year, the police had investigated the deaths of five children and two adults.

It was how it always started. On her way home from work the year before, she'd found a dog. Once she parted from her friends on the main road, her walk home had been a solitary one along a road which made its way between factories before abruptly turning into a country lane. On one side were the woods, on the other a landscaped park, which swept down to the motorway and the town beyond. The great house of an earl had once stood there. Now the council owned what was left of the estate and ran it as a nature reserve. The earl's home-farm had become a tourist attraction and the woods were a playground for local children and dogs. But though they worked the farm as it had been in Victorian times, and though they were bringing back old woodland crafts, the roar of the traffic on the motorway never stopped, night or day.

Lucy had climbed a stile into the woods, but had then turned aside from the main bridle path, which would have taken her in a direct fashion through a mile of woodland, past the abbey-ruins and the holy well, and to the farm. It was a path much used by horse-riders and walkers, and it bored her. Instead, she had taken a narrower, winding path that wandered through more over-grown parts of the woods, and at one point, had brought her to the edge of the lake. There, on a little sandy beach under a dark green holly bush, she'd found the dog torn to pieces.

This was how it started every year. A few animals died first, to be followed by the deaths of children. And nobody said a thing. Everyone knew about the tomtin but everyone ignored them, afraid to speak about them. As if vocalizing their concerns would make them stronger.

As Lucy made her way back to the house, she was certain she'd heard a scream. When she reached the house, she closed the door quickly behind her.

It started snowing at 12:01 am on December twentieth. Lucy—with her fiancé Leonard—were on their way home from a Christmas party from their friend Natalie, when Lucy noticed a few stray flakes as she turned onto Brook Road, and by the time she'd reached home, the snow was coming down hard.

"Oh, good," Leonard said, leaning forward over the steering wheel to peer through the windshield. "I've been hoping we'd have a white Christmas this year."

"Still a long way to go yet," Lucy told him.

At 1:37 a.m., on a late-night radio request show out of Barnstaple, the DJ said, "This just in from the National Weather Service. There's a snow advisory for everyone in the North Devon area tonight and tomorrow morning. Two to four inches expected." He then went back to discussing all the callers' least favorite Christmas songs.

Lucy looked out the window at the snow swirling around the farm. "I want a Christmas Eve wedding," she said. "All candlelight and evergreens. And I want snow falling outside the windows."

"I thought you wanted to get married next year? In the sun?" Leonard frowned.

"Why wait?" She looked at him. "Who knows if we'll be here next summer?"

"Why are you suddenly so morbid?"

"I just don't want to wait anymore."

"What if the weather doesn't cooperate?"

"It will," Lucy said. And here it was, snowing. She wondered if it was snowing in South Devon, too. She picked up a magazine and tried to read and then plugged in her headphones and listened to a CD of *Seasonal Favorites*.

The first song was *White Christmas* by Bing Crosby.

December twenty-third turned out to be a lot more exciting than Lucy expected. She woke early, and took a walk around the farm before the staff and visitors arrived. The early morning and the evening were the only times she could pretend that the farm was really theirs.

At night, with all the gates locked, the big farmyard with the tall buildings on all four sides became a fortress. With keys in hand, Lucy walked along the archway and unlocked the big door. That brought her out into the flower garden where the visitors sat over their 'farmhouse teas.' This morning they would have the chance to drink their teas surrounded by glistening, fresh snow.

A path led through the flower borders to the gate of the much bigger kitchen gardens. It was here, in the gardens, that her dog, Tom, spent his nights on guard. A small gate in the garden wall was usually left open, so that he could come and go to investigate any noise. Lucy called for him as she walked into the garden.

He didn't come to her call, but that didn't worry her. He might be anywhere, in the fields or woods. She walked over to the gate, meaning to take a stroll around the farm buildings, and perhaps go a little way into the woods before returning to breakfast.

Tom was lying on his back just outside the gate. She knew as soon as she saw him that he was dead: there was that peculiar, broomstick stiffness about his splayed legs. One of the dog's hind legs looked strange, and after staring for a long time, she realized that the flesh had been torn away from the bone. She turned and ran back through the garden, through the archway, into the yard and back into the farmhouse, shouting for Leonard the entire time.

A few minutes later, while Lucy remained at a distance, Leonard crouched beside the dead dog and turned the carcass over, examining it closely. He made Lucy feel cowardly.

"Still got the keys?" he asked and she nodded. "Then open the shed, will you?" There was a little wooden shed against the wall, just behind the garden gate. Lucy opened it, and turned to see Leonard carrying the dog's body towards her. She turned away hastily, afraid of what she might see.

Leonard put the carcass in the shed, took the keys from Lucy, and locked the door. "Can't leave him for the visitors to fall over, now can we?" He spoke while on the verge of tears. He took a spade from the shed, and turned over the blood-stained soil where the dog had lain.

"What do you think killed him?" Lucy asked, her voice strained and shaky.

Leonard glanced at her, knowing she already knew the truth. Then he said, "Tomtin. What else around here would take on an Alsatian? He was—no, let's not talk about it. Let's go and have a good hot cup of tea."

Ten minutes later, back in the house, Lucy drank a mug of tea but didn't feel much like breakfast. Leonard said that she needn't go to Barnstaple to collect supplies, but she wanted to. She drove through the woods, but didn't even get halfway. She felt shaky and upset, and couldn't bear the thought of trying to get through the day—and she couldn't stop thinking about the tomtin and what they did to Tom. These were gentle English woods, with broad paths, but they were also very lonely at that time in the morning. No walkers, no riders. The tomtin were about, though. They ran in the woods now, and if they could hunt down and kill a big, strong Alsatian, a dog who had been far stronger than Lucy, well…

She spun around and drove back home to the farm. When she turned off the engine, she leapt out of the car and ran into the farmhouse, thankful to get there without hearing the tomtin running behind her, without hearing their laughs and their growls. She spent the day half-heartedly helping in the shop, trying not to think of her dog or the tomtin, and envying the visitors who didn't know about them.

"Paul and his son Joe should be here soon," Leonard said and he was correct. They arrived at about three that afternoon and for an hour Lucy was happy and excited when a van drove up outside the farm and Paul and his fourteen-year-old son jumped out, shouting for keys. The big gates of the farmyard were unlocked, and the van was driven inside and pulled up beside the open-sided animal sheds that lined one side of the yard. A crowd of interested onlookers had gathered, Leonard and Lucy among them.

Paul led his son forward. "Let me introduce you to the best brother a man ever had."

Joe and Leonard shook hands.

Paul was six feet tall with blonde hair, and Joe was about five eight, and had mousey-brown hair. He had a nice, rather shy smile.

"Very pleased to meet you," Paul said.

"Pleased to meet you, too," Leonard replied.

"This is my son, Joe," Paul told Lucy.

"My pleasure," Lucy smiled.

"The pleasure's mine," Joe said.

After a couple of minutes of idle chatter, Lucy blurted out, "Our dog's been killed."

Paul came forward. "Your dog! I'm sorry to hear that!" He looked at Lucy with concern and she tried to be brave and smile.

"Was he hit by a car?" Joe asked

"No, the tomtin!" Lucy said, and Paul looked bewildered, especially when he saw Leonard's face, who looked totally and utterly embarrassed.

"Seems you're a veterinarian," Leonard said suddenly. "Why don't you come and have a look, Paul—give us your opinion, as a vet."

Paul still looked bewildered, but followed Leonard out into the yard. Joe went with them, and Lucy found herself trailing along behind. She didn't want to see her dog dead, and with bites all over him, but she didn't want to be left out either.

Leonard opened the shed and stood aside. He wasn't keen to see the dog again either. Paul and Joe went into the shed and squatted on their heels as Paul examined the carcass. Lucy stood a few feet away, looking at their bowed backs. She heard Paul say, "Bites?"

Father and son got to their feet and exited the shed. Paul pushed the shed door closed and looked at the ground.

"So, what do you think?" Leonard asked.

"The dog was attacked by—animals," Paul said. "By other dogs I would guess."

"A vicious dog?"

"Certainly."

"Not tomtin?" Lucy asked.

Paul looked from one to another of them. "Do you…"

"They're like…" she began but was cut off.

"Let him finish!" Leonard interrupted her.

"They're the undead! They look like elves…"

"And they have teeth like dogs," Joe explained, finishing her sentence.

"But claws like cats," Paul added.

Lucy saw Leonard raise his eyebrows in surprise and his expression quickened as Paul continued. "And they're red. Red as a fox but it's because they're covered in blood from those they devour."

"Yes, exactly," Lucy said.

"Let's go to the house and discuss this," Leonard said.

Once back in the house, Lucy made coffee, and they sat around the kitchen table and looked expectantly at Paul. "Here in Bucks Cross you have tomtin and this is a dangerous thing. There are many lonesome farms…and many tomtin. Did you know that tomtin in Polish is the same word for 'devil'? And as you already know, they're very fierce, and very clever. They're rare, but they kill sheep, dogs and even children. They're dangerous creatures. In Poland, the farmers get together every December and hunt and shoot them."

"This is a worldwide thing?" Lucy asked.

"Yes."

"So why did you deny that my dog was killed by tomtin at first?"

"We don't know that he was."

"But you…"

"Tomtin exist," Paul said. "The farmers kill them as soon as they find them—they say a tomtin is even smarter and fiercer than a grizzly bear.

Leonard laughed. "He's pulling your leg, Lucy! Paul always was a bit of a joker!"

"I'm not pulling anyone's leg," Paul said.

Leonard, sitting with folded arms, gave him a level stare across the table, waiting for him to admit that he was joking.

Paul looked calmly back. "They hunt in a pack, like wolves," he said.

"And they're led by Santa Claus."

"If by Santa Claus you mean Nacht Ruprecht—then yes. He's supposedly the one who created them. He was the first to beat a 'sinner' child on Christmas Eve. They were on the verge of death and as his ultimate punishment, he put together a concoction of tetrodotoxin, a chemical which when derived from the puffer fish produces paralysis and can mimic death. It's one hundred times as deadly as cyanide. After this initial zombification he created an army of undead."

"And how can you kill them?" Lucy asked.

Paul was only silent a moment, then said, "You ever heard of *lamping*?"

Lucy shook her head.

"You go out at night with a lamp or torch, and you shine it. If you catch a rabbit or a fox—or a tomtin—in the light, they freeze."

"And then you shoot them," Joe said. "Have you got a gun?"

Lucy shook her head.

"No," Leonard told them.

"Then I suggest you get one," Joe said.

"We don't like guns," Lucy said.

"Either do the tomtin," Joe said.

"If you don't kill the initial tomtin, Nacht Ruprecht will come on Christmas Eve and there'll be a massacre," Paul added.

"There will be no children left in Bucks Cross," Joe added.

"Then we really have no choice," Leonard said.

As soon as it was fully dark they were ready: Paul with his shotgun and his pockets full of cartridges; Joe with the big electric lamp with carrying handle and cover for the light. He gave his son a handgun and then offered one to Leonard, who shook his head.

"You may need it." Paul forced it into Leonard's ski jacket.

"You coming?" Paul asked Lucy.

She nodded.

"I'm not sure I like her going," Leonard said. "We're not hunters!"

"Joe is going and he's a kid," Paul said.

"And I think that's a stupid idea, too."

"It's better to be out there looking for them than waiting in here for them." Paul stared at him.

"I'm going," Lucy said, determined.

"Okay," Leonard mumbled, knowing to try and stop her would be futile. Lucy was as strong-willed as they came, which was one of the things that he loved about her.

However, she was less happy than she seemed as she followed them all through the farmyard and out into the woods.

It was easy enough to follow the tracks in the dark. Once they'd crossed the narrow plank bridge over the stream and were into the woods, the trees, meeting over their heads in a thick canopy, also made walls of dense leaves on either side, shutting out what little light there was. Unable to see the ground at their feet, they stumbled over every hollow or hump, staggered through roots, and were caught by briars. Branches lashed out of nowhere across their faces, or caught in their hair and jerked them backwards. It was impossible to move quietly. All around them was silence, but they thrashed, crashed and trampled.

Ahead of the others, Paul swore when his shotgun caught in branches. None of them, Lucy realized, had stopped to think of how difficult it was to move through the woods at night. To make it easier for them, she uncovered the lamp and allowed a thin beam of light to fall at their feet. It illuminated tangles of thin twigs and leaves, but made such deep, pit-like shadows that, if anything, it made them even more reluctant to risk another step.

"Cover the light," Paul hissed.

"Why?" she asked.

"It's ruining our night-vision," Paul said.

Lucy covered the lamp. Immediately, darkness fell and she stood still, blinded. The dark and the silence wrapped close around her, as did the slight dampness of the air. Ahead of her, seeming very far away, she could hear the crunch and thrash of Paul and Joe slowly making their way, step by careful step, along the narrow path.

But it was the other sounds that held her attention: the slight sound of a bird shifting in its roost above her head, the wind trickling through leaves, a stuttering in the bushes beside the path, to then fade into a deeper quiet.

From behind Leonard whispered, "Lucy!" She turned and, unable to see him, uncovered the lamp, shielding the light with her jacket. The beam brought a little patch of woodland out of the darkness--one quivering, emerald leaf, surrounded by thousand of snowy leaves and twigs of various grays, and then darkness again. She edged towards the sound of Leonard's voice, and bashed her head on a low branch.

Leonard was off the path, trapped knee-deep in a snow drift. Dazzling him briefly, she turned the light on the briars so he could untangle himself. He floundered back to the path and looked up into the dark, breeze-whispering canopies above them, hugging himself. Lucy thought she saw him shiver. He glanced at her in the lamp light, snowflakes spiraling all around them. It was beginning to snow harder.

They edged along the path, following Paul and Joe. Lucy covered the lamp again so as not to annoy Paul.

After a couple of minutes, she realized she'd lost them, and Leonard as well. Lucy stood alone still in the darkness, listening for the sound of Paul and Joe moving, but the woods were full of wariness and the silent falling of snow.

Paul must have noticed their absence, as he called softly, "Lucy, Leonard, where are you?"

From behind her came Paul's whisper, "Lucy!" She turned and, unable to see him and Joe, uncovered the lamp.

"I don't know where Leonard is," she said.

"Leonard!" Paul called out into the night.

They waited, their heads lifted up, but there was no answer. Lucy looked back, wondering if they should go back to the farm. But that seemed a stupid waste of time. Leonard would come back to them soon. They had the light.

A gun blasted in the darkness away to their right. An outcry of birds followed a second later. The three of them started towards the sound. It seemed, to Lucy, to come from further away than Leonard should be.

As the report of the blast died, birds cried out in alarm from every part of the woods. There were sounds of scurrying, wings clapping—and then all the sounds of fright began to settle into silence again, except for the sound of the howling wind and the falling snow. Lucy flashed the beam of light across the ground, hoping to see some path leading in the direction of the shot, but the only path seemed to lead away from it. So she left the path and struck out through the undergrowth. It seemed a good idea at the time, and Paul and Joe followed her, trampling through the snow.

There seemed nothing in the way except a few low-growing plants, a few bushes—but the ground sloped away suddenly, sending Lucy stumbling forward, half-running. Her feet slid from under her and she slithered downhill through the powdery snow.

In trying to grab at something to stop her fall, she let go of the lamp and left it behind.

When she stopped falling, she was nervous and bruised, and lying in darkness. The last reverberations of the noise she'd made were fading. Dozens of tiny scratches burned on her face and hands. Getting up on her hands and knees, she realized that she hardly knew which way was up, let alone how to get back to the path. The woods—where people walked dogs and jogged— suddenly seemed infinitely vast. Not wanting to raise her voice much, she called softly for Paul.

From somewhere came a sound that went through her like an arrow, and had her hugging the ground like every other terrified animal in the woods. It was a twisting, wailing shriek. Her breath came fast.

She wanted to call out for Leonard, Paul and Joe, but feared to make a sound. She lay flat in the snow, kept still, and tried not to breathe too loudly. Only when she was still safe minutes later did her brain begin to work again. She couldn't lie there all night. She shifted her position slightly and caught a gleam of light through the bushes. The lamp! Ignoring the branches and thorns in her way, she crawled towards it. As her hand was reaching out for it, she saw, at the edge of the light, a pair of pricked ears. With a lunge, she grabbed the lamp and turned the light full on it.

Nothing.

Filling her lungs, she shouted, "Leonard! Paul!"

"Here!" There as a shifting and rustling to her left, and Paul and Joe came crawling through the dark of the woods. She was glad to scramble over and sit next to them. She thought they seemed glad to see her.

"Did you hear that…noise?" she asked.

She saw him nod. "A tomtin." He peered about in the dark. "We shouldn't have come into the woods. It was a mistake. How do we get out?"

Lucy shone the light about. It showed them so little of their surroundings, and one suddenly-illuminated, gray-green tree trunk looked like another. "I don't know," she said.

Paul got to his feet, put his hands on either side of his mouth like a cone, and yelled, "Leonard!" His voice went clattering through the trees and the darkness. Birds roused, twittered, and fell silent. Lucy, still sitting, felt the woods grow tense around her. Everything out there knows exactly where we are, she thought.

Something darker than the darkness moved swiftly through the tangle of bushes near her, and she jumped to her feet and shone the light at that spot. Nothing. But the leaves were still quivering.

"Don't," she said, finding herself rather short of breath. "Don't shout again."

Paul was looking around. "Already they've separated us. Lucy, we need to stay together."

The fact that he was scared frightened her. "What about Leonard?"

"He has a gun."

True, but they hadn't heard anything of him since that last shot. Lucy listened. The woods weren't extensive, however endless it seemed in the darkness, and she thought that she ought to be able to hear Leonard moving about. He ought to have heard Paul's shout, too. Why hadn't he answered?

"We should try and find Leonard." She moved slowly in what she thought was the right direction, though she was no longer sure. Behind her, she could hear Paul and Joe following cautiously. With the help of the light, they picked their way around thickets, becoming more and more lost.

Suddenly, another long shriek pierced the darkness—a shriek that sounded like it might have come from a tortured child. Lucy leapt and spun, trying to see what had made it, her eyes darting back and forth.

Joe took her arm in a tight grip. "They're just trying to panic us," he said, gasping.

Lucy could feel her heart hammering in her chest.

"They want us to run and scatter," Paul said. He took a sudden step forward, waving his hands at the undergrowth and shouting, "Yah!"

Nearby, Lucy heard a flurry of movement, and turned sharply, shining her light at the spot.

Nothing.

They all came together and stood close. The trees towered around them, and the thick growth about their legs was full of slight sounds and movements. Bold gray tree trunks emerged suddenly from the darkness at the touch of the light-beam, and then quickly stepped back into the blackness as the light shifted.

"We need to get out of here," Paul said. "Which way?

"But Leonard," Lucy said.

"He has his gun, he should be fine."

Lucy stood still and tried to concentrate on the woods and its paths, and the one they had taken from the farm. "I think…if we go this way, we'll get to the main path."

It was slow going through the snow, even with the light of the lamp leading the way. Every step had to be felt for, and their faces guarded from the whipping wind and branches. "Why doesn't Leonard answer us?" Lucy asked, concern in her voice.

"He's…" Paul said. "He's probably…" Then he couldn't think of anything comforting to say. They pushed on, slipping, stumbling, without saying anything more. Lucy felt furious with the snow and the branches and the briars that kept getting in her way.

Anger wouldn't help, she knew, but it was hard to hold it down—or was it panic?

"I thought the path…" she said and trailed off. There was still no sign of any path. The falling snow had already started hiding everything from them. From their left came a sudden rising chain of quick little yelps—to then be answered from their right. Lucy almost started to run, but Joe held her arm. "We can't let them drive us," he said.

Lucy almost giggled.

"Keep calm," Paul said. "We have to keep calm. And get out of these damn woods!"

The ground began to slope again, and their feet slipped in the snow. They had to cling to trees and wedge their feet against the boles. Lucy slung the lamp on her arm, where it lit up her jeans and sneakers but left the snowy and tangled way ahead in darkness.

Behind them the tomtin yipped again. She began to sweat, with more than exertion. She was trying to think where this slope could be: where, *where* did the woods slope like this? In daylight she had never noticed.

They paused and Lucy shone the light around. It caught the red glare of eyes behind them, and she shouted. Paul and Joe looked around them wildly, wondering what had startled her.

The eyes vanished. The lamp shone ahead of them, lighting up a line of reddish stone. Lucy shone the light on a wall, a corner, and the remains of worn steps.

"It's the abbey!" she cried, looking up at them and grinning. She knew where they were now. They had come blundering out of the woods into the ruins of the abbey. "Listen!" she said, holding up a finger.

From the other side of the ruins could be heard the faint trickling of water in St. Braide's holy well. "The main path is by the well, it goes through the woods straight to my farm."

"Through the woods," Paul said doubtfully.

Hearing a sound, Lucy turned the light towards the woods behind them. There was a faint yip, and the sound of something moving away.

"There's no other way," she said. "But it's a clear path; easy going."

They slithered down the bank on their haunches, and stepped over the ruined wall into the abbey. "Sanctuary!" Lucy said, and then wished that she hadn't. There was no longer any safety in the abbey.

"I hate the woods," Joe muttered.

Outlined by its ruined walls, were big, loose chippings of stone, which crunched noisily under their feet and turned their ankles, making the going almost as difficult as in the woods. But at least they were free from the wind and snow.

"Look!" Lucy yelled. The light from the lamp had been streaming ahead of them, across loose stone and black walls. A running shape had suddenly darted across the light, and turned to run back—a jogging, child-like shape with pricked ears. It looked at them and grunted. It was answered by more calls and growls from the woods. The tomtin were on the path ahead of them.

They all moved back, away from the tomtin they could glimpse running at the edge of the abbey ruins, but Lucy and Joe broke to the left, back towards the woods they had just left, and Paul broke to the right.

Before they could realize their mistake and come together again, the tomtin ran between them. Lucy shone the light at them, and it glared red and green in their eyes, but they didn't freeze and they didn't run away. Two of them turned towards her and

Joe, jogging lightly, and although they weren't big, she knew they were strong and would try and kill them.

They were dead children; flesh gray and mottled. Their eyes dulled and their teeth razor-sharp.

Joe and Lucy ran forward, rattling over the loose chippings, jumping the walls and crashing down into the rocks on the other side. She could hear the well just ahead. From behind her, from the sanctuary of the abbey, she heard a man cry out.

"Paul!" She spun, and the lamp spun with her, illuminating fans of leaves, tree trunks, and a wall. Back and forth she sent the beam, at the same time turning her head constantly as she watched for tomtin near her. There seemed to be none. They had gone, left her. But something was moving out there in the abbey. She could hear the shifting of the stone chippings as something moved over them.

"Paul!" she called out.

Still no answer.

"What's happened to him?" She said to Joe, but he was gone. A terrible thought entered her mind. Had the tomtin killed Joe? Maybe if they had she would be okay. After all, didn't the tomtin hunt children? Maybe they were only after Joe, and now that they had him they would leave her alone.

"Joe? Joe!" She was on the verge of hysteria as she scrambled up the bank from the ruins and gained her way to a clear path. At her feet trickled the holy well. She shone the torch forward and saw that the path lead into a dark tunnel of leaves and tree trunks: the path to the farm. She started for it—and a tomtin darted before her. It laughed and giggled and snapped its teeth at her, playful as a child, and in the lamp light, its teeth and eyes were stained dark, the color of blood.

She took a step or two backwards, and would have turned and run unthinkingly back along the path into the woods, but a soft laugh made her turn and swing the light. Another tomtin was behind her.

Sheer terror gave her the courage to run forward on the path home, swinging the light at the tomtin blocking her way. The small zombie dodged the blow neatly and then, with a dancing step, darted in and sank its teeth into her forearm.

She couldn't believe it, and tried to pull her arm back as if nothing had happened, but the weight dragging down on her arm was greater than an active, strong weight, trying to pull her down. Her flesh felt as if it was on fire. She dropped the lamp. Another tug from her other side—the other tomtin had hold of her jacket! From somewhere close by came an eager yip as the others hurried to join the attack.

She clenched her free fist, and banged the tomtin that held her arm on the nose. The blow jarred the teeth holding her, and she figured it must have hurt her as much as it hurt the tomtin, but she punched again and the clamped teeth released their hold.

She was away, running, leaping from the path and crunching down in the loose chippings of the abbey. At first a weight hung on her—the tomtin that had seized hold of her jacket—but then it fell away and she bounded forward.

She had no light now and couldn't see where she was running. When she jumped, she couldn't see where she might land. In the fitful, overcast moonlight, the low walls were a dense black, the beds of stone chippings a paler gray. She didn't know if the tomtin were still after her—she couldn't hear them.

Her shin cracked against a head-sized stone, and she cata-pulted forward over the wall and went sprawling noisily and painfully into the chippings. Her teeth clashed together, catching the tip of her tongue and filling her mouth with blood and pain. For one second she lay still, winded, but then a distant pattering of feet sent her struggling forward again, stumbling over the chippings, panting for breath.

She bumped into something that was hard and yet yielding, that rolled a little with her impact…and sighed softly. She felt cotton under her fingers and a smell. A smell—not the smell of damp woodland earth or snow. Aftershave. She had found Leonard!

She grasped a handful of his ski jacket and shook him. His body moved slightly, heavily, but he didn't move or make a sound. "Leonard," she said. "Leonard." Her hand found his face, his nose, then her fingers slipped into his mouth. He didn't move. As her hand explored his face, his head tipped sideways…and, slipping lower, her fingers found another, wet mouth. She snatched her hand back, feeling the wetness turn sticky and thick, as only one liquid did—blood. Leonard might have sighed, but only because she had fallen on his chest.

For a moment, she was stunned. Then she saw a dark shape dash along the top of a black wall, and there was a terrible sound of tomtin laughter.

Leonard's gone, she thought. Paul's gone, Joe's gone. I'm on my own.

All the tomtin, she thought, all over the country…in the towns…in the cities in the woods… back-gardens, looking for children to make into new tomtin but killing anyone who stands in their way. Who knew how many tomtin there were right now all over the country, searching for new victims this Christmas, all very clever and *very* fierce.

The dark shape moved in front of her and she kicked out at it and yelled. One came at her with a quick, bruising, testing bite, which she shook off.

People will take them for elves—Santa's little helpers. How sweet, I'll put out some mince pies and milk, she thought. Noises on the roof at night. Soft muttering sounds in the living room. The sound of sleigh bells in the street, at night. People don't know who they really are—they need to be told. They need to know the dangers, she realized.

She saw movement—low and quick—out of the corner of her eye, then it was gone.

Jumping up, she ran. Something grabbed at her as she went by, but she was away, running for the path to the farm, refusing to care about the pain in her leg, the burning in her bitten arm.

The darkness sent her smacking into a tall section of the abbey wall. She slapped it with her hands, seeking its edge, a way around it. A weight fastened on her ankle, and pulled. She clawed at the wall, pulled against the weight, struggling to stay on her feet. Another grip clamped around her other leg, in the calf, pulling...

She went down. Saw the undead child's eyes, the evil in those dark orbs. It was covered in blood from head to toe. Whose blood? She didn't want to know.

Then there were two, three, many more.

She was certain she heard the sound of sleigh bells as the undead child opened its mouth wide...or was it just her imagination? After all, wasn't Santa Claus only supposed to come on Christmas Eve? And it wasn't Christmas Eve.

Lucy thought of Paul, Joe, Leonard and her Christmas wedding that would never happen.

And as the undead child clamped its teeth tight around her throat and yanked back, tearing out a large chunk and severing her jugular, to send hot blood squirting into the cold night air, she thought no more.

A VISIT FROM SANTA

DUSTIN STEVENS

The wooden floorboards creaked slightly beneath Logan Mannix's steel-toed boots, as he made a pass through the house, once more checking to ensure all the doors and windows were secured. Every few seconds he would stop and look out between the wooden slats nailed over the window openings, peering through the thick plastic that had replaced the long-since shattered glass panes.

The night was completely still, the earth shrouded in white.

Logan paused by the French doors in the kitchen and studied the backyard for a full minute, rubbing the back of his fist against his chin whiskers. Looking for any trace of footprints, his eyes focused on the fresh snow, even more for the tell-tale blood trails that followed the undead wherever they went.

"Anything?" his wife, Lena, asked, joining him.

He turned to regard her as she wrapped an oversized gray cardigan around her slight frame and leaned against the counter across from him. Her long blonde hair fell straight to the shoulder and bright blue eyes stared at him from the center of a face drawn tight from never having quite enough to eat.

"Pop always used to say snow was a blessing and a curse," Logan said, shifting his gaze back outside. "When it's on the ground, it makes for easy tracking. When it's in the air, it makes tracking impossible."

"And what's it doing now?"

"Both," he said.

"Another long night, huh?"

"Aren't they all?" he replied.

Lena nodded, unable to refute his simple logic. "Come on, the boys are waiting in the living room. It's almost time."

Logan grunted and pushed himself away from the doorframe, turned, and followed his wife into the living room. He was a big man, standing several inches over six feet, with broad shoulders and hands. Like Lena, his features were borderline gaunt, though a perpetual splash of beard across his face did its best to hide it.

Seated together on the couch were their two sons, Ben and Kurt. The boys were nine and seven years old respectively, both spitting images of their mother. The boys were huddled tight beneath two heavy blankets, staring up at their parents with solemn expressions. Behind them, a fire blazed in the stone fireplace, fighting a losing battle to heat the small home.

Lena walked straight to the far end of the couch and resumed her spot under the blankets with the boys. Once she was situated, all three pressed a little bit tighter together, a position they would hold until morning. On nights that were especially cold, Logan would join them, but for the most part he remained across from them in his old armchair, catching catnaps between trips to feed the fire and check the perimeter.

He hadn't slept more than four hours a night in years—not since before the zombies showed up.

Logan followed Lena into the living room and checked the fire, then took up a post behind his armchair. He leaned forward and rested his forearms across the top of it, then studied his family huddled together across from him.

It wasn't supposed to be like this.

Six years earlier, he was living the proverbial dream. He was young and virile, with a beautiful woman on his arm and two bouncing boys in the yard. Every day he awoke early and went to work at the sawmill, and each night he came home to give the boys their baths and put them to bed before sitting down to dinner with his wife.

It took only three days to change all that, for them and a million others just like them stretched across the country. It began with tainted chicken in Florida, turning harmless people into mindless, fresh-craving lunatics. Within twenty-four hours, the entire southeast corner of the United States had been crawling with zombies. By forty-eight hours, everything east of the Mississippi and after three days, it even reached his tiny corner of Oregon.

By all accounts, Logan and his family were considered some of the lucky ones. They'd raised an enormous garden each summer and Logan hunted relentlessly year round to keep them fed. Their remote location meant that the sheer number of undead they had to deal with was much smaller than in other parts of the country.

They were all still alive and together, to most that would be a win.

Logan swept his gaze across the three of them, not so sure they really were better off. His children had grown up almost entirely in a world controlled by roaming hordes of zombies. This was the fourth house they'd occupied in six years and all four of them were aged far beyond their years.

In truth, Logan was exhausted, and he could tell by the expressions on the faces of his family that they were tired, too.

"Is it time?" Ben asked, his small voice the only sound in the house save the crackling of the fireplace.

Logan shifted his gaze over to the wind-up clock sitting on the coffee table between them. "Yeah, it's almost eight." Without another word, he circled around the chair and turned on the a.m. radio that sat behind the clock, twisting the dial slightly until the sound of *Hail to the Chief* played out into the room.

There was no need to check the station number, it was the only program in the country that was still playing. Even at that, it only played from exactly 7:45 to 8:30 every night. Fifteen minutes for the President to broadcast any new information to the world from his personal bunker in Nebraska, which was sandwiched between pithy Americana music.

After years of the same tired songs and same inane updates, Logan wasn't sure which annoyed him more.

"You think he'll have anything new to say tonight?" Lena asked.

Logan settled himself back into the armchair and made an annoyed face, but said nothing. He didn't have to, Lena was fully aware of how he felt about these nightly broadcasts. They were little more than a pep talk to those who remained alive and functioning to keep battling to stay alive, that the government was doing all they could to find a cure for the epidemic and get things back to normal.

For the first year or so, people like the Maddix family had bought into it because there was little else for them to do. But by now, it was blatantly obvious that there was no cure forthcoming, the speeches just the hollow words of a man that had been President for nine years now with no worries of an election anywhere in the future.

At precisely eight, the music fell away to silence, followed by the sound of a microphone being turned on, then the rich baritone of Samson Howell, the forty-seventh President of the United States.

"Good evening," Howell began. "As always if you're listening right now then this message finds you alive, and I hope it finds you well. There's no denying the gravity of the situation we all find ourselves facing each and every day and I praise you all for your continued efforts and beseech you to push forward."

Logan snorted softly and shook his head. The gall of a man sitting a mile beneath the ground in a concrete bunker in Nebraska to ask them to keep fighting the good fight.

"Take hope in knowing that each passing day brings us another step closer to finding a cure to this heinous disease that has gripped our great nation. Even as I speak, teams of scientists are working tirelessly to find a cure that will allow us all to soon get back to the lives we once knew."

Logan's eyelids slid closed as he settled a little lower into his chair. It was important he try as hard as possible not to let the boys see his open disgust at the President's message, the same exact message he'd been hearing for almost six years and counting.

"Beyond that though, we have an extra cause for celebration tonight, for it's Christmas Eve. A night for us to draw close to the ones around us, whether they be family by birth or by circumstance, and to say thanks for the things we do have. For the fact that we are all still alive, that a new year is just days away, that we have the ability to communicate with one another each night like this."

Logan's eyes popped open and he stared straight across at his wife. Her gaze met his, both with the same thought running through their minds.

"So tonight, I ask that you maintain hope and that you continue to persevere in these seemingly dark times. There's a light on the horizon and I assure you, little by little, together we are moving forward. I also want to wish you all a Merry Christmas, from me and my family to you and yours, and I look forward to speaking with you all back here tomorrow. Good night."

The voice of the President fell away and the microphone clicked off, followed not by another round of *Hail to the Chief*, but instead by an instrumental rendition of *O Holy Night*.

Logan kept his eyes locked on his wife, barely hearing the music. It was Christmas. Somehow they, two people that used to live for the holiday season and the parents of two young boys, had missed one of the most important days of the year. It was one of the few things they could still do as a family that maintained some tiny connection to the normality of a life they once knew.

"It's Christmas?" Ben asked, his voice completely void of enthusiasm or anticipation.

Lena offered a pleading look to Logan and said, "Yes, sweetheart, it's Christmas."

"Oh," Ben said. "I knew it was cold out, but I didn't think it was that late already."

The even, resigned way his son spoke of the holiday jabbed at Logan's stomach. Still, he remained silent.

"Remember when Santa used to come visit?" Kurt said. Youth was plainly apparent in his voice, though it too was completely void of overt excitement.

"Yeah," Ben replied. "I remember."

Silence fell over the room for a moment. Logan pressed his eyes tight together and lowered his chin to his chest. Neither of his boys were even ten years old, yet already he had asked them to become men. To handle guns, chop wood, hunt for food. It always pained him to do so, but there had been no other way for the family to survive.

Still, somehow, this hurt more than all of that combined. Santa Claus was one of the most fundamental images of childhood. Hearing his children speak so candidly about it as a thing of the past was wrong on every level.

"What do you mean, you remember?" Logan asked. "You act like Santa doesn't exist anymore or something."

Lena looked at him questioningly, but said nothing.

"Does he?" Ben asked. "He hasn't been to see us in a long time. Not since he brought me a baseball bat when I was five."

"Of course he does, son. You just have to keep in mind that Santa is a very busy guy. He has to keep track of where all the kids move around to these days. Why, just think how many places we've been in the last year."

The boys exchanged a quick glance, a bit of contained excitement beginning to grow on their faces. Beside them, Lena made a disapproving face.

"Besides, think about how we spend most of our time now," Logan continued.

"Yeah, working," Ben grumbled.

"True, but what *else* do we do with our time?" Logan asked.

"Fight zombies?" Kurt asked.

Logan pushed himself from the back of the chair and leaned forward onto his knees. Beside him the radio transitioned from *O Holy Night* to *Jingle Bells*, though no one was paying attention to it. "That's right," he said. "We fight zombies."

"So Santa hasn't come the last couple of years because he's been fighting zombies, too?" Kurt pressed.

Logan pursed his lips and twisted his head, making a show of debating the question. "I can think of no other reason why he wouldn't be here, can you?"

The boys both smiled and exchanged anxious glances, though said nothing.

Logan matched the smile and pushed himself to his feet, leaving the radio on to play the Christmas music throughout the house. Slowly, he circled around the couch and dropped another log on the fire, then went on another perimeter check.

He made it as far as the bedroom before Lena caught up to him, her stocking feet shuffling quickly across the floorboards.

"What the hell was that?" she hissed. "Telling the boys that Santa's hasn't been to see them because he's off fighting zombies?"

Logan leaned past her to make sure the boys were still in the living room and pulled the door closed behind her. "Honey, we forgot Christmas," he said evenly.

"I didn't *forget* Christmas," Lena spat. "There was just nothing to do for it anyway. There's nowhere left to get presents, and no money to buy them with if there was. What little we have to barter with we need to survive."

Logan let his wife finish her rant, then raised a hand to calm her. "I know. Believe me, I know. But there was just something about hearing those boys in there talk about Santa like that."

Lena's face softened. "Almost like he was dead."

With a shake of his head, Logan said, "Not him, he was never alive. Them, their childhood. The way they were talking made it sound like *they* were dead."

Lena opened her mouth to respond, but closed it just as fast. A small cloud passed over her face, the anger fleeing as she looked up. "I hadn't considered that. All I heard was you filling them with false hope."

"Not false hope," Logan said. "Just hope."

Lena nodded. "What are you going to do?"

Logan cast his gaze around the room, taking in everything around them. They had stumbled upon the house just a few months ago while driving through the countryside and had stopped to check for survivors. From the moment they arrived, it was evident the place had not been lived in for quite some time.

Whoever had lived there before them must have fled in a hurry, as very little had been taken from the house. Closets were still filled with winter clothing and the cabinets had held canned goods that were only a couple of years outdated.

Where they now stood had once been the master bedroom. An overstuffed queen-size bed dominated the room, flanked by a dresser on one side and a nightstand on the other. A closet stood off to the left, it's door sagging open to reveal a bevy of brightly-colored clothes within.

"What year did we give Ben that baseball bat?" Logan asked.

Lena made a face and focused on the wall opposite them. "He was five, meaning four years ago."

"Four years," Logan repeated softly. "I'd say it's about time the boys got a visit from Santa, don't you?"

"I'd love a Whopper and a milkshake, too," Lena said. "But that doesn't mean we can just wish for it. How in the world are we going to get Santa here tonight? And what will *he* bring the boys even if we do?"

"You just leave that to me," he said, his mind already devising a scheme. "I'm going outside for a little while. Can you find me a pair of scissors and some string or rope?"

Lena stepped back, her jaw open. "You're going outside? Now? You know what could be lurking out there."

"Actually," he said, already reaching past her for the door, "I'm kind of banking on it."

Icy crystals hung in the air, filling Logan's lungs as he strode across the backyard. His boots cut a heavy path through the fresh snow as he walked a direct line from the porch to a small storage shed standing fifty yards away. Thick snowflakes continued to fall from the sky in waves, sticking to his bare head and shrouding his parka and jeans in white.

Both of his wrists rested alongside his chest, each gripping a weapon. In his right hand was the walnut stock of a Winchester double-barreled shotgun, in his left the treated hickory of a number 7 axe. A Ruger P-Series was strapped to his hip should he need the extra firepower, though he doubted he would.

Not for a little while yet anyway.

When they first arrived a few months before, he'd made an inventory of the grounds and knew exactly what he was looking for. Feeling a small bounce in his step, he crossed into the shed and slipped inside. He gave a quick once-over of the place to make sure he was alone, then dropped the shotgun and the axe and went straight for the corner.

Tucked beneath an old gray tarp dotted with bird droppings, was a massive box labeled **Xmas Decorations**. The first time he saw it he hadn't thought much of it and didn't bother to look inside. He now prayed it held what he was looking for.

As quietly as possible, he dragged the large box back out to the door of the shed and tore open the top, tossing aside a handful of wreaths and plastic reindeer before finding what he wanted in a tangle at the bottom.

Christmas lights.

Leaving the axe and the shotgun where they were, he touched his hip to make sure the Ruger was still firmly affixed to his side before stepping back out into the night. Holding the oversized ball of lights in his left hand, he made a quick trip around the house, looping the lights over low-hanging branches with his right hand. By the time he was finished, a light sweat was on his brow and his nerves were on end from staring into the darkness.

The wad of lights left him with a few extra feet that he dropped onto the ground by the front of the shed. On the other side of the door was a generator he'd stowed there in the Fall, already gassed up and ready to go, just waiting for him to start it.

Logan stood with his hands on his hips and did a quick survey of his handiwork. Strings of white and green plastic lights hung in misshapen loops from the various trees, all ready to be turned on and bathe the house in light.

The outside was ready.

It was time for him to get into costume.

The house was quiet when Logan tapped the snow from his boots and stepped inside. He checked to make sure the fire still burned brightly in the fireplace and saw that the boys were both asleep on the couch, their heads thrown back and their mouths hanging open. Lena sat curled into Logan's armchair, her knees tucked up under her chin with a blanket wrapped tight around her.

A pair of sewing shears and some white yarn sat on the table. A worried look stretched across her face.

Logan rose onto his toes and stepped into the room, his footfalls barely perceptible as he lifted the shears and yarn from the table and retreated towards the bedroom. Lena followed close on his heels, the blanket still enveloping her body.

"What are you going to do?" she whispered as they walked down the hallway.

Logan waited until they were both inside the bedroom with the door closed before responding. "Just what I said I was going to do, I'm going to give the boys a visit from Santa."

A look of confusion passed over her face. "What? How? You aren't Santa, and you don't have the first thing to give them."

Logan peeled back the thick down comforter from atop the bed and tossed it aside to reveal a set of bright red satin sheets with matching pillow cases. Unceremoniously, he snatched up the sheet, chose a spot roughly in the center of it, and hacked out a large circle. "Remember the conversation I had with the boys earlier? About Santa being busy right now?"

"Yes. You said it was too hard for him to find all the children with them moving so much. So?"

Peeling his coat off, he lined the rough-hewn hole up with his eyes and tossed the sheet around his neck, his head protruding through the opening. The rest of the sheet hung down around him in heavy folds, stretching almost to his knees. "What else did I tell them Santa was busy doing right now?"

Lena made another face and started to reply, the look just as suddenly evaporating as realization set in. "You're going to dress up as Santa and fight zombies. *That's* your plan?"

Logan rolled out a length of yarn almost ten feet in length, looped it in half, then cinched it tight around his waist. The bottom half of the sheet bunched tight against his hips, allowing his legs and arms to swing free. "Yes, it is," he said simply.

Taking great pains to avoid eye contact, he grabbed a pillow from the end of the bed and peeled the case from it. He tied the bright red material tight around his head like a bandana, letting the remainder of it fall down his back. The pillow itself he sheared open and grabbed out an oversized handful of stuffing from within.

"You're seriously going to draw the zombies in to where we live and fight them in front of the boys?" Lena asked. She was doing her best to keep her tone even and volume low, though her exasperation at the plan was obvious.

Logan wound another length of the yarn through the stuffing and pressed it against his face, then stretched the yarn tight and tied it behind his ears. "So, how do I look?"

"Like a damn idiot!" she seethed. "An idiot that's liable to get his family killed for no good reason!"

Logan untied the beard for a moment and pulled it back from his face. When he spoke, his voice was just as earnest as Lena's, though it lacked the same vitriol. "Look, I know how dangerous this could be. And I know you think I must be stark-raving mad. But to those boys in there, who are clinging to any last shred of childhood they might have, this could make their year."

"You, dressed as Santa, fighting zombies in the backyard?" Lena said. "What if something happens to you? Then what?"

Logan pressed his palms flat against Lena's shoulders and said, "Nothing's going to happen to me. We've been here three months and seen a dozen zombies total. I don't even know if any are going to show up. All I know is I'm going to go out back, turn on the lights, and yell a few Ho-Ho-Ho's. You'll bring the boys out, I'll tell them I've been busy fighting zombies, and wish them a Merry Christmas."

Lena stared back at him hard for a full minute, her blue eyes boring into his. "Why are you really doing this?"

Logan returned the beard to his face and tied it tight. "When my mother died, I was ten. I didn't realize it at the time, but that one day changed how I viewed the world forever. I was no longer a child. I was no longer innocent or oblivious. For all these years, I have done everything possible to put off that moment for the boys. It hasn't been easy, not with the damn world coming to an end and the dead crawling over the countryside, but I've done it. Tonight though, for the first time, I saw a little bit of that feeling I remember having in Kurt's face."

Lena said nothing so he continued. "Look, I get it, Lena. I understand that me dressing like this and potentially inviting in a horde of flesh-craving zombies doesn't make the most sense, but if it helps maintain those boys belief in something as fundamental as Santa Claus for even a little bit longer, then at least I have to try."

Lena stared at him for several long seconds as a single tear slid down her cheek. After several seconds she whispered, "What do you need me to do?"

* * *

It took three pulls to get the old generator to turn over. The first one elicited no response, and the second gave a small sputter before the machine fell silent. On the third, he was greeted by a small black plume of oil vapor followed by an uneven cadence of pistons turning before it settled into an even din.

On cue, the lights around the house sprang to life, illuminating everything in a yellow-tinged glow. Grabbing up the shotgun and axe, Logan ran around behind the shed and waited, then snow continuing to fall in heavy flakes around him.

A few moments later, he could hear the backdoor swing open. The excited sounds of the boys' voices floated out through the air, and with a large smile in place, Logan stepped out from behind the shed. "HO-HO-HO! *Merrrry* Christmas!" he called in his best imitation of Santa.

His sudden appearance froze both Kurt and Ben in place for several long seconds before realization set in and they both reached for each other, smiling broadly and bouncing lightly on the balls of their feet.

Walking in a slow and even gait, Logan marched across the lawn and stopped several feet from the back porch. His costume was poor at best; there was no need to get any closer than necessary. "Well now, who do we have here?"

The boys exchanged looks with one another. "I'm Kurt," the first boy said. "And this is my brother Ben."

"Why hello there," Logan said. "My name is Kris Kringle, though most of my friends just call me Santa."

The smiles grew a little larger on their faces, matched by a begrudging smile on Lena's face behind them.

"You boys have been rather tough to find," Logan said. "If it wasn't for a letter from your mother telling me where you were, I might never have found you."

"You've been looking for us?" Ben asked, his eyes wide.

"Of course I have," Logan said, hefting the axe and the shotgun from either shoulder. "When I wasn't busy fighting off zombies of course."

"So you've really been fighting?" Kurt asked. "That wasn't just something our dad made up?"

A small tinge passed through Logan. "I should say not. Sometimes children ask me for toys, other times they ask me to keep them safe."

"But has anybody ever asked you to fight a snowman?" Kurt asked.

For just a moment, Logan broke character and made a face at his son. "What?"

If either noticed the sudden change in voice, neither let it show. Instead, Ben raised a finger to the woods behind them and said, "Look! Snowmen!"

Logan subconsciously gripped the weapons in his hand tightly and rotated to face the woods behind them. There, emerging through the trees, was a band of zombies marching straight for the house. The Christmas lights had drawn them in like moths to a flame, just as he'd hoped.

There were eight of them in total, all of them staggering forward with bloody spittle hanging from their mouths. The thick snow that continued to fall had blanketed them all in white, making them look like snowmen, as they emerged through the trees.

Logan rotated back to the house to see a pale Lena standing behind two very excited little boys. "Would you like to see Santa fight some zombie snowmen?"

"Yeah!" the boys yelled in unison.

Without a word, Logan turned back to the encroaching undead and drew in a deep breath. Over the last six years he'd killed over a hundred zombies, but that didn't mean his heart didn't still race a little faster each time he encountered them. He cast a quick glance down to his hip to make sure the Ruger was in place, then cast his gaze around the house to make sure there weren't any more coming.

It was Santa against eight zombies, with two little boys watching, waiting to see a good show.

"Well, this is what you wanted," Logan said, then turned and walked quickly towards the zombies. Their bodies were nearly completely wrapped in snow as they closed the gap from him, streaks of blood the only variance of color on their pale faces.

With a shrug of his shoulders, Logan pushed the axe head and barrel of the shotgun forward and extended them both in front of him. He walked straight at the zombies, picked out the leader of the pack, and sighted in down the length of the shotgun barrel.

The weapon bucked wildly in his hand as the first blast struck a zombie right in the mouth just as it let out a thunderous moan. The report of the shotgun echoed through the quiet woods as the zombie's head exploded, everything above the neck turning into a plume of red jelly.

The momentum of the blast tossed the zombie's body backwards into the snow as Logan continued to move forward. He let the momentum of the blast raise the barrel of the shotgun almost directly up into the sky, then brought it back down and sighted in on his second target. This time he bypassed the closest zombie, a diminutive one that looked to have been a female at one time, in favor a massive male just behind her.

Using the axe as a makeshift stabilizer, he leveled the shotgun at the bridge of the male's nose and let loose another round. The shot struck it directly between the eyes and carved out a thick groove through the pale face, rendering the head into the shape of a canoe, as brains and bone matter spilled out onto the frozen ground.

Behind him, Logan could hear the boys cheering loudly.

This time, as the barrel of the shotgun kicked high into the air, Logan let the momentum carry it up and over his shoulder. For a moment he considered pulling out the Ruger and mowing down the remainder of the zombies, but instead decided to put on a show for the boys. The thick layer of snow on everything kept the gore to a minimum, and their cheers told him they were enjoying everything so far.

Logan dropped the axe down in front of him and slid his right hand into position above his left. The small female zombie continued pressing in on him, her face contorted into a mask of hunger beneath the snow covering it as Logan stepped forward and slashed the axe blade across her throat. He was going for a clean decapitation blow, but he missed the last inch of the neck as her skull swung backwards, streams of dark, congealed blood spewing up into the air. The back of her head came to rest flat against her shoulder blades as she stood still for several seconds before crumpling into a ball, blood pouring out onto the cold ground.

Sweat bathed Logan beneath his makeshift costume as his heart rate picked up and the remaining zombies closed in around him. With the axe dripping blood and poised in his hands, he shuffle-stepped forward towards the next one and raised the axe high over his head, smashing it down as if chopping a piece of firewood. The razor-honed blade sliced easily through the rotting flesh, splitting it clear to the sternum.

The zombie seemed to melt to the ground in a wave of blood and bodily fluids as a pair of zombies lunged for Logan, their arms outstretched in front of them. Dropping to a knee, Logan spun in a tight circle and swung the axe. It struck the thigh of the closest zombie, snapping its leg off just above the knee. A torrent of blood and bone fragments splattered onto the ground as the zombie teetered for a moment, before falling into the snow face first.

Allowing his movement to carry him forward, Logan gripped the axe in an underhand fashion and swung the blade up through the second zombie's chin, the steel point tearing out the soft underside of its throat and ripping away the entire bottom half of its face. For a moment the zombie wobbled and attempted to continue its pursuit, then Logan slashed it across the stomach with his axe. A writhing mash of intestines spilled onto the snow-covered ground with a wet smack, followed soon by the rest of the body.

His heart racing, Logan stood between the zombie snowmen in a circle of snow painted red and searched for his next victim. On either side of him were two more rotting corpses bundled in snow, both fighting to get past their fallen counterparts to reach him. Ahead of him, a lone zombie had broken off from the group and was headed towards the back porch.

A surge of anxiety filled Logan as he watched the zombie make a slow, steady pace towards his family. Beyond the creature he could see fear on Lena's face as she grabbed the boys tight and tried to pull them towards the back door.

In their excitement, neither one could be moved from their spot.

No longer concerned with putting on a show, Logan slid the Ruger from his hip holster and extended it to his right. In practiced fashion, he put two quick shots into the zombie's chest, then two through its skull in a move he called 'dotting the eyes.' The back of its head exploded into two equal puffs of red mist as it fell backwards.

Rotating at the hip, he pushed the gun out to his left and fired the same quartet of shots, the result much the same as the one before.

"Get him, Santa! Get him!" Ben cried excitedly from the porch, completely oblivious to any potential danger as the eighth and final zombie closed the gap between them.

"Yeah!" Kurt called beside him.

Adrenaline surged through Logan as he moved forward, the Ruger extended in front of him. The zombie was exactly equidistant between him and the porch, its uneven gait pushing a meandering path through the thickening snow. From where he stood, Logan could easily shoot it down, though he ran the risk of bullets passing through the body and hitting one of his family. He could try and chase it down or get a better angle, but there was no telling how much the thick snow might slow Logan down.

Glancing down at the hickory axe handle in his hand, he drew in a sharp breath and raised it over his head. His hands slid easily over the polished wood and came together as the axe stopped its backswing behind his head, before surging forward in an overhead toss.

The Christmas lights glinted off the blade as it rotated end over end through the air before burying itself into the base of the zombie's skull. The force of the blow pitched the body headlong into the snow, and Logan was there a moment later to wrench the blade free and cleave the head clean from the rest of the body. Dark blood spewed from the exposed veins of the neck and out onto the snow as the boys cheered wildly from the porch, both extending their hands high over their heads in exultation.

"Yay, Santa!" Ben yelled.

"That was amazing!" Kurt called.

Logan posed for a moment with the axe dripping blood in front of him, searching to make sure no stragglers remained. He waited until the boys calmed enough for him to talk and said, "I have to be going now, but I want you boys to promise me two things, okay?"

They both nodded in unison.

"I want you to both be good boys and listen to your parents."

More nodding.

"And I want you both to have a Merry Christmas. Can you do that for me?"

"Yes, Santa!" Kurt said.

"Merry Christmas, Santa!" Ben said.

Logan raised a hand to the boys. "Merry Christmas!" He stood like that, rooted in place, for several long minutes as Lena shuffled the boys back inside and the world fell silent again.

Logan left his homemade Santa suit wadded up at the bottom of the box of decorations, hidden beneath the wreaths he'd put back and the lights that he'd taken down from the trees earlier. He then put the box back into the corner of the shed and stretched the tarp over it, so that the boys wouldn't stumble upon it by mistake.

Not that they were going to be living in the house much longer anyway. The eight bloody, putrid lumps of rotting flesh dotting the backyard and buried beneath another inch of fresh snow were reason enough to ensure that he and his family moved on soon. If six years of fighting had taught Logan anything, it was that where one group of zombies was, more were sure to follow.

He made no effort to be quiet as he stamped the snow from his boots and stepped into the house by the back door, pulling his coat from his shoulders as he passed through the kitchen and into the living room.

"Dad! Where have you been? You missed it!" Ben cried, leaping up from the couch.

"Yeah! It was awesome! Santa totally took down the zombie snowmen!" Kurt said while standing and swinging an imaginary axe through the air.

Behind them, Lena stood by the fire, smiling and shaking her head.

"I was out getting some more wood," Logan said. "What's this about Santa? And zombie snowmen?"

"Yeah! Santa came to see us, and he brought lights and everything…" Ben started.

"And while he was talking to us, a bunch of zombie snowmen showed up," Kurt finished.

"He took them all down!" Ben exclaimed.

"Really? All that happened in the last half hour?" Logan asked.

"Yeah, it's true!" Kurt said earnestly. "Right, Mom?"

Lena continued smiling and shaking her head. "You should have been there, Logan, it was something to see."

Logan stared at his wife for several long seconds. "It sounds like I really missed out," he said. "But I'm glad you guys got to see Santa."

"Me too! This is the best Christmas ever!" Ben yelled happily as he and his brother began a reenactment of the fight.

Watching the entire time, Logan looped around the couch and slid his arm around Lena's shoulder. She leaned in tight and whispered, "I still think you're crazy."

Logan smirked softly, watching Kurt take off the leg of an imaginary zombie snowman, the same move that Logan had used just a short time ago. "Probably, but sometimes crazy makes for the best Christmas ever."

CHECK THE HALLS
(FOR BRAINS AND ZOMBIES)

DENNIS FINOCCHIARO

Zach Ward ran from the large number of blood-coated un-dead as fast as he could, but his legs were sapped of strength. He knew he couldn't last much longer and lunged for the first build-ing with a door ajar. Crashing through it, he probably attracted the attention of more zombies with the noise, but he didn't care. Now it was just about getting himself to the roof, blocking the door, and regaining his strength. Unfortunately, his pack only had one more piece of food left, and he wasn't even sure it was edible. Added to the fact that he'd ruined his favorite Iron Man t-shirt with zombie guts—which, try as you will, do *not* come out in the laundry—it wasn't his best day. His only weapon left was an old axe he'd been carrying for days since temporarily leaving his van behind.

The building he entered had once been apartments. It was clearly a space where people had holed up when it had all started, based on the old dressers, bed frames and other assortments of furniture that had once acted as a barrier—now all destroyed. Hurdling a smashed oak wardrobe, he reached the stairs as one of the zombies reached for his jacket, narrowly missing it.

Taking the steps two at a time, Zach made it to the fourth floor before he became exhausted and they had caught up, one grabbing his ankle and tripping him. He turned with hatchet in hand, and swung at the zombie's wrist, severing it enough that the creature fell backwards, slowing down the others that were making their way up the stairs. Zach was without energy and knew it was time to either take a stand or barricade himself inside an apartment. He decided on the latter.

The nearest room was 412, so he dove into the doorway, but he didn't close it in time. Four arms reached in and kept him from closing the door. He hacked and hacked, blood splattering the faux-wood door and the orange walls, creating what looked a bit like what passed for modern art before all this zombie stuff started.

After taking off two more arms, the owner of the fourth limb got her head into the crack of the door. He turned the axe backwards and hit her so hard in the skull that she went limp immediately and fell backwards. He slammed the door closed, throwing the lock and placing the chain in the little slot.

Exhausted, Zach flopped to the floor, panting. He took note of a metal slot screwed into the hardwood and recognized it as one of those slots that included a heavy bar that would block the door. He found it and slid it into place as the scraping started from the hallway. He was safe—for now.

The only furniture in the room was an old, ratty couch, but it looked like home to him as he rose, walked to it, and passed out from exhaustion.

By the time Zach woke up, night had fallen. The scraping, unlike the sun, was still there, and he knew that the door wouldn't hold forever. Cracks had already started to form. A quick inventory of the room found a can of beans, which he quickly devoured, and a butter knife—nothing else.

He ran to the bedroom, hoping to find a window that would lead to a small roof or something similar, but when he pulled the dusty shades up, something else caught his eye. About a half mile away, a small lit up plastic Santa Claus could be seen lighting its way to other survivors.

It didn't take long for Zach, once he noticed the fire escape, to get to the holiday decoration. When he arrived, he could hardly believe what he saw. The building itself was fenced in and appeared to be an old inner city school. He pushed on the fence and it held; the rattle brought two survivors with guns running in his direction.

"I'm alive!" he yelled quickly before he ended up being shot. This was one of the many things he'd learned to do in the time since *they* had taken over. The pair, a man and a woman, ran up to him. They both wore dark green pants and black winter jackets that made them look like security guards. One held a gun, the other a walkie talkie.

"We've got a survivor," the woman said into the two-way radio.

Zach relaxed a little.

"You bit?" she asked.

"No, I'm not."

"Strip," the man said as he pointed his gun in Zach's direction.

"Could I possibly come in first? I might have been followed."

The couple whispered to each other and finally the woman pushed a button that opened the gate.

"You guys still have power here, huh? Generators?"

The woman nodded.

"The name's Zach. Zach Ward."

The woman smiled. "I'm Janice and this is Hector. I've heard of you. You actually saved a few of the people here. They talk about you like you're a hero. Right, Hector?"

Hector scratched at his beard and looked at Zach. "I thought you'd be taller."

"I get that a lot," Zach said with a smile. "So should I just strip here?"

"Not necessary," Hector said. "You're practically a celebrity. I'm sure you're good." He didn't try to hide the sarcasm. "Are you on foot?" He looked past Zach at the road as if a car might drive up.

"Nope. I have a van, but I left it behind—temporarily. I'll head back there in a day or so, as long as you guys don't mind me resting up a bit."

"Not at all," Janice said. "We'd love to have you. Nobody's been through here in quite a while. Let's bring you up to the group. Show you ar…"

A scream echoed through the yard and the trio turned to the fence to see an outline yelling to be let in.

"It's Franklin. Better see what the bastard has gotten himself into this time!" Hector said as he cocked his gun.

They ran to the gate in time to see a horde of zombies chasing after what looked to Zach to be a kid. The kid's dark complexion made it difficult to see his face, but Zach figured he was around seventeen or eighteen.

"Open the gate! Quick!" the kid yelled.

"There's too many of them, Janice! Don't open it!" Hector yelled.

Zach pulled the axe from his belt. "Open it just enough for me to go out. I'll get him." Janice ignored Hector's plea and pushed the button, quickly hitting it again once Zach was through.

Zach turned and looked at Hector through the fence. "Cover me."

Hector nodded and held the muzzle up towards the upcoming creatures.

Franklin ran to the gate and quickly realized it was closed. Zach turned and yelled, "Franklin. Franklin! That's your name, right?"

The kid turned and nodded, his large, white eyes about as wide as they could get.

"I'm Zach. You got a weapon?"

The kid nodded and held up a baseball bat.

"Great." Zach assessed the situation and went for the closest zombie, splitting its skull in two. Some of its brains squirted out and landed on Franklin's hoodie.

Zach turned to him and gave him a sharp shove. "Franklin! Help me out, man! There's five more in close range. You take the two on the right, and I'll get the other three!"

Franklin woke as if from a dream, shook it off, and gripped the bat.

As Zach kicked the middle zombie in the stomach, Franklin took a swing at the one on the far right, what used to be a woman, wearing a red and white striped cashier shirt. He clipped her on the side of the shoulder, stunning her, but she recovered and continued towards him.

Meanwhile, Zach finished off another zombie, this one a man in a tattered business suit. Franklin focused and hit the woman again, taking her out, then swung a home run hit right into the other one's skull. It dropped fast, and he turned to see Zach facing a zombie dressed as a milk shake.

"Hey, Franklin! This one's almost funny, isn't it?" Zach called as he shoved it away from him. Suddenly, the milkshake exploded red all over the street, and they turned to see Hector lower his gun. The rest of the zombies slowly made their way towards Zach and Franklin, but the immediate area was clear.

"Maybe you can let us in now?" Zach asked with a grin.

Franklin was excited when Hector told him to give Zach a tour of the campus while the leaders were informed of the new arrival. Hector was already looking up to Zach as a hero, considering he'd become somewhat of an urban legend in the area. Their fight together would be a great story to tell. As he took off the splattered hoodie, he immediately started to shiver a little in the cold.

"So, did you find anything good out there?" Zach asked him, gesturing to the backpack Hector wore.

"Oh yeah! But I want to show everyone. Let's check out the school," Hector replied as he threw the soiled shirt into a nearby trash can.

The structure which used to be an elementary school, included the building that housed the classrooms, a giant metal barn, a cafeteria/kitchen, and a bell tower in the middle that was part of a historic landmark that someone was forced to build the school around. In one of the clearings was a garden, but the cold had hardened the soil and frost now covered it.

The tour took a while since the school seemed to have at one time been rather wealthy. The entire place was surrounded by solid, chain-link fencing, except for one spot where a car had crashed into it and was still there. Zach stared at the car while Franklin explained.

"We were going to move it when we got here," Hector said, "but the car blocks the hole, so we aren't too worried. The only way it would be a problem is if we had a ton of zombies trying to get in at once, and so far that hasn't happened. Knock on wood," he said and tapped the hood of the car with his knuckles.

After that area, which was right next to the gate and the two small security buildings that lined the entrance, they came up to a large building that looked like a warehouse made of aluminum sheets, almost like a barn.

"This is where we keep the vehicles and other larger stuff," Hector said.

"Are they for a quick getaway?" Zach asked.

"Oh no, they're just the ones people came in with. Jason hangs out in there a lot, too. You'll meet him. There's a lot of dried meat hanging inside, so I don't go in there much. He hunts and dries it out, which is our main source of meat through the winter. Jason is...interesting."

In the middle of the compound stood a large, old stone building that looked like a lighthouse. From the bottom, Zach could hear voices up top.

"Sentries? Lookouts?" Zach inquired.

Franklin listened. "Oh no, that would probably be Gary stargazing up in the bell tower. He's the one who knows you, right?"

Zach nodded.

"Let's go up and pay him a visit!" Hector said.

They climbed circular stairs to the top, where Gary sat in a raggedy-old armchair with his wife and two kids. He wore a weathered flannel shirt, khaki pants and gloves. Zach smiled as eight-year-old, Julie, jumped up to greet him, leaving her toys behind. She looked like she was wearing a marshmallow in her puffy purple coat.

"Zach!" Gary looked up and smiled as his little boy looked on.

"Hey Julie!" Zach said as the child ran up and hugged him. "Gary, Karen, how are you?" he asked the couple.

They smiled. Karen, a little bit taller than Gary, wore similar flannel and jeans.

Karen left a telescope pointed to the sky to come over and say hello. "Great, thanks to you. We never would have survived and found this place," she said. Gary stood and walked over to Zach, who put out his hand.

"Oh no," Gary said with a huge grin as he hugged Zach. "I want a hug!" He let go and turned. "And of course you remember Steven. He was a bit younger last time."

Zach walked over to the little boy, who wore a jacket similar to Julie's, and watched him with interest. He sat on the floor with beaten up blocks stacked like a wall, protecting little soldiers.

"You probably don't remember me, do you? I met you a while ago. You were much smaller then."

Steven frowned a bit when Zach tousled his hair.

"It's great to see you, Zach," Gary said. "We found this place a short while after we left the old folks home where you left us. It'd gotten too crowded but by then we'd met Franklin, who brought us here. Pretty neat place, huh? This tower is perfect for checking out the stars. You know, since Karen used to work for NASA. She misses it."

A gunshot echoed by the gates and Zach ran to the edge of the tower. A quick look down showed a small collection of zombies at the gate; while Hector and Janice were yelling to each other with guns pointed at the creatures.

"I gotta go help!" Zach yelled and turned and ran down the steps, skipping every three, to land hard on the grass in the yard. He ran to assist the two guards as they took shots at the zombies, missing more than they were hitting.

"Hold on, guys! All those shots might attract others!" He walked up to a space between fence poles and lured one in, then pulled the hatchet from his backpack and smacked it right down the part in its hair.

"Boy oh boy, that'll mess up his hair for good, that's for sure," Hector said from behind.

Zach did the same once more, and then Janice followed suit and took out two more, clearing the area.

"Good job!" she said to Zach, patting him on the back. "We'd never thought of that. Gunshots attract them?"

"Yup," Zach said, panting a little.

"Thanks for the help," Hector said, looking at Zach with a hint of admiration.

"It's nothing," Zach said. "I just wouldn't use those guns unless you have to. You never know how many are lurking out there between all those buildings. This is a city, after all. I found out the hard way that one or two quickly becomes thirty."

Franklin ran up to the group. "Everything under control here?"

"Yeah," Hector said.

"Great! Come on, Zach, let's finish that tour," Franklin said.

Beyond the bell tower was an old-looking brick house, something out of an old fairy tale, with a sign that said, **Headmaster** behind a white picket fence. A wreath hung on the door by wire and a few plastic deer stood in front of a sled with an inflatable Santa.

"That's Harrison's place." He's our leader, Franklin said. "He sleeps there, but really doesn't use it much. It's a fully functioning house; even has a principal's office in it."

"I hate those places," Zach said.

"Me too. When we pass by it you can hear the genny running between his place and the cafeteria. It keeps us with power when we need it. They must be cooking dinner since it's running, otherwise it's usually off. Harrison hates wasting the gas on just himself, so he mostly works by candlelight at night. The caf was half-stocked when we got here, so there's still some canned goods that are edible, plus a huge kitchen and an eating area that seats about a hundred. Guess that's how big the school was in its day. Christina is in charge of the kitchen; you'll meet her soon, too."

The cafeteria was a giant stone building with many windows and double doors that led to the courtyard. It reminded Zach of his elementary school cafeteria. They passed the hum of the generator soon enough. The school itself loomed high, and Zach could see the glow of the Santa that was on the roof. The school had two large buildings, one on each side, with an enclosed walkway and entrance in the middle that attached the two. In front of it, in the middle of the courtyard, was a gigantic fir tree loosely decorated with ornaments and lights, which dimmed off and on to the sound of the genny running.

"Each side of the classroom building has about twenty classrooms that we're slowly converting into bedrooms as we need them," Franklin said. "Right now we have twenty-four people here, well twenty-five including you. Some are couples and some are families. For now people can have their own room, but eventually, if we add people, that'll have to change. Mine is that one right there." He pointed to a window.

"What do you mean 'if' ? Why wouldn't you let people in?" Zach asked.

"That's the big debate going on right now. The adults are arguing. I'm staying out of it."

"Shhh! Did you hear that?" Zach heard a slight scratching sound and ran for the fencing to the left of the classroom building. He looked out in the waning light and then saw it. A female, armless zombie, veins and loose skin hanging from her sides, was walking in their direction on the other side of the fence.

"Can I try to kill it?" Franklin asked.

Zach nodded and handed him the hatchet. Franklin walked up to the fencing, found a space between the chain-link and the pole that held it, and waited. After another minute, the zombie finally made it to the gap and tried to bite Franklin, who grabbed her shirt, pulled her right up against the fence, and split her face open.

When the job was done he turned to Zach, smiling. "Don't get me wrong, I've killed them before, but usually with this." He pulled a handgun out of a holster in his jacket. "I ran out of bullets or I would've used it, but I'll get more."

* * *

Franklin ended the tour in the cafeteria, the size of which made Zach's jaw almost hit the floor. In the middle of the huge eating area lined with long tables and stools, was a giant Christmas tree that reached the ceiling, covered in ornaments, some real but most handmade by a few of the children from the compound. At the very top was a large star that was actually too big for the tree; it was likely stolen from a tree in the city. It weighed down the top a bit and the points looked sharp.

Under the tree were piles of presents, mostly wrapped in old newspapers, comics, and food wrappers. Some were big, some small, and a few were obviously weapons by the way they were wrapped.

All over the cafeteria were decorations, including many meant as lawn ornaments such as plastic Santas, reindeer and snowmen. The walls were adorned with strands of lights, mostly multi-colored, but some were just blue and others were only red.

None of this was what really surprised Zach, though. It was the fact that it was somehow Christmas and he didn't even know it.

"I had no idea it was Christmas," Zach said to Franklin. "I hadn't even thought of it. I mean, maybe if I had thought about…"

He was interrupted by screaming from the other side of the cafeteria.

"Oh no, Jason. You are *not* bringing that in here!" a woman yelled.

A man in a denim jacket with the sleeves cut off and dirty jeans, entered the room, followed by a woman in khakis and a button down shirt that looked like it was for a man. The man's boots made a clomping sound as he stormed through the cafeteria. The item in question was a stuffed and mounted deer head with huge antlers.

"I brought it as a decoration!" the man yelled. "I hauled this mother from across town through two giant crowds of zombies, just to give us another decoration. So shut the hell up, woman!"

She stopped and looked around the room for help.

"That's Jason," Franklin told Zach. "He's one of our hunters. He goes out to the woods on the outskirts of the city for a few days at a time and usually comes back with deer meat, rabbits, stuff like that. The woman is Christina. She's a vegan and runs the kitchen, but will still cook meat so long as she doesn't have to eat it. She used to be a chef in a restaurant. They don't get along."

"I gathered that," Zach said.

Jason, meanwhile, had found a spot to hang the deer head near the Christmas tree.

"There, that's perfect, huh? It's as close to a reindeer as we're gonna get! The kids'll get a kick outta it, too. Don't you think?" Jason asked.

He was talking to Zach, who wasn't aware he was being dragged into the middle of the argument.

"Hey! New guy! You gonna talk or just stand there like some sorta mute?"

Zach realized he was being addressed and looked over. "Um…er…I'm new. I don't want to get involved."

"Well, I got a word for you, buddy. But I've been asked not to use it within the confines of the fence, so I'll just call you a wuss." Jason looked back at Christina. "It's stayin'. I want to contribute to the celebration, and I'll be damned if you're gonna stop me." He stomped out the door he'd entered.

"Sorry about that. I'm Christina," she said to Zach as she walked over. "I don't like seeing things like that poor deer like that. It's wrong. But maybe it was also rude of me to try to push my feelings on him. He really was trying to contribute, and he doesn't do it much outside of the food he brings in. And well, people here love the fresh meat."

"Christina, this is Zach," Franklin said. "And don't worry about it. He's already over it, I can promise you that. Just don't go tryin' to apologize to Jason…men like that don't understand apologies and all. Reminds me of my dad. Just let it be."

She smiled at him, then Zach, and headed towards the door in the back. "See you two later! I have work to do. Oh and Zach, this really is a great place. Welcome!"

"As I was about to say," Franklin said. "Yeah, it's the Christmas season. As far as we can tell, we're ninety-eight percent sure it's tomorrow. All the electronics ran out of batteries a while ago, but we've got a guy who's a bit obsessed with numbers, and swears to us today is the twenty-fourth."

"Well then, merry Christmas Eve," Zach said.

"Same to you," Franklin replied.

Zach pulled off his pack and was about to reach in when Jason came back in, distracting him. "Hey, Franklin. Harrison's ready to see the new guy. Move it."

A few minutes later, Zach was sitting in a room that looked like a principal's office. The mahogany desk was huge and had multiple kinds of desk-like paraphernalia on it, including a blotter, one of those in and out filers—which had a few papers in the out box, but was otherwise empty—post-its, and a mug that said *I Brake for Zombies* filled with pens. Zach reached for the mug and turned it to find a drawing of a zombie being run over by a truck. He laughed out loud a bit.

"Funny, isn't it?" asked a voice from behind him.

Zach jumped in his chair, then stood and offered his hand.

"It's a bit ironic these days, too. I'm Harrison. Please, have a seat," he said after they'd shaken hands.

Zach observed Harrison. He was tall with graying hair. Though his face showed wrinkles from age, he still had a lot of youth in his eyes. He wore a plaid, tucked in button-down shirt that was a bit small for him, and corduroy pants.

As the older man walked behind the desk, he tripped over a box that tipped over and spilled out a good amount of fake plastic icicles. After composing himself, he sat behind the desk.

Zach couldn't help but notice that the man was about Zach's height when sitting.

"So you're the famous Zach Ward, huh? I thought you'd be bigger."

"Well, I was bigger, but in a world like this you lose weight fast," Zach replied.

"Not exactly what I meant…"

Zach laughed. "I know. Anyway, this is a great place you have here. Seems pretty safe and locked down. Are you looking for more survivors? I met a farmer a while back who might be able to help you with your gardens come springtime…"

"Well, right now we accept new people on a temporary basis and see how they work out. Interested?" Harrison asked.

"Oh no, I'm just stopping by. I'm more of a…loner. I like being out there, traveling, surviving. I was a bit of a homebody when this all started, and I've been kind of on a roll."

Harrison looked down at Zach's bloodied Iron Man shirt. "I used to read about heroes, now you're living as one. I imagine sitting in one place would cramp that."

"I'm no hero. I just go where I go, and do what I can, " Zach said.

"Well, please understand, to the people here, you are one. You saved the Jenkins family, and they're here now. The way they spoke of you, you could have been ten feet tall and I still might have expected you to be bigger."

"Anyway, if I find anyone around, would you want me to direct them to you?" Zach asked.

Harrison stood up and walked to the bookshelf behind him to look at a wreath hanging there. "Well, that farmer sounds like a great find. We have the space, as Franklin probably showed you. With the classrooms turned into bedrooms, we could easily fit more. Our food stores are adequate, and with Jason and his crew we get a decent income of fresh meat. With Franklin and the others who patrol and search for supplies, we get by. I'll talk it over with the board and see what they think, but I'm leaning towards *yes*."

Zach stood up. "I think that's a good idea. Do you have an emergency plan in place? I find that a lot of the places I visit don't. They get bunkered in and start to feel safe, kind of forget how dangerous it is out there. The ones that do prepare tend to still be there when I return. Some of the others…"

"Stop. No offense, son, but I didn't ask for your help. These fences have held strong, and will continue to do so." He sat down behind the desk and steepled his hands—to Zach, he looked as if he was praying. "How long do you wish to stay?"

Zach frowned, feeling a less welcome. "Uh…just long enough to recharge. A day or two. Maybe, since it's Christmas, if you wouldn't mind, I'll hang around for that. I spent many Christmases with just my grandmother, so I think it would be nice to be with others here. If that's okay with you. As a matter of fact…" Zach went to reach into his bag when Christina knocked on the door.

"Hey, Harrison, Zach. Dinner time," Christina said.

Harrison rose. "Thanks for the advice, Zach. I'm sorry I overreacted. Let's go grab some dinner."

* * *

The tables were cleared of food, for the most part, and Zach was helping Christina and Franklin with the dishes. Zach had met more people in the last hour than he had in the last few weeks combined, and he was a bit overwhelmed. The only ones he could really remember were Emily, a geologist who was a bit taller than him but a pretty gal, and Oliver, a mildly-overweight man who had worked in a fast food chain. The two had talked his ear off at dinner, and it was pretty obvious Oliver had unrequited feelings towards Emily. Besides that, Zach couldn't put another name to the faces he'd met at dinner.

"How'd you get stuck doing the dishes?" Franklin asked. "It's my night, but you're a guest!"

Zach laughed. "I was raised to always help in the kitchen...it's just a habit I guess. So that's how you do the chores? A schedule?"

"Yeah, we all take turns," Christina said. She was still slumped over the sink, scrubbing a pan that had contained baked deer meat at dinner. "Except the guards, scouts and the hunters, they work hard enough. And I'm always in the kitchen. It's like my second home."

Zach agreed about the hunters. Hunting in the cold winter was probably no fun, and it would only get colder, considering it wasn't even January yet. "So whose idea was it to decorate?"

"Oh, that was some of the kids' idea. Mostly Gary's kids. I think they just want presents."

"What kid doesn't?" a gruff voice asked from the doorway.

Zach turned to find Jason standing there.

"Why, Christina, I never knew you cared," Jason said. "Givin' me credit for huntin' when you won't even eat it? Wait till we run out of beans. Then you'll care."

"Oh shove it!" Christina said. She placed the pan in the drying rack and returned to the cafeteria, pushing past Jason as she went.

"What's her problem?" Jason asked as he turned and left. His quiet chuckle echoed through the halls.

"Man, they hate each other, huh?" Zach asked Franklin.

"Yeah. Come on, we're done here. Let's go see the final decorations!"

Zach and Franklin entered the cafeteria to find Emily and Oliver bringing in a few more boxes.

Zach helped them open the cardboard containers to find glass ornaments. "Wow, these look old!"

Oliver smiled. "Yeah, Franklin brought them in a few weeks ago. It was you and Stephanie going out tonight to search for stuff, right? Where is she?"

Franklin pulled out a schedule and ran a finger down it. "She's supposed to be back tonight. Actually, she's a bit overdue...but I'm not worried or anything," he said more to Zach than the others. "My crew knows what they're doing. We take turns heading out scrounging for items we need. Tools, canned goods, weapons, the usual."

Jason walked through the front door with his rifle and smiled. "I'm thinking of headin' out for some night huntin'. Just letting someone know so Harrison doesn't get his panties in a twist like last time."

Everyone stopped and looked at him. Franklin was about to say something when the bell in the tower started ringing. "Why in the hell is the bell ringing?" Franklin asked.

A sound came from the door behind Jason. Before most of them even turned to look, it was kicked inward, and three zombies rushed inside to grab onto Jason, forcing him to the floor.

"What the..." Jason began to say before he was buried under the three bodies, with more coming in. Now that the door was open, the bell was louder and they could hear Gary yelling from the tower.

Franklin quickly drew his gun and started shooting, taking out two zombies and hitting two more harmlessly in the arm and shoulder before hearing the click of an empty chamber. Zach went for his axe, realizing he'd left it in his pack in the kitchen. Christina entered the room, saw the creatures, and ran for the tree and the presents beneath it.

"Franklin!" she yelled, throwing him a wrapped box. "It's your gift! A new bat!" He tore through the wrapping quickly and pulled it out of a long box.

"All right! Aluminum!" he yelled. Smiling, he went for the closest creature.

Emily, meanwhile, took Christina's cue and grabbed another box. "Oliver! Shotgun!" She threw it to him and as he opened it Emily started cursing.

"I can't find the shells! Christina! Help! They're wrapped in an old Ziggy comic!" Emily called.

Meanwhile, the three zombies on top of Jason fought to bite him, as one of their heads exploded. Zach ran to Jason and kicked one off him, just as Jason reached up and broke the last one's neck quickly with a loud snap.

"I didn't need your help, kid," he said to Zach.

"I know," Zach said as he looked around. "But you got it anyway." A zombie was coming at him, so he grabbed a small plastic Christmas tree near the wall and shoved it into a bullet hole already in the zombie's stomach, making the small hole larger. The tree went in up to the stump and the zombie toppled over, unable to balance itself with the tree through it.

"Nice! Watch this!" Jason said and shot another one in the head, then dropped the empty rifle. He ran to the wall and grabbed the deer head he'd placed there just hours before.

"Found it!" Christina yelled as she spotted the box wrapped in a comic of a little bald guy saying something about life sucking. She tore it open and threw the box of shells to Oliver, who began loading his weapon as the zombies poured into the room. He started shooting the creatures as they came in, taking out as many as he could.

Meanwhile, Jason was gouging them in the head with the antlers of the deer, laughing as he did it. "Slobber on me, will you?" he screamed and took out zombie after zombie. Zach grabbed a nearby wreath and slammed it over another creature, trapping its arms in the wreath, keeping it harmless until someone could take it out. It helplessly toppled over onto its side.

"Guess that's workin', hero," Jason said, then jumped a table and shoved an antler right through a zombie's left eye socket. The eye popped as he shoved, and as the antler went deeper into the head, the body dropped.

Franklin took out one after another with a swift swing of his new bat. Emily and Christina grabbed one of the tables that was folded up against the wall and pushed it into the doorway so no more could get in while the others took the stragglers out as quickly as they could. Once they'd regained the cafeteria, they went to the window to see the damage outside the school.

There was literally hundreds of the undead just wandering around the parking lot. The compound was overrun.

The small group assessed the situation as quickly as they could from the windows. The zombies had broken down the door to the bell tower and could be seen wandering downstairs. One or two attempted the climb up the spiral staircase leading to the bell but toppled back down. The Jenkins couple seemed safe for now.

Zach grabbed his bag from the kitchen. Pulling out a small set of binoculars, he looked to the tower. He could see Gary and two of the people he'd seen at dinner watching the yard. One of them had a rifle and was taking out one zombie at a time, but he soon stopped after running out of bullets. Zach checked the classroom building to see that the people inside were barricading the front doors.

As Zach scanned the grounds, he saw that the zombies were coming in the hole by the car that had crashed through. A bunch of them had shoved on the broken fencing until it had opened up a bit for them. He felt grief, knowing there was a good chance that this horde had followed him here and that this was all his fault. He had to fix it.

He looked at Jason. "Do you have any extra fencing over in that barn where you dry the meat?"

The large man nodded.

"Good. I'm going to go get some of it and then try to close the hole. I think the zombies may have followed me here. I need to stop this. If we can close the hole, then we just have to pick off the ones inside. The hole in the fence is small right now, and only one or two can fit through at a time." He frowned as he tried to come up with a way across the parking lot.

"But there's too many out there," Emily said. She looked at him with big brown eyes, possibly eyes that had a bit of a crush on him. He shook it off when Oliver gave him a dirty look.

"I have to do it," Zach said.

"I'm in, too," Jason added. "Best bet might be to go through the kitchen window, out through Harrison's place, then follow the perimeter of the fence. Maybe Hector and Janice are out there and can help if we get close enough to the gate."

They all ran to the kitchen, except Oliver, who decided to stay and keep an eye on the makeshift door. A quick survey of the generator showed it was still running, there were no zombies between the buildings yet. Zach opened the window, tossed his bag out, and went to climb when Jason grabbed his shoulder.

"Hold on there. What the hell is that?" Jason asked, still holding the deer head in his hands.

Something was moving past the candlelight inside Harrison's house. As Zach watched, he realized the home had been penetrated.

"Shit. We can't go through there to the fence!" Jason yelled and kicked at the table, knocking a pan to the floor with a loud clang. "Damn it!"

"Shhh," Christina said. "Why don't you just let them all know we're in here while you're at it?"

He gave her a grim look and then nodded at Zach. "What now?"

"Well, Harrison's in there. We need to save him, then go from there. Look." He pointed to the back window where they could see Harrison and Grace, his companion, quietly holding the door to his office closed. Harrison turned and made eye contact with Zach through the window, pleading for help, but shaking his head no. Clearly, the man didn't want them to endanger themselves for his sake.

Suddenly, Franklin threw open the other kitchen window and jumped out of it. He brandished the bat, now splattered with bits and pieces of zombie, and ran to the front door of Harrison's house. "Hey, you bastards!" he yelled, smacking the front metal shutters with the bat. "Come and get me!"

Not only did some of the zombies in the house turn towards the noise the teenager was making, but many in the parking lot turned as well. He smiled at Zach and the others through the window and yelled "Go!" to them as he ran in the other direction and out of sight.

Not wanting to waste a moment, Zach jumped through the window and was blasted by the cold night air, followed by Jason, who barely fit through. Emily grabbed the largest knife she could find.

"I'll go check on Oliver and meet you!" Christina said and turned to leave.

Zach tried to yell to her to stay behind, but then heard a crashing sound from the cafeteria that he could only assume was the table in the doorway giving way to the zombies.

Zach heard Oliver scream and turned to the others. "I think we just lost Oliver and Christina."

"We can mourn for them later," Jason said. "Let's go!"

As they ran to the front of Harrison's, Jason cleared the path with the deer head, which was starting to get heavy due to the blood and guts hanging from it.

As Zach reached for his axe, he turned to find that it had hit the window on his way out and fallen to the ground, which was now surrounded by the undead, who were attracted by the sound of the generator.

Emily threw him the knife she'd taken from the kitchen as a zombie came up on her and she backed into an inflated snowman. She almost got caught in it, then realized she could use it.

She lured the zombie towards it, then unplugged the little motor that gave it life. As the zombie fought against the deflating snowman, it surrounded the creature and pinned it to the ground.

She grabbed a brick and hit it on the head until it stopped moving.

Jason swung the deer head straight up into two zombies' faces simultaneously, but each antler broke off as the two bodies fell to the ground. He dropped the now useless head.

Zach stabbed another in the skull, but the knife got stuck and he was forced to abandon it. The way was clear enough and they made it into Harrison's house. They closed the door and locked it, but knew it wouldn't last long. The small group ran to the office door and started yelling to be let in. It opened.

The front door began to splinter as the group ran into the office and Harrison slammed the door. Zach immediately began looking around the room for weapons.

"Has anyone died?" Harrison asked them.

"Do you have any weapons in here?" Zach asked.

"No, the weapons cabinet is in the basement."

"A lot of good it does there, huh?" Jason said. "We're real prepared for this shit, Harrison. Great leading."

Harrison puffed up his chest as Zach jumped between them.

"Forget it!" Zach said. "There must be something we can use in here." His eyes landed on the box of fake icicles behind the desk. He ran to it, opened the flaps, and grabbed the long, fake plastic icicles. "These could work! We have to get out now, before there are too many and we're trapped!"

He threw a few icicles each to Emily, Jason, Harrison and Grace, pocketing a bunch for himself, too. One in each hand, he nodded to Jason, who flung open the door.

Zach ran directly at the closest zombie, pushing the icicle through its eye socket and yanking it back out with enough speed to stab another in the eye as well. Jason followed him, swinging upward into one of the undead, squishing the icicle into the soft skin under the creature's jaw.

Emily stuck one right into a zombie wearing a Hawaiian shirt that was to her left, but then she couldn't pull it back out again. She left it and pulled a spare out of her pocket while Harrison took out another zombie.

They then made their way to the front door and ran towards the fence.

Grace was panicking and not much help, and Harrison had to drag her along behind the rest of the group.

Zach was in the lead when he tripped over something and landed face first.

Jason stood over the object, shaking his head. "Damn. They got Hector."

What was left of Hector was torn to shreds. Jason went through the corpse's pockets and found a knife, so he dropped his remaining icicles. He picked up Hector's gun and checked it. "Just one more bullet." He aimed it at Hector's head and squeezed the trigger.

"Damn it, Jason!" Grace yelled at him. "You're just attracting attention!"

Zach turned to see a cluster of zombies face them and start moving in the group's direction.

"Come on!" Zach yelled to them, heading for the closest building—the bell tower.

Harrison followed quickly, pulling Grace along, who was still crying over the loss of Hector. Emily gripped her icicles tight and trailed him with Jason taking up the rear. Jason went out of his way to reach one of the undead and stabbed it in the head. "Yeah!" he yelled as he turned to catch up to them.

Ignoring Jason, Zach dodged as many zombies as he could, taking out a few on the way to the entryway, all the while yelling up to Gary to let the man know they were coming. As Zach approached the door, the largest zombie he'd ever seen suddenly blocked his way. He looked up to see the towering creature, fresh blood pouring from its mouth from a kill as it looked down at him with glazed eyes.

"Wow, you're a big one!" Zach said to the giant, which grabbed at him. Zach ducked away from its arms and narrowly escaped as Harrison bumped into him from behind.

"Zach, what in the hell is the hold up? Whoa!" Harrison yelled as he hit the ground, saving himself from being grabbed. Grace, Emily and Jason caught up in time to see the large zombie and just froze.

"Wow!" Jason yelled. "That's a huge mother!" He ran to it and stabbed it three times in the stomach, but the zombie swung an arm into him, throwing the hunter ten feet. Zach stabbed it twice in the side, leaving the icicles there, as Emily and Grace, who finally snapped out of it, did the same from the other side. Harrison, unable to get up in the commotion, stabbed one in the creature's bare foot. None of this even slowed it down.

"Guys! We have to hurry!" Harrison yelled from the ground as he turned to see twenty more zombies heading their way. The wall of undead shuffled towards the group as Zach and the others continued to attack the behemoth.

Jason jumped onto its back from behind, wrapping his belt around the neck of the creature and stepping on its back. "This isn't working!" he yelled as it spun and tried to reach him with its large hands. Zach jumped and embedded an icicle in the eye of the zombie, which just seemed to anger it more.

"Hold it steady!" a voice yelled from the shadow of a nearby tree. Jason ducked as the zombie's brain splattered out of the back of its head, showering Jason with a spray of blood, brains and bone matter. As the zombie went to its knees, Janice came out of the shadows and threw her empty gun to the ground.

The other zombies renewed their attack, and the small group ran through the doorway of the bell tower. Janice couldn't make it in and had to run in another direction.

Inside, five zombies were trying to get up the spiral staircase. They turned and started to come at the survivors. The group made short work of the small number of undead, then they searched for more weapons.

Unfortunately, the room was destroyed and there wasn't anything of use. A few trampled gifts sat by the fire, and as Zach went to grab them in the hopes they might contained weapons, the others made for the stairs. After opening a bunch of toys and useless items, he picked up the last package wrapped in an old cereal box. The smell of a pot of chestnuts roasting on the fire inside caught his attention.

The cereal box rattled when he shook it, and Zach had a good idea what it was filled with, so he threw it into the fireplace and ran to the door. After making all the noise he could, most of the zombies in the courtyard turned and started in his direction again. He waited as long as he dared and then turned to run up the staircase.

He tripped twice as he took the awkward spiral stairs two at a time. He made it to the top and ran to the lookout, ignoring everyone's questions. The zombies were all piling in the doorway downstairs.

"Everyone! Get away from the stairs and get down!" Zach yelled.

The entire group hit the floor, but nothing happened. They all waited, some of them holding their ears as if expecting an explosion, but still all was quiet.

"Hey, what was in that cereal box-wrapped gift?" Zach asked.

"Bullets for Gary's gun," Karen answered.

"That's what I was hoping. I threw them into the fire but I guess it didn't work."

Then came the sound of the bullets all firing like crazy. Easily fifty shots went off, and the echoes of ricochets against the stone walls and splintering wood came up the stairs.

When the noise finally stopped, Zach spun and spotted Gary covering Steven on the ground. "Do you have any weapons up here?"

"We have the sword over there. Our guns are out of ammo. That's about it," he said while nodding to the corner. Zach picked up the sword and weighed it.

"Not really my thing. Hey, Jason, trade?"

Jason nodded and smiled as he threw the knife at Zach's feet, the point sticking into the wood floor.

Zach didn't even flinch as he tossed the sword, handle first, to Jason, who caught it.

"Great," Zach said. "Now those of you who're coming with me to the shed, we have to go now. I think I cleared us a path but the zombies outside won't give us a lot of time."

Harrison went to leave when Grace grabbed his arm. "You're our leader. I don't think you should be risking yourself."

He looked at Zach, who nodded approval.

Jason gripped the sword tighter and followed Zach down the stairs. Emily and Gary went down after them.

The downstairs of the bell tower was clear, and besides the new carpeting of fresh bodies, they made it through without a problem. And while there were easily a hundred zombies roaming the courtyard, Zach, Jason and the others made it to the giant metal barn-like shed without issue.

When they got to the entrance, the door was off its hinges and on the ground.

"What's inside?" Zach asked the group. "I've never been in there, but I want in fast!" Emily said as the nearby undead started to take notice of the small group. She shivered but it was unclear if it was because of the situation or the bitter cold of the oncoming winter night. "Jason's the expert."

Jason spit on the ground. "Long hall leads to the main building."

Zach looked inside and didn't see anything. "Should I check the hall?"

"I'll lead, damn it. It's my place," Jason said. He gripped the sword and started down the long, dark passage.

"Check the halls, for brains and zombies..." Jason started singing with a smirk. One zombie came up on him without warning and Jason sliced it in two. "Fa la la la laaa...fa fa fuuck youuu," he sang as he swung the blade into its head.

"Funny," Zach said and nodded for Emily and Gary to go next. He took up the rear as they made their way down the hall and into the larger area. It had two trucks, a motorcycle and a hundred zombies inside.

"We may need a new plan, buddy," Jason said, looking at the large number of the undead. "No way can the four of us take that many. No way...not when two of us are only armed with plastic icicles. Shit," he said with another spit to the ground.

Zach agreed and they turned to leave, only to find the hall blocked with zombies. "Well, we need to get out! What do we do?"

"Whattaya think we do?" Jason asked rhetorically. "We start chopping!" The two took the lead and started killing the undead as fast as they could, but as they did, more fell into the doorway at the far end of the hallway.

"Shit! We're getting outnumbered!" Zach yelled.

"And more are noticing us! They're coming from this way, too!" Emily called from the other end of the hall. A small window, about seven feet off the ground, let in enough starlight for them to see.

"Could we all fit through there?" Zach asked, pointing to the window.

"Sure we can. We just lift people!" Jason yelled. "Ladies first," he said to Emily. Zach and Gary helped her up to the window, which she opened and pulled herself through. Zach put his hands together so Gary could climb up, and then he was out. Zach jumped up and tried to pull himself up but couldn't.

"Hold on," Jason said. "No upper body strength, eh?" He sliced a zombie's head off at the neck, swung at another one, giving it a haircut, then lopped the top off it's head, knocking it to the ground.

"Alley-oop!" Jason said and grabbed Zach's foot and practically threw him out the window. Jason then jumped up; he had the upper body strength to pull himself out to the relative safety of the courtyard, as the undead poured into the hall.

As Zach and the others attempted to head back to the bell tower, it was easy to tell that the building was lost to them. So many of the zombies now surrounded the doorway that they knew it would be impossible to gain access. Harrison's house was overwhelmed as well, as was the kitchen and cafeteria. Zach looked over at the hole in the fence, where zombies still continued to pour into the once safe schoolyard and parking lot.

That only left the school-turned-dorm, which was clearly barricaded. They went for it anyway, hoping they could find a way inside. The group raced through the straggling zombies, staying away from the larger crowds.

Zach spotted his axe on the ground on the way and ran for it. He stabbed a zombie in the neck and watched it fall. Dark blood splashed him, soaking the sleeve of his shirt. "Damn it!" he yelled and stabbed another one in the eye and continued towards the axe. When Zach was close, he tripped and found himself face-down in the grass between the buildings as Emily and Gary yelled for him. He turned over to see one of the zombies clutching his pant leg. He kicked at it, but it held strong until Emily ran up and stabbed it in the back of the head, just above its neck, from behind. Her icicle got stuck and as she tried to free it, another zombie came at her, so Zach threw her the knife. She used it, sinking the blade into the creature's ear until the body fell to the ground.

Grabbing the axe, Zach felt better now that three of them had actual weapons, leaving only Gary armed with the icicles.

Zach blew on his hands to warm them from the cold as he led the way to the school building. Each of the others followed, taking out any zombie that came too close, but mostly the group just weaved through the undead crowd on their way to the front door. As they ran, a window opened from above and a head popped out.

"It's barricaded!" the man yelled. "We can't let you in or they'll get in, too! It took us forever to get all that furniture in front of the doors. I'm sorry."

Jason stopped and looked up. "Freddie! You get down here and let us in, damn it!"

Freddie shook his head no and his head disappeared from the window, but a second later he popped his head out once more. "Meet me around back! I'll try to drop the fire escape down to you! And here, use this!" He dropped a shotgun and a box of ammunition to the grass. "Good luck!"

Gary ran and picked them up, dropping the icicles he still held.

Now fully armed, the group started to thin out the number of undead as they ran around the perimeter of the school. A few close calls were taken care of and they'd just made it around to the back when they heard the clanging of the metal ladder.

Emily climbed up first, then Gary, who had to move slowly since he was carrying the shotgun and only had hand free. As Jason started to climb, a loud car horn started going off from the opposite side of the building.

"What the hell is all that?" Jason growled.

Zach was curious, too. "I'm going to go around and find out. You guys stay here."

He turned and had run back the way they'd come when Jason jumped down from halfway up the first ladder. "To hell with it, I'm going, too. Pull this thing up but stay on the escape so we can get back up!" he yelled up to Gary.

As he followed Zach, he saw at the front gate, all the way across the schoolyard, an armored car with its headlights on. When he and Zach came into view, it started honking again. "Who is it?" Jason asked.

Zach held his hand over his eyes to block out the headlights. He recognized the person driving instantly. "Holy...it's Franklin!"

The teen rolled down the window and waved triumphantly to the men. He reversed the truck and began driving towards the side of the fence with the hole in it.

"He can use the armored car to block up the hole!" Zach said to Jason as he ran in the direction of the hole. A small group of zombies got in his way, one still wearing an iPod. Zach swung the axe right through its neck. As its head rolled to the grass, the others were on him. Jason sliced through two of them while Zach took out the last one by hacking a hole in the side of its head.

The tide of zombies in the yard noticed the action and started to head Jason and Zach's way, but the two men were already on the move towards the hole in the fence. There was a temporary break; no zombies were trying to get into the compound through the hole.

"Now's our chance!" Zach yelled to Jason. "If we can just move the car out of the hole, we can get the armored car in front of it to block anymore from getting in."

Jason stopped. "Yeah, but they can still climb under it!"

"Not if we take the air out of the tires! Look how low to the ground it'll be then!"

Zach ran to the wrecked car and slipped through the fence, jumping inside it. There were no keys. "Where the hell are the keys?"

"Why would we ever move it? I dunno...they're gone! I can push it!" Jason said.

Zach put the car in neutral and released the emergency break. As he jumped out of the car to help push it, a zombie came at him, shoving him against the door.

"Zach!" Jason yelled.

"I got it...just try to move the car! Here comes Franklin!"

The armored car was low to the ground. Too low. As Franklin jumped the curb and the front wheels hit the grass, the undercarriage got stuck on the curb and the tires spun uselessly in the air.

"Shit!" Franklin yelled as he pressed on the gas pedal harder, which did nothing.

The zombie was too close to Zach for him to swing the axe, so he started punching it in the face. The punches were landing but the zombie kept clawing at Zach. A gash opened above Zach's eye and blood momentarily blinded him.

Jason started pushing the car with all he had, and it began to roll very slowly, knocking Zach and the zombie to the grass. Zach rolled away from the creature and quickly swung the back end of the axe at its head. With the sound of crunching bone, he put it down for good. As quickly as he could, he joined Jason and started pushing the car away from the fence. The nearby undead quickly saw the gap and began cantering towards it as the men pushed the car further away.

Meanwhile, Franklin was revving the engine but getting nowhere. It was useless with all four tires in the air, and he knew he was stuck for good. An idea hit him, and he stood on the gas pedal and leaned forward into the windshield. His extra weight on the front end was just enough to push the front tires onto the grass. The vehicle began moving forward once more.

"Yahoo!" Franklin yelled out and drove in front of the opening a second before anymore zombies could sneak through. As he jumped out of the passenger side, Jason was already stabbing the tires, bringing the vehicle down into the grass.

"We did it!" Zach said.

"Yeah, that's great and all. But now how do we get back inside?"

F ranklin had an idea. He told them to wait and he ran off towards the front gate. There were a few zombies creeping up on the two men, so Zach and Jason took them out.

Then Franklin came around the corner at a fast pace, carrying a weather beaten ladder. "Guys! There's a large group of them coming! Hurry!" He leaned the ladder against the fence near the giant shed. "We can climb this and get onto the roof of the garages! Then we just have to find a safe way down!"

Zach and Jason looked at each other, then followed Franklin up the ladder and onto the roof of the metal building. Jason used his foot to kick the ladder back down. "At least it'll be there next time we need it," he said.

The trio moved to the front of the building and looked out over the schoolyard. There were still eighty of the undead roaming around. A gunshot from the school building grabbed the zombies' attention away from the three survivors. Then one of the zombies dropped and another shot went off, killing one more.

"Wow, that may take a while. Is there only one gun in there?" Franklin asked.

Jason watched as the gun barrel was aimed at another zombie. "Yes, looks it. A rifle. So it'll be slow going. Might as well see what I can do," he said, and went to the edge of the roof, dropped his sword to the ground, and started lowering himself down.

Zach and Franklin followed.

Once on the ground, the trio got into a circle and started moving into the crowd of zombies. A bat, axe and sword were close combat weapons, and they'd taken out a few when the sound of struggle came from the bell tower. Harrison, Grace and a few of the other adults came out of the tower with what weapons they had and started helping. Harrison was still using the icicles.

After about an hour, they had cleared a majority of the grounds, and only a few undead stragglers were left. The people in the school finally came out and helped finish off the undead. As the sun rose and began to warm them from the bitter cold, they started to check the corners of the property.

"Would you look at that," Jason said as they looked under Harrison's deck. "You gotta see this shit." He reached under and grabbed something, and it was easy to tell that he had the zombie by the foot. First out was a black boot, followed by another boot, then red pants and finally a red coat and hat. He turned the zombie around and it was still wearing a white beard.

"Don't that beat all," Jason said. The beard was covered in gore and dried blood, but sure enough, they'd found zombie Santa. Slung over its back was a sign that said *Please Give*.

"Merry *effing* Christmas," Jason said as he pulled back his sword and put it right through zombie Santa's head. Once dispatched, Jason turned to everyone and sighed. "What a day."

As the group gathered in the courtyard by what was left of the giant Christmas tree, they did a head count. Losses weren't as bad as they would have thought.

"Zach!" Franklin said. "I found your bag."

Zach laughed and took the backpack from Franklin. "You know," Zach said. "I kept trying to give you this earlier, but I have something to add to the festivities." He approached Harrison and pulled a metal tin out of the bag.

Harrison took it and shook the tin. "Is this what I think it is?"

Zach nodded. "A fruit cake."

As the small group laughed, Harrison opened the tin and held up the stale cake that was as hard as a rock. "You know, we may just have to eat this."

Zach suddenly grabbed the fruitcake from Harrison's hand and the older man thought Zach was going to hit him with it, but then Zach pushed Harrison aside and smacked one last stray zombie on the head with the Christmas cake, killing it dead with a caved-in skull.

"Huh, how 'bout that," Zach said with a grin. "I knew these things were good for something."

If you enjoyed this story, then check out
"The Z Word,"
for more of Zach Ward's adventures—written
by the author and published by Living Dead Press.

A ZOMBIE CHRISTMAS

CHAUMA SMITH GUS

Sitting on the stone walkway of a house, Bonnie Chiarella twisted the tourniquet tighter around her calf, whimpering a little as the phone cord bit harder into her flesh and the muscle beneath. She paused a moment, listening to the heavy silence of the big house before her. Her foot was swollen taut and ugly, black streaks running up her ankle and down to her toes. She'd taken off her shoe and sock yesterday, hoping that the cold would kill the infection, praying she would lose the entire foot to frostbite.

Better to be frostbit than monster bit.

"Good morning, Phil." The smartphone in her pocket lit up, playing a cheerful alarm jingle, and she clapped her hands over her mouth to keep from shrieking. "The time is now six forty five a.m. on December twenty-fourth. You have an appointment scheduled with Mom at eleven thirty a.m. Later, Phil!"

The phone went silent again. She didn't know who Phil was, but he was certainly ruled by his gadget. The phone would light up again later when it was close to the time of his appointment, the GPS ready to direct Phil to his mother's apartment, the shopping mall, the attorney's office, or the hair salon, depending on the day and the errand.

She'd found the phone inside a shopping mall three days ago. She'd numbly picked it up off the floor for no other reason than the idea that cell phones don't belong on the floor, because they might get broken. Its Auto-Assistant program faithfully plugged along, every morning turning on briefly to wake Phil and tell him about his appointments for the day, offering GPS directions and last night, even a recipe to cook for Jane— whoever Jane was. It was a dangerous gadget, something that would randomly light up and make noise, attracting attention to itself. Even so, Bonnie couldn't bear to put it down and limp away, just in case someone might call her or she might finally get through and call someone— so far service was non-existent.

She picked up a handful of snow and ate it carefully, thirsty from fever. Falling against the brick gate post, she pulled herself up until she was sitting with her back to the post, out of sight of the road. The gate itself had been opened wide after the last heavy snow, a drift pushed aside, and fresh snow on the smooth pavement of the driveway. The house seemed untouched by fire. A lot of the old brick fireplaces in the neighborhood inside the elegant older houses had been abandoned to burn out or burn until the house caught fire.

Thrusting her foot into a bitterly gray pile of snow, she pulled her coat tighter around her shoulders. She scooted the bottom edge of the coat under her backside so the snow and ice wouldn't melt into her jeans. In the house, a light upstairs came on, then the kitchen, and the porch light went off as the people in the house started stirring. There was no movement in the windows, but after a few minutes an explosion of colored lights scattered over the windows in and above the door. After a long moment, the colors started to move, and Bonnie relaxed as she recognized the peaceful blinking of Christmas lights. As the sun started to brighten the snow around her, Bonnie noticed newspapers piled up against her snow drift, three plastic wrapped paper relics with bright red and green holiday ads boldly peering through.

She closed her eyes for a moment in relief. If nobody's home, if they were away on vacation with the lights on a timer, then maybe the house was empty. If she was going to die from the wound on her foot, at least maybe she should be warm.

After she died, it wouldn't matter anymore anyway. These images caught her unawares, exhaustion ambushing her the moment her eyelids slid closed.

It was December twenty-first and the world was ending. She'd fought with her mother about whether her daughter, Lindsey, would participate in the Christmas Pageant, followed by a lengthy lecture about Lindsey's dead-beat dad. Delores rounded out the trifecta by delivering the latest variation on 'you really need to come to church with her on Christmas, you know it's better for her to grow up with Jesus in her life.' It was almost too much. Bonnie had finally found the courage to leave her ex, but had lost the fight about church once more. Her mother took Lindsey to the pageant 'just to watch,' generously giving Bonnie a chance to do some last-minute shopping, since Lindsey's father wasn't around. Her mother's thinly-veiled criticism was almost as bad as the argument about why Bonnie didn't want to take Lindsey to church.

Upon arriving at the mall, it was a riot of desperate shoppers. They juggled bags and packages from the department stores, streaming past the sporting goods shop and the food court. Santa's Chair and the Winter Wonderland filled the atrium outside the home improvement store. The living nativity and the barnyard smell of a few live reindeer only added to the chaos. People were edgy because of the flu bug that was going around, but no one seemed to see the wisdom in just staying home and shopping online.

Bonnie had edged away from the man behind her in the toy store, the heat of his fever radiating off of him even through his coat. His eyes were red-rimmed and watery as he stiffly pulled the last *Marry Me Kate* boxed set off the shelf.

She'd left the store as quickly as possible, navigating the roped sections of parents and children waiting on the harried-looking mall Santa and runny-eyed elves.

The home improvement store was festive and twinkling with its tasteful white lights and faux garland, and she'd debated over the poor selection of extension cords versus the two remaining power strips when the screaming began.

Curious, she stood on her tiptoes to look around a tired display of small, artificial trees. The families waiting on Santa were struggling against the velvet rope, tumbling over each other to escape the Living Nativity. One of the Wise Men was grappling with a shepherd, and a fountain of blood suddenly spilled in a crimson torrent down Mary's white veil and blue robe. The woman was clutching a wound in her neck and had dropped the swaddled bundle in her arms. Meanwhile, Joseph had vaulted the rope and was trying to escape with the rest of the crowd, flailing his arms and flinging gore into the crowd.

The crowd grew more violent, people punching and scratching. Bonnie saw a small child trampled by the surge of uncaring feet. She stumbled back and turned, trying to remember where the nearest outside exit was located. She knocked over a display of gardening equipment, tucked out of the way behind the fake Douglas firs and ladders. Tripping over a fallen shovel, she twisted her ankle and went sprawling. A man stepped on Bonnie's hand as he rushed past her, uncaring of the fallen woman on the floor or the scattered shovels, clippers and pitchforks. Someone else tripped over her legs, dropping shopping bags and keys right in front of her. Pulling in her arms and legs to protect them, panicked thoughts darted through her mind as trowels were kicked around her.

She stayed that way till the crowd finally cleared.

A calm distant part of her looked critically at the equipment nearby. Deliberately, she dismissed the shovels, hoes and hay forks as cheaply built, but upon turning her head, she spotted a machete hanging on a middle peg. Gathering her legs under her, and clumsily slinging her handbag over her shoulder and abandoning her purchases, she grabbed the machete off the peg and started towards the back of the store.

Walking carefully, she was passed by other stampeding shoppers, and she clutched the machete and its cardboard backing that it was tied to against her chest. An expensive smartphone lay on the tiles between displays, and she automatically bent down to pick it up, thrusting it into her pocket without thinking about it. By the time she reached the door, her head was clearer.

Traffic was locked outside the shopping mall, and she dismissed the subway as a possible option when a bloody man stumbled out of the entrance, pursued by a thin man in a Salvation Army volunteer Santa suit. The volunteer's fake beard was stained red, pulled askew, and his arms and legs were stiff as he walked, uncoordinated. A bus careened onto the sidewalk and both the volunteer and the bloody man were hit straight on, then run down to quickly disappear under the vehicle.

"You now have GPS signal," a light feminine voice announced from within Bonnie's jacket.

Ducking down an alley, she cut across the block and then another, dodging hysterical pedestrians and insane drivers, angling towards the church and the stupid Christmas Pageant where her mother and daughter were hopefully safe and unaware of what was happening.

A police car was parked sideways across the avenue ahead, the officer firing from behind the driver's door. Bonnie started to emerge from the haze of her own fear, and she listened to the gunshots, trying to figure out what was wrong with the tableaux ahead. She realized that the only gunshots she heard were from the officer's gun, and that the shrieks of sirens, car alarms, distant shouts and gunfire were beginning to fade.

Then a different sound began to rise from the din, a low mumble rising into a breathless moan.

Two people—a man and a woman—walked up to the black and white squad car, the officer pausing only to pull a second gun from an ankle holster. A woman wearing an expensive but now-ruined fur coat jerked sideways as the bullet tore into her, but even as she stumbled against him the man with her kept coming, reaching for the officer. The gun clicked, empty, and the policeman screamed and threw the useless weapon at the oncoming couple. The last Bonnie saw of any of it was the couple's hands reaching, fingers bloody, for the officer, and the last she heard was the cop's scream as they grasped him.

She backtracked and took a second alleyway, wishing that the screams would stop, but they haunted her retreat for more than a block, the growing silence a showcase for the cop's pain.

It took hours to cross town. Caught in her own horror movie, she felt foolish. More than seeing people die around her, more than the chaos around her, or Bonnie's continuing freakish fortune in avoiding all of the hellish scenes as they occurred, her chief complaint was that her hands were painfully cold. She saw more people overcome, and as her nauseated fear was replaced by dreadful apprehension, she began to realize that she was walking by blood—so much blood—and sometimes body parts, but only a few bodies, most burned horribly or with smashed faces or dreadful head wounds.

Somewhere along the way she tore off the cardboard backing on the machete, but she couldn't break the plastic ties around the handle. The handle and ties blistered her palm, but she clung to it anyway.

She stumbled down the block, the church finally coming into sight.

"Checking you in at Pete's Pizzeria, placing your to-go order," the phone said from her pocket.

A dozen people were wandering around in front of the grand double doors. Sunday-suited men and women in heavy coats and pearls, and a small girl clinging to a mangled doll, all milled about on the landing at the top of the broad stairs. Smoke rose from a broken window in the Sunday school annex, and the shriek of the fire alarm came into focus.

Bonnie huddled against the corner of the pizza shop. "Oh, no... Where are you?"

Her pocket answered after a moment, "I'm wherever you are, Phil. Right now, we're at Pete's Pizzeria. Your order will be twenty one dollars and thirty eight cents," the phone said.

"No, shut up, I'm looking for Lindsay or my mom," she said and pulled the phone out of her pocket, looking for a power button to turn it off.

"No contact information for *Lindsay Ormymom* is listed in the directory. Sorry," the phone said.

Bonnie found the button and held it until the phone turned off.

"Later, Phil!" the phone said as it powered off.

Bonnie stayed at the corner of the pizza restaurant, watching the crowd of people. As dusk settled, Father Mark burst from the side door of the church and tried to make a run for it, his long robes flapping around his skinny legs. The people milling around the front of the church began to moan, which grew louder and louder as they pursued the priest.

Bonnie ducked into the doorway as they went past her, but then almost cried out in shock when she recognized her mother's ragged halo of blue, high-lighted hair, her stockings ripped and one shoe missing. Delores Elizabeth Chiarella chased after the priest with blood on her face and dress.

Another man with a bloody face shambled past in slower pursuit.

"Hello, Phil, you will be dining with Mom-in one hour," the phone cheerfully announced, buzzing in her pocket. As she jerked it out of her pocket, it turned itself back off with another cheerful "Later, Phil!"

The bloody man turned towards her and Bonnie slumped back further into the doorway. He seemed to see her for a moment, then turned to follow after Father Mark and the ghoulish Delores.

Bonnie eased out of the doorway, walking slowly, her feet and ankles sore, her knees and hips stiff, her clothes filthy with gore and mud. None of the crazy people in front of the church paid her much mind, but she couldn't get inside without pushing through the crowd of them.

"Crap, crap, crap," she muttered under her breath, worried beyond rational thought by the idea of her daughter trapped inside the building, mauled, dead or even worse. *I should just go*, she thought, despairing, and then the fury finally surfaced. "Fucking mother of the year, Bonnie. Put on your big girl pants and go find your daughter," she whispered.

She circled the block, walking slowly, unsteadily, and it seemed that the mad people that she had once attended pot-luck dinners with were willing to ignore her if she didn't make any sudden moves, if she just moved on by them. There was another squad car parked half on the sidewalk across the intersection next to the church playground. She walked around the car slowly, looking in the windows. It had been abandoned, the front doors open, the windshield bloody.

She ducked into the driver's seat, fumbling with the computer mounted against the dash, digging through the glove box until she found what she was looking for: a heavy revolver. It was icy in her hand, the metal cold. By some sort of miracle, a cold cup of coffee sat in the cup-holder. She gulped it down greedily. There was nothing else she could use. The trunk was locked and she couldn't find a release for it. Realizing she was procrastinating again, she pulled herself back out of the squad car, tugged her jacket down, and held the machete in her left hand and the gun in her right.

The single door to the church school wing was open, hanging askew on its hinges. She slipped inside, hearing the shuffling of feet wandering the halls. A muffled curse from the kindergarten room drew her across the foyer to open door. A policeman lay on the brightly-colored carpet, the cheerful blue and yellow pattern stained darker with his blood. He looked up when he saw her movement out of the corner of his remaining eye, and she found herself facing down the muzzle of his service pistol.

"Jesus, Andy," she whispered. She recognized him. It was Andy Wilson. They'd gone through confirmation classes together and even dated a little in high school. When he graduated, he'd enrolled to the police academy and was accepted immediately.

"Bonnie, you gotta get outta here, babe, they're coming back." His voice was slow and slurred. "I want you to pick up this gun in a minute, there'll be one bullet left. You'll know what to do." He looked past her legs into the hallway, as she heard the footsteps coming closer. He dragged himself closer to the door and she saw that his bulletproof vest was askew, and bloody, slippery things slid out of him as he moved towards her. When he was close enough to touch her, he looked up at her again, a bright blue eye and the red ruin of a socket in his once-handsome face. "Don't wait around for Lindsay, babe, you don't want to see her."

Bonnie stood frozen as he brought his gun up and placed it against his temple.

"Sorry, Bonnie, I'm sorry I let you marry that jerk," he said, coughing and spitting blood. Then he pulled the trigger. Blood and bits of bone spattered her face and shoulder, and the top of his head was just gone. The hand holding the gun dropped to the floor, limp fingers loosening on the handgrip. She picked it up just as the soft moan began to rise from the children filing out of the other classrooms to stumble towards her.

She looked at the crowd of small children, searching their faces. She began to walk slowly away, pressing her hands over her ears so she didn't have to hear the slurping and tearing coming from the kindergarten classroom, knowing the children were feeding on Andy's corpse.

Once free of the church, she started walking quickly north towards one of the bridges, hoping to find something different in the neighborhoods on the other side of the river. Twice she had to defend herself, the first time by using the revolver from the squad car. There were only three bullets in it, and she missed twice. When the faceless thing finally lay still, she threw the empty revolver at it in helpless fury. The second time she'd used the machete to hack at the face and head of the vaguely familiar-looking man trying to grab her. She used the machete to pry body parts and debris out of her way when she couldn't pass. More than anything, she tried to move slowly, working hard to shamble along with the same gait she'd seen the people using.

The phone turned on and Bonnie heard it telling her that Phil missed a massage and an appointment with his shrink.

She spent the first night in a furniture store. Wrapped in a thin comforter, she raided the employee break room for someone's abandoned lunch and some ginger ale. She didn't meet anyone else alive on the second day.

Rounding a corner on a side street, she tripped over the legs of a police horse, its uniformed rider trapped by one leg under the horse's body, all of the dead man's exposed flesh eaten away. There were other pedestrians, though, walking in circles or milling around in groups. She passed the entrance to the zoo late in the afternoon, the gates tightly shut. A howl from deep in the zoo made her walk a little faster.

The next night was even colder. According to Phil's phone, she was almost to the bridge, and almost out of the city. She wanted to scream in frustration. How could it have taken her two days to cover such a short distance, no matter how often she had to stop, or wait for it to be clear?

She spent the night of December the twenty-second in an attorney's office, curled up and miserable on a couch in one of the offices, with the door locked between her and the rest of the world. There was a small Christmas tree in the corner of the office, the blinking lights now dark, a small ceramic angel for a topper.

The next morning she found a shower in the executive bathroom, and by some miracle, there was still hot water in the water heater somewhere in the building. The hot water ran out just as she was finishing up.

Which was why she was barefoot when one of the *things* found her.

As soon as it sank its teeth into her foot, rolling its single pulpy eye up at her as if it could actually see her, she knew she was done for. She grabbed the machete and hacked at its skull anyway until finally its head broke open and the brains spilled out across her foot and ankle, splattering her other leg with dark gore.

No hope, no redemption, was there as little chance of getting medical help. Hell, even if she managed to tie a tourniquet tight enough to stop the blood from flowing out of the wound, she'd probably die of shock and exposure.

She had one bullet left in Andy's gun, and she hoped Andy was right: she hoped she would know when to use it. She put on her clothes, tied a tourniquet of telephone cord around her calf, and limped back out into the street, hoping to find people, to find help, across the bridge.

As she sat in the snow-covered yard of the house, its Christmas lights beckoning cheerfully in the gathering gloom, Bonnie woke with a start, clutching at the smartphone. Darkness was falling over the neighborhood, and the pain in her foot was a throbbing counterpoint to her awful thirst. Shadows ran deep blue across the yard, and suddenly the house lit up like a dream, golden lights from most of the windows, silent and still except for the colored strobes from the Christmas tree in the living room.

She scraped some of the snow out of the drift beside her to eat, but it was grimy and tasted like gravel and dirt. She looked around, almost hoping she would see something moving in her direction. Fumbling in her pockets, she found Andy's gun and slid it out onto her lap. The bitten foot suddenly flexed on its own, the phone cord digging hard into her calf. She doubled over, retching. The dry heaves left her shaking from more than the cold and a fever. Sobbing, half insane with hunger, she almost missed the noise. Softly into the silence, the snow began to come down again, and she heard a racket approaching on the road behind her. She couldn't turn far enough to see, as the noise sorted itself out into the sound of hooves muffled on concrete, and a man's low voice talking to the animals.

The beat of hooves and the soft ,gravely-grind of wheels stopped at the gate, hidden from her view behind the gate post. She held her breath, hearing muffled footsteps on the sidewalk.

The man was short, smoke-streaked and covered with ashes. His boots were black, his trousers and coat a far darker red than they had started at the beginning of the night. He was thinner than she would have imagined, and he walked lightly through the gate, puffing on his pipe and glancing over at her. He took in the bare, oozing foot, feverish eyes, and the pistol Bonnie held but had not raised against him. The horses—or what she thought were horses—snorted behind her and he glanced back warily. He continued on up the walkway and broke the thin rectangular window next to the front door. Reaching in to unlock it, he then simply walked into the house. There was a long moment of silence, and she saw movement in the living room and kitchen through the windows, then heard the sharp retort of gunfire and saw blood splatter against a picture window.

He came out again ten minutes later, a heavy plastic garbage bag slung over his shoulder. He stopped in front of her, easing the bag off his back. He reached into the top of the bag and pulled out a blanket, then gently spread it over her. Standing and picking up the bag, he produced a bottle of water, twisted the top to break the plastic ring, and tossed it onto her lap. He hitched the bag up on his shoulder again and started to move on.

"Wait," she began, and he whirled to look at her again, now holding his finger to his lips for her to be silent. He smiled like a demented elf behind his bushy white beard.

With a flourish that sounded suspiciously like sleigh bells, he was gone. She heard the hoof beats fall off into the distance as she greedily drank the clean, cold water. When the silence returned, she listened to the falling snow again for a few minutes. She startled out of a doze when the first moan rose from the house. Her foot jerked again in response, and the muscles in her thigh cramped hard. A man shambled out of the front door, followed by a woman in a nightgown and a pair of children in pajamas. The moaning came louder, and she finished the last of the water, throwing the bottle away from her and placing the gun under her chin. A single tear rolled down her dirt-streaked face.

The phone came on, the screen lighting up. "Merry Christmas, Phil! The time is now," the muffled voice said from inside her jacket.

If there had been anyone around to hear it, the sound of the single gunshot was deafening.

THE SON OF SANTA CLAUS

SHANE KOCH

The ocean liner *Sea King* smashed into the arctic ice shelf, a tiny manmade dagger wedging in the massive frozen shore, glinting in the weak morning sun.

Suddenly, the bow crumpled and folded in on itself with a screech of twisted metal, and the ship dug in and ran aground, chunks and shards of ice exploding from the point of impact. The ship continued forward, blasting the snow into a massive cloud.

The sound of the massive liner beaching itself like a screaming whale echoed for miles through the polar expanse, a symphony of destruction filling the air.

The entire structure of the ship shuddered and contorted, writhing in one last metal crunch before the vessel finally ground to a halt. Hull debris rained down, leaving little explosions of white powder before being swallowed by the deep drifts.

The ship stood stories high, half out of the water, half mangled on the ice. The white cloud of snow was carried away quickly by the howling wind. Nothing moved on the deck of the *Sea King*. All was still, except for the loosened bits of destroyed ship that twitched in the grabbing wind.

Gusting snow was already beginning to claim the deck, wind rattled the chairs, the once-heated pool began to freeze, and ice collected in every crevice. The cracked window of the darkened bridge reflected nothing but a white vista, the dim sun sliding from the snow in the distance.

A man burst from the window holding a fire axe. He landed heavily on his feet on the deck below. He rolled to absorb the jump and came up on his feet, none the worse for wear. He was a large man, thickly built, young but with premature white hair and a square jaw. His sky-blue eyes scanned the horizon, as the wind whipped his Hawaiian shirt and Bermuda shorts. He wasn't bothered by the slicing cold wind; his sandaled feet carrying him across the snow-swept deck. He swung the fire axe loosely as he ran.

He stopped at one of the mangled railings that had once overlooked the ocean, and he looked down at the ice far below. Then glancing back at the window of the bridge, the things started streaming out, as if on cue. The entirety of the crew and passengers of the *Sea King*—all zombies now—leapt and tumbled through the broken window, shattering the rest of it. Meanwhile, an undead horde that had once bottlenecked the barricaded bridge door now gushed forward in a rotted mass.

The blob of grasping hands and snapping teeth slammed into the deck below. The leading zombies were crushed, their broken and oozing bodies providing a bloody cushion for the second and third waves.

Still they issued forth from the dark bridge. Upon seeing the white-haired man in the distance, resembling a cartoon character, they seemed to hang in the air for a moment before falling into a squirming pile of zombies on the deck.

Rippling pineapples on the man's loud shirt flapped in the wind, and his white hair trapped snowflakes as he watched the zombies fall and collect on the deck. Slowly, some of them began to dislodge from the pulsing mass and they started to move to him, intent on gorging themselves on the last warm morsel that existed on the dead ship

The man snorted derisively at the oncoming horde of the dead, then hopped over the railing, easily landing on the ice shelf below.

He began to put some distance between himself and the *Sea King*, jogging lightly through the drifts. He turned and looked over his shoulder from time to time as he moved steadily along. The zombies had followed over the railing, smashing their bodies on the ice below and making a gory landing pad for the next zombies that continued to hurl themselves into space like lemmings.

Soon, the zombies were chasing after him, trudging through the snow, hundreds of them, all seemingly annoyed that their meal was giving them so much trouble.

A cacophony of moans and groans drifted through the air, a sound of desperation and hunger that chilled the man far more than the climate. The zombies relentlessly pressed on through the wind and the snow, the sun shining on their backs as their feet began to collect with ice and freeze.

When the man gauged the speed of his pursuers, he figured he could outpace them with a steady, fast-paced walk. He continued into the polar landscape, a white world of nothingness. On and on he led the army of undead through the snow, staying a hundred yards ahead of them, the arctic weather passing over him.

He looked back periodically, and finally his suspicions about the zombies and their reaction to the climate began to bear fruit. The dead were slowly beginning to lessen in number.

Some of the moaning throng began to peel off and stall in the harsh conditions. The slowest and weakest of the dead faltered first, slowing under the hammer of the Arctic wind. Their legs betrayed them, the snow like molasses, and they started falling to their knees like confused animals, their flesh turning gradually into rancid ice that crept ever upward from their solidly-frozen feet to their seizing calves and thighs.

Into the drifts they dropped, one by one, never to rise again, twitching to an icy standstill on the white flypaper of the frozen plains. The stronger zombies still struggled forward, but they wouldn't last long. Though unnatural, the living dead would have no choice but to succumb to the laws of nature. Alive or dead, they were still made of flesh and would freeze solid soon.

The white-haired man watched the advancing zombies for a moment, then continued on his way, his loud shirt a lone dot of color in the white wasteland. He didn't look back again.

The austere, frozen landscape stretched out before him, showing no landmarks, nothing but a blank void. Still, he stomped purposefully through the snow, the fire axe swinging by his side, his face showing no clue of any hesitation or doubt. Through drifts that varied from knee to chest height, he continued unabated, the frigid cold and snow not bothering him in the least. For he was a man of the Arctic, a man of snow. He was Toby Claus, son of Santa Claus, and he was going home.

Earlier that day, the *Sea King* cruise ship was just as it should have been, gliding along on the Chukchi Sea. It was a ship full of happy people on an Alaskan cruise. Passengers lined the railing on the promenade, dressed warmly and armed with their binoculars and telephoto-lens cameras, hoping to see the whales. Every now and then, a dark mass would break the water's surface, and a hail of appreciative 'oohs' and 'ahhs' would come from the crowd.

The passengers that preferred to remain inside and out of the cold, spent their time eating at the buffet and the many fine restaurants, shopping, seeing movies and shows, or joining in any number of other shipboard activities that filled the daily calendar. Toby Claus was one of these people.

Toby was eternally thirty and a generally decent sort of guy. He whiled away most of the year abroad, sticking to beaches, deserts, jungles, and just about anywhere there wasn't snow. He liked the ladies, made friends, had some fun, and stayed out of trouble. Right around September he always gravitated back towards home, as did most of the Claus children, to make sure all of their father's business was sorted out and he wasn't running behind. Santa never was behind actually, but to Toby it was always a nice excuse to zip back up to the North Pole for a few weeks to visit. Toby's mother always appreciated it the most, and he sometimes wondered why she never ventured out from the Arctic for a vacation. Either she couldn't leave, or she wouldn't leave, and Toby figured the latter.

He sat on the upper level of one of the buffet dining rooms. It was a pretty good spread, and every once in a while he would amble down for another plate of food. He'd been eating for about four hours, and he was just about getting full. He couldn't pack it away like his father, but he could get close, and enjoyed trying. All the Claus children had a pinch of their father's magic in them, not enough to bend time and space once a year, but definitely enough to make it interesting.

Toby could sense his siblings if he concentrated, scattered around the world, walking their odd paths, feeling them in some unclear empathic way. He could find them eventually if he ever wanted to. But they never really tried to find each other. He'd spent several hundred years in the company of his siblings, and seeing some of them once a year was plenty. He knew his brothers and sisters felt the same. They loved each other, but they didn't need to be with each other.

He sat back in his chair, and out of curiosity, let his mind branch out, just to see how many of them were on their way home. But there was something wrong, something skewing his mind's vision—there was a dark shape that clouded and obscured. He came back to himself, relatively unconcerned. The *group think* of the world sometimes made things hazy, but he had to admit to himself that it had never been quite as garbled before. He thought for a moment that he'd felt some of his brothers' and sisters' panicked thoughts, but he couldn't be sure.

Over at the buffet, several people suddenly keeled over, dropping their plates, while others fell out of their chairs, or bounced heavily off tables on their way to the floor. Toby leaned over the railing and watched, interested at the novelty of so many people afflicted with something. Food poisoning, perhaps? Toby couldn't be poisoned, so he wasn't personally worried, but the part of him that was kind of human was certainly concerned for the welfare of those collapsed diners. He watched closely as onlookers rushed to the aid of the sick or injured. The ship's medical staff were summoned.

Toby began to feel strange. There was something calling to him from that little magic place inside him, something whispering, warning him. He continued to watch the tableaux below. The general consensus among the onlookers, and the ones taking pulses and administering CPR, was that the people who had collapsed were now dead. So Toby was relieved when the fallen diners in question began to stir. His relief didn't last long.

Unbelievable as it sounded, the passengers had apparently died, but were now back on their feet, screaming, biting, grabbing and attacking the ones who had been trying to help them. Toby watched the fight, not knowing what to make of it. It looked as if the people had been afflicted by some strange malady and had woken up and become insane and violent. Toby hated to meddle in human affairs, but it looked like he had no choice but to get involved.

He leapt the railing and landed next to the buffet line easily. One of the crazy people was biting into a woman's neck, an arterial spray spewing across the sneeze guard of the salad bar. The television sets in the dining area, previously showing various satellite sporting events, switched to the emergency broadcast system as Toby watched people ripping each other apart in an orgy of blood and violence.

Then the people began to eat the flesh of their victims. One of them spotted Toby, and with a grunting moan, the manic-eyed man ran at him, the man's face contorted into an almost orgasmic-looking hunger. Toby punched the attacker in the face, and the crazy man flew backwards, falling over a table. Then a screeching woman loped at Toby from his right, her dressed ripped, her breasts bouncing about in shameless, blood-dripping nakedness. He backhanded her, knocking her for a loop against a tray of gore-spattered desserts. He heard screams from everywhere, at various distances, coming from all over the ship. Even gunfire could be heard somewhere. He continued hammering away at the crazies with his fists, chairs, tables, anything he could get his hands on. He was hitting them very hard, easily hard enough to knock them out given his strength, but he saw that they didn't stay down for long, and he ended up having to knock the same people down more than once before they finally stayed down for good.

The dining room was quickly degenerating into a slaughterhouse. The crazies were everywhere, and Toby saw that the people who were attacked also became violently cannibalistic after being taken down. After a few minutes, Toby was the only normal person in the room, and he was surrounded by a crowd of killers, their mouths spewing rabid foam and blood.

He had no choice; Toby had to get rough with them to protect himself. He sighed, grabbed a chair, and he began swinging it at the people hard enough to cause real damage. With every swing bones broke, skulls were caved in, and teeth were sent rattling across the floor. But even injured, the crazy people kept coming at him. That was when Toby decided to look a little closer at the group encircling him. Some of their throats had been torn out, but they weren't bleeding anymore. Their eyes were glazed over, and their broken bones didn't seem to bother them. They were dead—he realized it was true. They were zombies, like in the movies.

Toby started swinging the chair again, and the zombies' heads burst and popped at the impacts. They started to fall and stay down, their skulls broken wide open and leaking globs of brain matter like some awful and hellish cornucopia. After a while, Toby stopped fighting, seeing that he was the only one standing, the carpet covered in blood and destroyed zombies.

He ran from the dining room and found the neighboring hallway was much the same as the room he'd just vacated. Zombies were attacking the living, and the zombies winning. He put his hand through the glass case of a fire axe box and pulled out the bright red axe. He was strong, endowed with magic. But though he was unaffected by cold temperatures, he still wasn't invulnerable. He figured that these creatures could probably bite through his skin. He didn't know if he would become one of them if he was bitten, but he had no intention of finding out. He decided to make for the bridge. At least there he might find someone still alive, or he'd be able to call for help. He hacked at anyone who got in his way if they looked undead and ran through the blood-drenched corridors of the *Sea King*. The fire axe cleaved the zombies well enough, and just like in the movies, if he destroyed their brains, the zombies stayed down.

He'd intended to save anyone he could, but on his way to the bridge, he never laid eyes on a normal person. Everyone he saw was a zombie, or dead and on their way to becoming a zombie. He charged onto the bridge, which was awash with blood, and he split the undead captain's head in two with the axe. Then he barricaded the door.

The zombies had chased him all the way to the bridge, and he was starting to get the feeling that he was the only person left alive on the ship. But that couldn't be possible. Or at least he hoped it wasn't. He tried all the channels of the communication system, and he broadcast his voice all over the intercom, looking for any other survivors. No one came to the bridge. There were no more screams or gunfire, just the incessant moaning and groaning of the zombies as their fists beat against the bridge door.

He tried calling the Coast Guard, running through the emergency channels, anything he could think of, but either his transmissions couldn't get through or he was getting no answer. He feared that this zombie thing might be happening everywhere on the planet. He familiarized himself with the controls of the ship, reading the manuals he found in one of the computers, then pointed the *Sea King* north, hoping he could make it home before the zombies broke down the door to the bridge. He really didn't want to have to swim the distance home.

The zombies had become frozen solid in Toby's snowy wake, as he continued onward through the ice field, the rapidly-waning daylight letting the temperature drop even lower than it already was. He walked for days, always at the same steady pace. At night, the moon shone bright in the cloud-scattered sky, giving the rolling drifts an unearthly glow. He walked until he finally skirted the veil to his father's small, hidden kingdom. Toby closed his eyes and concentrated, slipping through the invisible fabric of ancient magic, until he stood again in the land of Santa Claus.

As his eyes took it all in, he saw that the land had most certainly seen better days.

His father's cottage and workshop were visible in the distance, through the howling, white winds. The gingerbread house-like cottage was under siege by scores of zombified elves and reindeer. The stables were a dark, smoking ruin, and the elf barracks were ablaze in the night, the fire casting a harsh light on the stumbling and lurching blood-faced elves that shuffled to and fro.

Gone was the ring of jaunty, toy-building songs that used to hang in the air all year round, now to be replaced by the high-pitched moaning and wailing of the diminutive zombies. The elves, their colorful little clothes caked with gore, beat their tiny fists against the heavy, wooden door of the cottage ineffectively, single-mindedly fixed on whoever remained alive inside. Toby found himself horrified by the ghastly, final state of all his little friends, the once joyful and proud makers of toys now reduced to mindless zombies.

The reindeer, their brown hides marked with blood-encrusted bites, flew through the air, circling around the cottage, a zombie rush of tornadic horror. The undead animals banged their bodies angrily against the red shutters of the cottage, destroying themselves in mad hunger, their broken legs dangling and twisting unnaturally under their fleeting, airborne forms. The fiery nose of Rudolph the Red-nosed Reindeer spun in the swirl, a hateful semaphore that signaled the pitiful end of everything Toby knew in a bright, bloody glare.

Suddenly, strange black lightning crackled from around the side of the cottage, arcing and spitting, laying waste to handfuls of the undead elves and reindeers. Then from behind the cottage Toby's father limped into view. Santa Claus teetered through the horrible scene, black electricity crackling around his slack-jawed face. His black boots struggled forward through the bloody snow, his red pants held fast by one straining suspender. His large belly was ripped open, and glistening ropes of intestines spilled and hung down between his legs, to drag behind him in a tangled and shiny mass of coils. His undead eyes were black and his beard soaked with chunks of meaty flesh. Santa dragged the corpse of Toby's sister, Greta, through the snow by her red-stained white hair. Greta had been freshly killed, stripped naked, and her torso was a splayed bowl of swishing gore. Elves clung to her dragging legs, clutching at her flesh with their child-like hands. They were attached to her naked white thighs like leeches, and they dipped their greedy faces deep into the holes in her flesh, resembling pigs at a trough.

Every now and then, the lightning would lash out from Santa's body like an evil Tesla coil, stabbing into any unwary zombie in range, to burst them open like rotten meat balloons. Santa's magic had become twisted in his death, uncontrolled, and Toby could feel the evil emanating from his undead father in a sick, mental cloud.

Greta reanimated then, writhing about as she was dragged, a strangled moan escaping her once beautiful mouth. A black pop of energy flicked out from Santa, and Greta's head exploded, cutting her zombie life short. Santa stumbled around to the front of the cottage, still holding Greta's bloody scalp in his hand, leaving her twitching body behind. Lightning continued to annihilate the ranks of the undead that surrounded the little house. Elves exploded in clouds of red mist, and reindeer were blown from the sky. Santa began to beat his ham-hock fists bloodily against the front door of the cottage. Toby heard his mother scream from inside the house, and that sorrowful sound compelled him to act.

He flung the axe at the back of his father's head, and the blade embedded itself there perfectly. Santa stumbled backwards a step or two, turned, and fell face down into a red-splattered snow drift. His body convulsed and jiggled, and one final burst of black lightning reached out, hissing and sizzling, tearing through the zombies like jittering saw blades. Then Santa ceased in his bucking and the dark energy fizzled out, dissipating into the howling wind in a smoky whine.

Toby dashed to the actual North Pole itself, a twenty-foot tall, candy-cane-striped wooden rod, thick as a small tree, with a round, white wooden ball on top. He ripped the pole from the ice and dug his powerful fingers into the cracking wood. He ran toward the cottage and his mother's anguished cries. Toby swung the North Pole back and forth, smashing elves and the darting, flying reindeer into piles of quivering, spoiled jelly of red meat. Rudolph swooped down from on high, his straight, cow-like teeth snapping, and Toby knocked the undead reindeer from the air with a mighty swing, breaking Rudolph's spine with a loud snap. He then made short work of any zombies that were left after his father's electrical storm, before tossing the bloody pole aside after making sure there were no undead stragglers.

He ran to the front door of the cottage and pounded on it. When there was no answer he kicked it in. Toby recoiled in horror at the sight of his mother being eaten alive by three of his brothers. She looked at him with panicked eyes that were wet and terrified, like a farm animal on the slaughterhouse killing floor. His brothers ripped handfuls of spurting flesh from her. Her clothes were ripped away, and their powerful hands popped her breasts to pull strands of muscle and tendons out of her bloody body, the elasticity resembling taffy. They gorged their blood-red mouths as they bit off their own tongues in the teeth-gnashing, gore-slick orgy of feeding.

It was in that horrible moment, while Toby watched his mother being eaten to death, that she choked one last spewing death rattle and became nothing more than a pile of dripping meat.

He went and retrieved the fire axe from Santa's head. Then walked back into the cottage, easily striking down his flesh-hungry brothers, and splitting their white-haired heads with his flashing weapon. He did the same to his mother, before she had a chance to come back. Then he would burn all the bodies, and wait to see if any more of his brothers or sisters would make it home, either alive or dead.

ABOUT THE WRITERS

Mariah Deitrick is a wife, mother of four, and writer. She's a graduate from the Institute of Children's Literature, and is the author of the adult novel, "Deadly Hunt," with Undead Press. Her work has appeared in a variety of markets including, Spaceports and Spidersilk, Knowownder!, Super Teacher Worksheets, Stories That Lift, StoryTeller Tymes, and Living Dead Press.

A complete list of her work can be found at her website www.mariahdeitrick.weebly.com

Dennis Finocchiaro lives in the suburbs of Philadelphia and writes constantly. He's written a few books, including the zombie novel "The Z Word" published by Living Dead Press, which the story in this anthology was inspired from.

Anthony Giangregorio is the author of 45 novels and novellas, most about zombies, and has edited over 50 anthologies and novels. His work has appeared in Dead Science & Metahumans vs. the Undead by Coscomentertainment, Dead Worlds: Undead Stories Volumes 1-7, and Wolves of War by Library of the Living Dead Press. He also has stories in End of Days: An Apocalyptic Anthology Vol. 1-5, the Book of the Dead series Vol. 1-6 by LDP, Zombie Zoology by Severed Press, and two anthologies with Pill Hill Press. He's also the creator of the ten book action/zombie series titled Deadwater and the apocalyptic series Warriors of the Apocalypse. His action/horror novel Dead Rage is being optioned for a movie at this time.

Michael D. Griffiths is from Flagstaff, Arizona. He focuses on Horror, Dark Fantasy, Sci Fi, Humor, and Reviews. His "Eternal Aftermath" novel is set five years deep into the Zombie Apocalypse. His "Chronicles of Jack Primus" series is released by Living Dead Press. He also works for The Daily Discord and SFReader.

Chauma Smith Guss lives and works in Birmingham Alabama, and will tell you about her dogs if given any opportunity. She is a not-so-closet fan of horror and dark urban fantasy, serial killer trivia, and her husband Sam. Outside her passion for reading and writing, her hobbies include speaking at church, teaching Sunday school, and participating in a wedding ministry. No, really.

Kelly M. Hudson is the author of over two dozen short stories published in a variety of anthologies as well as the author of two horror novels, "The Turning" and "Men of Perdition," both available though all retailers. To find out more about Kelly and his work, please visit his website at www.kellyhudson.com

Julie R Kendrick is an English author living in Northamptonshire. She writes horror and dark fantasy. Her stories are published in various US and UK anthologies. She is currently working with a number of publishers and is in the process of writing her first book.

Marc Shemmans is a writer from Birmingham, UK who has had several stories published in a variety of magazines and anthologies from both sides of the Atlantic. He's hoping they will find homes as soon as they're finished.

R P Steeves is a former teacher and a writer who specializes in the fantastic. His most recent novel, an urban fantasy tale of paranormal detection, The National Maul is now available, and is the 2nd book in the Misty Johnson series. Follow his blog and learn of his upcoming horror, fantasy, sci-fi and pulp adventure titles at http://www.rpsteeves.com

Dustin Stevens is the other of Zombie Kill: Predator or Prey, Just a Game, and several short stories. He holds a BA from Harvard University and a JD from the University of Montana. He currently lives in Honolulu.

For more Christmas/zombie horror, check out:
Christmas is Dead from Living Dead Press
Christmas is Dead...Again from Living Dead Press
Dead Christmas from Open Casket Press

VICTORY OF THE DEAD
ANTHONY GIANGREGORIO

UNDEAD PRESS
UNDEAD PRESS
Where the Dead
Never Sleep
UNDEADPRESS.COM

ETERNAL AFTERMATH

A ZOMBIE NOVEL

MICHAEL D. GRIFFITHS